Maisey Yates is a *New York Times* bestselling author of over one hundred romance novels. Whether she's writing strong, hard-working cowboys, dissolute princes or multigenerational family stories, she loves getting lost in fictional worlds. An avid knitter with a dangerous yarn addiction and an aversion to housework, Maisey lives with her husband and three kids in rural Oregon.

Check out her website, **maiseyyates.com**,
or find her on Facebook **/MaiseyYates.Author**

T0383920

By Maisey Yates with Headline Eternal

Other People's Weddings

Deacons of Bourbon Street
Strip You Bare

You can find a full list of Maisey's titles at maiseyyates.com.

OTHER PEOPLE'S WEDDINGS

MAISEY YATES

HEADLINE
ETERNAL

First published in 2024
by HEADLINE ETERNAL
An imprint of HEADLINE PUBLISHING GROUP

2

Cataloguing in Publication Data is available from the British Library

ISBN 978 1 0354 1376 8

Typeset in 11/14.5 pt Granjon LT Std by Jouve (UK), Milton Keynes

Printed and bound in Great Britain by Clays Ltd, Elcograf S.p.A.

Headline's policy is to use papers that are natural, renewable and recyclable
products and made from wood grown in well-managed forests and other
controlled sources. The logging and manufacturing processes are expected to
conform to the environmental regulations of the country of origin.

HEADLINE PUBLISHING GROUP
An Hachette UK Company
Carmelite House
50 Victoria Embankment
London EC4Y 0DZ

The authorised representative in the EEA is Hachette Ireland, 8 Castlecourt
Centre, Dublin 15, D15 XTP3, Ireland (email: info@hbgi.ie)

www.headlineeternal.com
www.headline.co.uk
www.hachette.co.uk

To Jackie
Things will always work out just as they should

OTHER PEOPLE'S
WEDDINGS

PROLOGUE

The Fourth Wedding
South Lake Tahoe
Eighteen Months Ago

I looked at the empty cake platter, and the emptying dance floor, and smiled. The bride and groom were on their way to the absolutely beautiful lodge they'd rented for their first night as a married couple, the guests were happy, and I could finally breathe after a long day of wedding cake presenting, serving duties and one near disaster involving the photographer.

Not a feat I'm in a hurry to repeat. But the end result was worth it.

I wouldn't call myself a romantic. But I do love weddings.

Weddings are, fundamentally, not about *romance*, anyway. Not really.

They might start out that way, but they evolve. When a person proposes to another person that they love very much (this has never happened to me, and I'm not in a hurry for it to, but I've had it recounted to me by many friends, brides, grooms and maybe I've watched the occasional flashmob proposal on YouTube) it's about *them*. The couple.

Unless it's a flashmob, then I usually assume it's about someone's ego.

But generally speaking, the *proposal* is between two people. The *wedding* is about two people, their competing tastes, the influence of their friends, and all their familial issues coming home to roost.

That's the part I like. The whole glittering tapestry of connections between all the people involved. Which can often devolve into spectacle, but I enjoy that too.

I love what a wedding says about – not just the people getting married – but everyone in their lives.

Like when a couple chooses to get married in New Orleans during Mardi Gras but don't want their Baptist grandmother to know they drink. Or are having premarital sex.

People are fascinating. And very, very strange.

I love to bake because I loved my grandmother with my whole heart. I love to bake wedding cakes, because I love the strangeness, romanticism and uniqueness of other people, and the parties they choose to throw when they optimistically promise themselves to another human being for all eternity.

I might not be a romantic, but I'm not a cynic either. That doesn't mean I can ignore the glaring stat that more than half of the happy unions I bake cakes for won't last.

So far, though, only six of the two hundred and eighty-eight wedding cakes have gotten divorced. That I know of.

One of them did recently change her profile picture to a selfie, along with a quote about seasons, so it's possible we're at seven now.

Yes, I do friend everyone I bake a cake for. Or they friend me. But it would be weird not to. This is a very small town.

Personal and professional lines get very blurry when you frequently run into clients in the grocery store. And at the dentist. Or at your gynecologist.

Worse when it *is* your gynecologist.

It's unnerving, to say the least, when the nurse looks at you with very large eyes and says: *Poppy, if you could bake my cake, I'd be so honored and I know it's short notice but . . . well, I'm pregnant but you can't tell anyone.*

Possibly the worst place I've ever been asked if I'd bake a cake for someone. Also, though, I could hardly say no to a pleading pregnant woman while I was laid up in stirrups.

I didn't want to say no anyway. I love my job.

And all its perks.

A common thread between brides in my hometown is the desire to get married anywhere *but* the town. It's too common. Everyone has the same pictures. No out-of-town family wants to spend time in a tiny Oregon town whose population hasn't grown since the gold rush era, et cetera.

That's how I end up traveling for work. Often. Not a complaint.

This particular wedding was staid compared to the New Orleans wedding I'd gone to the year before, but it wasn't quiet by any stretch of the imagination. The outdoor dance floor at the lodge had cleared hours ago, and the bar was packed now.

I was buzzing on the triumph of how smoothly everything had gone, how gloriously the cake had blended with the theme and how good it had all tasted. I wouldn't be able to sleep for hours. Quinn had been a bridesmaid and I'd been the baker, and I was effervescent with the way it had all gone. In spite of the earlier kerfuffle.

Caitlin had been a beautiful bride. And if I ever had a tendency toward being a romantic it was in these moments.

It's impossible to resist the glow of a newly married couple.

Because the event itself is behind them, and life stretches out before them in all its infinite possibility, unspoiled yet by reality.

Moments like that, I can admit that I want that. *Someday*.

I don't need it right this second, but if I didn't want to get married, I wouldn't be in a long term relationship. I'm in the dress rehearsal phase. Can we cohabitate together without killing each other? Can I imagine this man living alongside me like this every day forever?

That's the thing. I'm not going to get married if I can't be reasonably certain it will last.

I need certainty.

Though now wasn't the time to reflect on my own issues. Everyone was happy, the wedding was through and it was time to celebrate.

Quinn was still in her berry-colored bridesmaid gown and her hair still twisted into an elaborate updo with two strands pulled out to 'frame her face' (the hair stylist's words) but Quinn was the sort of person who could pull off any look simply because she decided it worked, and she projected so much confidence no one would dare question her.

I was in black, which was not best practices at a wedding if you were a guest, but I wasn't really a guest. I was the cake lady. And the cake lady worked best when blended neatly into the background.

My cake was the star, not me.

I was okay with that.

"Drinks are on me, Poppy," she said, making her way toward the bar. "Because you did exquisite work today, and should I ever get married I'll need you to make my cake."

"Should you get married, I'll be the last one standing."

"You'll probably get married before me," Quinn said. "You and Josh have been together forever."

Seven years. Four of them cohabitating. And yes it was beginning to feel like if we didn't get married soon we might not ever. But I also felt . . . paralyzed. I didn't want to disrupt what we had if he was happy. I didn't want to take something that worked and make it *not* work.

But I wanted . . .

I craved the stability of marriage. After my childhood, no one would blame me, I knew that for certain. My therapist had confirmed it was wholly understandable given the circumstances. So . . .

It also made me feel wary of projecting my own issues too aggressively at Josh.

"I'm not in a hurry," I said. It was maybe a lie. I felt much more in a hurry than I had for a while. But maybe that was just because of . . . well. I wasn't going to ruminate on that. "Besides, I go to more weddings a year than anyone I know."

"I'm sure he goes to as many as you do. If not more." Quinn's left shoulder shifted outward, a gesture in a direction I was trying to avoid looking in.

Because I already knew who *he* was. I already knew where *he* was.

He being the wedding photographer.

He being Ryan Clark.

He being . . . a complication. A scowly, recalcitrant entirely-too-compelling complication.

One who hated me nearly as much as I hated him. Or perhaps hate was too strong of a word.

But then, after today's events, maybe not.

"Sure," I said.

It was like her statement conjured him up. Out of thin air.

Because there he was, striding toward the bar – and maybe us – with intent and intensity. A hallmark of his entire . . . thing. It irritated me. We were at a wedding. Well, the afterparty. It wouldn't kill him to smile.

Except then he did, and I'd never be able to explain the reaction I had to it.

It shifted his whole face.

I'd known him since sixth grade. It wasn't like I'd never seen him smile.

But on his thirty-year-old face, it seemed new.

And I found myself smiling back.

Only to realize he hadn't been smiling at me. Or heading my way at all.

He stopped at the bar and clapped a man sitting there on the back, who stood and greeted him like they were long lost brothers.

"Who is that?"

Quinn was looking over at Ryan and his friend with very intense interest.

I wanted to say something cutting and clever about the fact that he was clearly someone important because he'd made Ryan, of all people, smile, like an actual human man and not a robot, or maybe something about how I couldn't possibly know if Quinn didn't know.

Instead, I managed a shrug.

And Quinn marched right over there as I shrugged, so I had to hurry and follow along.

"Hi, Ryan," she said.

This time, Ryan did look at me. And then back at Quinn. "Hi, Quinn." He looked at me again. Then at the man sitting at the bar. "Quinn," he paused for a beat, "this is Noah."

And Quinn looked lit up. "It's nice to meet you."

CHAPTER 1

Present Day

*E*ven if I believed in fate, and I don't, I would *never* subscribe to the belief that Ryan Clark was the master of it.

Quinn would tell me – and anyone listening – that he was, in fact, the architect of her romantic destiny. The arranger of her stars. *The very hand of God.*

It makes me want to die.

But I can't die. I have a wedding cake to bake.

The cake I'm making for my next wedding is the most important cake I've ever been asked to bake.

I'm assuming I'm baking her cake, of course. No one else would be able to make a cake that is as quintessentially Quinn as I would.

Nobody knows Quinn better than I do. Well, arguably her fiancé does, I guess. But in the scheme of space and time, I feel that Quinn barely knows him.

They've been together *ten months*. And are now engaged.

In contrast, I lived with the same man for *seven years* without even a discussion of marriage, before it all fell apart last winter.

I don't believe in destiny, or *the one*, or anything like that. That's the sort of mindset people who don't want to take charge of their lives buy into. An excuse for why they don't have to make a relationship work, an excuse for drifting along in life, waiting for love, wealth or otherwise to come slap them in the face.

You have to go looking for special things in life.

If you want to chase your dreams you have to run.

To LA if need be.

At the expense of your child, *if need be*.

Though, this wasn't about my mother. Who was certainly better known for playing a mother on TV than being one in actual real life.

But she'd succeeded in her dreams after she'd left me behind. Because we make choices. And that's okay. How can you argue with a choice that hurts for a while but results in a person's dreams coming true?

I mean, you can't. Or at least, I can't.

Given my personal viewpoint on the whole subject, I can't really claim that Josh and I weren't 'meant to be'. In the end, I think it wasn't a relationship we wanted to do the work for. And that's fine.

It hurt when he broke up with me. Especially given I'd thought we were on the cusp of a proposal, not an ending, but I'd grown since then. Painfully, and with great effort.

But that's my perspective on love in general. It isn't a matter of 'meant to be' or 'not meant to be'. You work at a relationship, and then you work to get over it. I wish things were as easy as fate.

Quinn says that kind of thing all the time, because Quinn is a romantic. With eleven months between her first meeting of Noah and their engagement, she kind of has to be.

Quinn would say that she and Noah were *fated*.

How could they be anything else?

After that chance meeting in the Lake Tahoe bar, it had to have come from something bigger than them. Bigger than *all of us*.

I looked at it this way. If you think a guy in a bar is hot and fin-agle your way into an introduction, is it fate, or are you horny? No judgment.

And if you then decide that this is going to be the thing you make work, because he makes you smile and he's handsome and you have an easy time weaving your life into his, great.

I think *fate* is a very strong word for what are really mundane, daily occurrences that you choose to apply meaning to – or don't. And once you've given something meaning, you tend to hang onto it a lot harder than if you hadn't.

So maybe it's more than fate that has Quinn and Noah rushing to get married. Not that I think she *shouldn't* marry him. He's a great guy and she's the happiest I've ever seen her. I just think it's more choice than magic, that's all.

She'd asked me out to dinner tonight and I was sure it was going to be the will-you-be-my-maid-of-honor will-you-bake-my-cake dinner. Which meant I needed a truly stunning outfit, because honestly, it made more sense to dress up for your best friend than for a man.

Men didn't care what dress you had on, in my experience.

Your best friend was the one who would be delighted by effort put into hair, makeup and the perfect shoes.

I'd rather dress for Quinn than some guy any day.

I was half ready when my doorbell rang.

I frowned and wondered if I'd forgotten I'd ordered something I had to sign for – I ordered a lot of kitchen gadgets online during late night doomscrolling sessions before bed and I often had no memory of it.

But when I walked toward the front door, in a clingy red dress, barefoot and with red lipstick on, and saw the top of a familiar head in the high windows in the oak door I froze for a second.

This was not fate.

So there, Quinn.

But as I moved to the door and jerked it open, I realized that Quinn had never even implied that Josh might be my fate.

Which was the prevailing thought in my mind as I came face to face with my ex-boyfriend.

He smiled. Boyishly. I'd always liked his smile. He had dimples and pale blue eyes, blond hair that often fell into his eyes. And I felt a rush of warmth. Familiarity. I missed feeling this comfortable.

But that dissipated when I remembered he wasn't my boyfriend anymore, he'd hurt me, and I didn't know why he was here.

"What are you doing here?" I asked.

"Hi. I . . . realized I left some things here."

"Six months ago?"

"Yes."

"I . . . yeah come in."

I stepped back and let him walk inside the house he'd once lived in. An unexpected guest now and not a cohabitant.

Weird.

It felt destabilizing and uncomfortable and I hated it.

I didn't hate him though. That was the tough thing. I never had.

He'd gotten me through such a hard time in my life. When I'd lost Gran I'd really felt like a part of me had died with her, and Josh had been so good to me. But even outside of the bad times, he'd made me feel important. Needed. And I really, really liked that.

But it was like I couldn't find that feeling now either. Any more than I could find hate.

He was looking at me like he expected me to say something that would make this situation less awkward, and my brain started to do a desperate tap dance, trying to find the right words because I still wanted to make things easy, I wanted to make him comfortable, even if I shouldn't.

It was ingrained in me.

After all, why would anyone want to stay with someone who made life harder?

He didn't want to stay with you.

My mental tap dance ended on a thud.

"I haven't gone through the closet in your game room," I said.

"That's probably where it is. Just . . . my sheets and some stuff from school. My D.A.R.E. t-shirt."

"Your . . . D.A.R.E. t-shirt?"

"Drug abuse resistance edu—"

"We were in D.A.R.E. together, I know what it is. I didn't know the shirt was important to you."

He lifted a shoulder. "I don't do drugs."

"Well. I think statistically the program wasn't very successful, but yay to us outliers, I guess."

He smiled. "I guess."

He shifted his weight from one foot to another and it was like I felt it inside my chest. A shift, a weird longing. I didn't want to kiss him or anything but I wanted to hang onto him. For just a second. Because in the six months since we'd broken up it had felt like I was in a storm with nothing to hold onto. Everything I'd thought about myself and my life and my future had changed, and for a moment I just wanted it to go back to how it had been.

Quinn was getting married.

I felt like a sad, lonely cliché. Gazing at my ex like the past had the answers because the future was a blank space.

"You can go look in the game room," I said. "I'm getting ready."

That was so firm. I was proud of myself. I was trying to rescue myself more than I'd been trying to be firm, but whatever.

He nodded and headed back toward what had been his game room. Where he'd had his PC set up for gaming, and a table for D&D sessions – which I'd sometimes participated in too. Dungeons and Dragons was maybe my favorite thing I'd learned from Josh. What wasn't to like about a few hours of total escapism where you could pretend to be a Druidic Wood Elf instead of a regular girl?

Nothing, that's what.

I wrinkled my nose and went into the bathroom to finish

putting my makeup on. I was getting nostalgic. Nostalgia felt dangerous right now.

I looked at myself and tried to make a stern face at my reflection before I walked back out of the bathroom and practically ran into him in the hallway.

"Sorry," I said, feeling silly and awkward as I walked quickly into the living room.

He followed me. "Poppy."

I turned around and looked at him, standing there holding a cardboard box filled with stuff that was apparently very important to him. "We can be friends, Poppy," he said. "We were together too long to just be nothing."

I blinked. "I . . ."

Maybe he was right. I'd been angry when he'd broken up with me, of course I had been. I'd been blindsided. Who would respond to that well?

But we had been together so long.

We'd known each other since elementary school.

Maybe that was part of why I wanted to sink into him now. Because he'd been one of the steady things, one of the constant things, and losing him entirely was absurd.

"Would you think about it?" he asked.

He looked hopeful, and entirely different to the image I'd constructed of him in my head, pasted together from moments during our breakup. I'd fashioned him into a brand-new Josh in my mind, who was only the one that had hurt me because that made it easy to never regret it and never miss him.

"Yeah," I said. "I don't . . . hate you."

That was the truth. It surprised me a little.

His shoulders sagged with what looked like relief and my previous statement became even truer.

I didn't want an enemy wandering around the streets of Pineville anyway.

Well, not another one anyway. I already had the one.

Ryan.

I did not need to think about Ryan now. Anyway, thank God I hadn't seen Josh's best friend/my professional nemesis in six months. Not even randomly on the street.

A minor miracle in a town this size.

Which was why what Josh was suggesting was the dream, really. If you had to break up in a small town, wasn't it better if you didn't have to cycle through the stages of grief every time you saw your ex?

Friendship was potentially the best solution.

"I'm glad you don't hate me. I know I said . . ." he winced. "I said some things I wish I hadn't."

"Did you not mean them?"

"I did. But I think I might have . . . sometimes it's hard to know what you actually feel."

He looked at me expectantly and I realized I didn't know what he expected. I'd been an expert on that, once upon a time. I'd taken great delight in it. In knowing just what to do. Just what to say. Just how to be.

I chewed on the inside of my cheek. "Right."

I wasn't sure I agreed. I'd known what I felt.

But then I was reminded of times when I hadn't known and hadn't been my best self at all and I felt like I didn't have the right to say anything at all.

"I'll get out of your hair. But maybe we can . . . see each other again sometime."

"Yeah," I said.

He was gone before I realized he hadn't said anything about my dress. Proving my earlier internal musings a little too well.

I felt unsettled and weird. He seemed regretful, which was very, very strange considering he'd been the one to break up with me because he'd wanted to see what else was out there.

Sometimes it's hard to know what you actually feel.

I shoved that thought aside and went to go choose my shoes because I didn't need the specter of my past romance hanging over tonight.

This was about Quinn. Not Josh. And not the weird tug I felt toward the safety he'd once represented for me.

When Quinn rolled up in the driveway I was a little surprised to see Noah in the passenger's seat. I'd imagined the dinner was just *us* celebrating.

It wounded me just slightly that Noah would be here for this, which was silly because it was about Noah and Quinn.

I waved and tried not to telegraph my emotions as I made my way to the backseat.

And stopped.

Ryan Clark was in the backseat.

Like this was a double date.

Ryan. Clark. Who I hadn't seen since the fifth wedding.

The fifth wedding in four years where I made the cake and he was the photographer. We hadn't seen each other because I no longer lived with his best friend. Because he didn't come to my bakery and I didn't go to his studio. Because we hadn't worked a wedding together since.

We hadn't seen each other because we had no reason to see each other.

Unlike with Josh, I didn't feel nostalgic looking at Ryan.

And this was not fate.

This was *Quinn.*

I was very aware that I was standing outside the car for far too long, being far too still, with my arms held loose at my sides like one of those dopey, bargain bin cat pillows you could pick up at a truck stop.

I also couldn't move.

Until he did.

He shifted. Inside the car. Just a little. Not a smile. Just . . . his shoulders lowered. He sat back – just a small movement – and his eyebrows went slack rather than being held tight together, pinching his forehead.

So . . . I took a deep breath like I was diving off a cliff into freezing cold water and opened the car door, got in and closed it in one quick movement. I grabbed my seatbelt and tried to buckle with the same fluidity but found myself fumbling to get the mechanism into the actual buckle and it took three tries. Three impotent clicks. When I looked up my eyes met his. And I know I sneered.

I did know it.

I didn't mean to.

I meant to smile.

The result was, I could imagine, more like when my grandma's old Australian Shepherd used to get caught doing something wrong. Just my lips lifted over my teeth.

I stopped. Quickly.

He looked away.

I was going to say hi to him. I was about to.

"Good to see you, Poppy." That came from Noah who was looking at me in the rearview mirror, and I did manage to smile at him.

"Good to see you too." I like him. Really. He's a great guy. My issue isn't with Noah at all. It's more timelines and of course fear for my friend's heart. And the possibility she might choose New Zealand over the US and leave me forever, tapping into all my childhood trauma around abandonment that was recently compounded by the death of my grandmother.

That's all.

"It's been a while."

It had been. Which was a given, since Noah had been in New Zealand the past few months, and that meant the tension in the car was so noticeable we'd been reduced to soap opera speech that barely rose above the level of *as you know, Bob.* Anything to fill the silence.

"Well," I said, because if there was one thing I knew it was how to make conversation with a recently engaged couple. "Tell us the whole story!"

"I told you everything," said Quinn, lifting her hand from the steering wheel very deliberately so that her ring sparkled.

"I want to hear Noah's point of view."

And as I thought they would be, they were off. Telling the whole story and stepping on each other's sentences. It made it a lot harder for me to be worried about it, and them, timelines notwithstanding. They were in love, and it was beautiful.

I just needed to push off the weirdness that I felt from my earlier visit with Josh. That was why I felt so . . . off.

I did not look at Ryan to get a gauge on his reaction. I didn't care what he thought.

I might not be a romantic, but he was the most anti-romance human being to ever come near the bridal industrial complex. I couldn't imagine him getting starry eyed over an engagement story.

Or, indeed, anything.

Thankfully, we were close to the restaurant, and I all-but tumbled out of the car when we pulled up to the curb.

Then we walked into the restaurant, and down the stairs to what was a rather cave-like dining room that had been the epitome of class and fanciness back in the 1960s, with its stone walls and red lamps on the tables. I had always been fond of the retro nature of the place.

"You can't see anything in here," Ryan said after they sat down at their table.

"I like it. It makes me want a fancy cigarette case and a martini," I countered, not even being contrary for the sake of it.

"This is why I like Poppy," Noah said. "She's a hard case."

Noah had called me that before, and I was sure he was doing it again just because I'd been so amused by it last time.

I looked at Noah. "Try to explain what that means again."

He did try, but when the waiter came to take our drink order it got lost in the shuffle, and then we spent the next five minutes talking about wine until the drinks arrived and the appetizer and dinner order were taken.

I reached into the bread basket at the same time as Ryan and our fingers brushed, and I took a half breath and made the deliberate choice not to respond like an angry cat who'd gotten her tail stepped on.

I let our hands stay touching. I *lingered* even.

His eyes caught mine, and I knew whatever game I'd been playing . . . I hadn't won.

I pulled my hand out.

And forgot my bread, dammit.

I couldn't reach for more bread now. It would look like touching Ryan's hand had flustered me.

I couldn't have it looking like that.

I watched him butter the bread he'd gotten and felt a little salty about it.

The appetizers arrived, which felt like a blessing because then I got to pretend I'd been waiting for the blue cheese crème brulee rather than awkwardly avoiding the bread.

I attacked it with relish, enjoying the crispy-topped, creamy cheese and trying to ignore that my hand still felt warm.

"Have you thought about theme, Quinn?" I asked. "I think a naked cake would be so good for you. With pines and fresh berries . . ."

"I don't know," Quinn said. "I might want something more traditional. With a cake topper."

That did not please me.

"Oh . . ." I frowned and then tried not to.

"But we haven't really . . . committed to anything yet."

I nodded. "Sure. Of course."

Maybe Quinn didn't want me to make her cake? It would be okay if she didn't.

Maybe.

But Brittney Keller had me make her wedding cake and she'd hated me in high school so it would be a little weird if Quinn didn't want me to make her cake, that was all.

But I was distracted from my cake worry when Noah and Quinn took each other's hands and gazed meaningfully across the table at Ryan and myself.

"We wanted to bring you both out tonight," Quinn said, her eyes shining in the dim light, tears shimmering there and making my throat tight even though I didn't know why she was crying, "because you're our best friends. Ryan, you brought us together. You're our North Star." Noah shot Ryan a rueful smile that seemed to be apologizing for Quinn's dramatization. "And Poppy, you've been there for me always. We don't have sisters, we have each other."

Well, that really made me want to cry.

"Poppy, I want you to be my maid of honor."

"Ryan, I want you to be my best man."

Ryan and I turned to look at each other slowly, very slowly. Our eyes caught. And held.

"We're going to get married in Queenstown, New Zealand," Quinn said. "And we really want to have the wedding party and family there for two weeks. For excursions and sightseeing and just . . . hanging out."

Quinn's voice faltered, and I knew why.

She was having her wedding in New Zealand. She wanted us all there for two weeks to spend time together because she was leaving.

She really was leaving.

I'd been worried about this. It had been sitting in the back of my mind, gnawing at my brain for weeks. *Months.* As she'd fallen harder and harder for Noah and I'd found myself vacillating between joy at her joy and fear over the inevitable change it would bring.

Where would they live?

I asked myself that question a lot.

I'd deliberately avoided asking Quinn.

Oregon was beautiful. My understanding was that New Zealand was one of the few places that rivaled it for beauty.

Noah was from Queenstown, and though I'd never been I had googled it extensively and I, who had never considered leaving Pineville in my life, could even imagine being very happy there.

So I worried.

My worry was founded, it turned out.

Very founded.

She wanted to spend quality time with her family and the bridal party for two whole weeks because she was leaving us forever.

I couldn't handle it. I couldn't actually handle hearing the words come out of her mouth.

The cake didn't matter.

Nothing really did.

"I need to . . . excuse me. I need to use the bathroom."

I hustled up the stairs and down a long hall, and ducked into the tiny bathroom that was in bad need of an update.

I looked in the mirror and silently called myself a coward. My dark hair was askew, my blue eyes red even though I hadn't shed a tear yet. But I looked shell-shocked. I looked like someone who was afraid of losing her best friend.

"Get a grip, get a grip, get a grip," I muttered, running cold water over my wrists and splashing some onto my neck.

I just couldn't figure out how I was supposed to live without Quinn right down the street from me. She'd been my best friend since I'd moved here in second grade and we'd only ever been separated temporarily by college. Even then we'd seen each other here when we were on break.

When I'd come to Pineville I'd clung to people. My grandmother. Quinn. Later to Josh.

I'd lost my gran and Josh. Losing Quinn felt unbearable.

It felt like being a kid who didn't know when she'd ever see her mom again.

Someone walked into the bathroom and I took a deep breath, and walked back out.

And nearly tripped over Ryan, who was coming down the same hall in the opposite direction.

He reached out and steadied me, his eyes meeting mine. I overcorrected, I admit that. I pushed him. I didn't mean to. I meant to sort of push off of him like a spring board, to get away from the solid wall of his body, but it really was more of a shove.

"Well. Watch where you're going," I said.

It was like I was in sixth grade all over again, when I'd accidentally dropped the bowling ball from my gravity-themed science project onto his solar system.

I'd tried to be nice to Ryan when we'd first met and I'd been given nothing but hostility in return.

The way I coped with my life, with my maternal abandonment, with everything, was to make myself the brightest ray of sunshine around. I was a people pleaser, I knew that. I'd done a stint in therapy in college. I had great reason for my issues.

My mom and I met up with Gran in Lake Tahoe when I was seven. We spent three lovely days together and then she sent me home with my grandmother. She hadn't told me that's what she was doing. Hadn't told me I wouldn't be going back to LA with her. I'd just been . . . sent off. With a backpack that only contained a few of my possessions.

I'd only seen her a scattered, handful of times since then. The last time was five years ago when I'd been in LA for a wedding industry convention and it had been . . . fine.

I did the thing with her I did with everyone. I was smiley. I never asked her why she left me. I didn't want her to cut off contact with me altogether.

The point is, I try. I've always tried. And nine times out of ten, it works.

It had never worked with Ryan.

With him, I'd always managed to be wrong.

"She's happy," he said, his voice hard. "And so is he. Don't ruin it by making it about you."

My jaw dropped. "Excuse me?"

"I get that you don't want to make a traditional cake, and you don't want her to move to New Zealand."

"*Christ Jesus our Lord,* are you really putting the cake on par with them moving to New Zealand? And did you know about them moving to New Zealand?"

"Noah talked to me about it."

Quinn had not talked to me.

And he knew.

"Why didn't Quinn talk to me? She hasn't even actually told me – it's just so obvious and . . . and . . ."

"She doesn't want to hurt you."

I hated him right then. He had no right to give this news to me so casually, acting high and mighty and above it. He had his family here. I didn't have *anyone.*

Maybe, just maybe, my reaction was affected by my earlier encounter with Josh. Or maybe it was just the Ryan of it all. When I'd seen Josh earlier, I'd felt this deep need to smooth it over, and with Ryan . . .

I never felt that.

Ever.

"Well . . . she should treat me like an adult and speak to me, then." And I was determined to act like an adult and not a wounded child, so I walked past him, down those stairs and back to the table with my chin lifted high.

My heart was breaking.

The only thing that softened the blow was the slow realization that seeped through all the shattered cracks.

Two. Weeks.

In New Zealand.

I was the maid of honor.

He was the best man.

Two weeks.

Ryan sat down at the table, and we looked at each other as if we'd both had the same thought.

We were going to be stuck with each other, in a foreign country, for fourteen days. Like the awkward car ride, but for three-hundred thirty-six hours.

It was going to kill me.

If I didn't kill him first.

CHAPTER 2

The First Wedding
Joshua Tree
Five Years Ago

*J*had never been so nervous in my life as I was driving the disparate layers for what would be a three-foot-high cake, nearly nine hours southeast to Joshua Tree for Sarah and Derek's wedding.

Poppy, I saw this gravity-defying inverse wedding cake online and if you could actually do that instead of what we discussed a few months ago . . .

Of course!

I'd said that with great confidence, and I had absolutely no evidence I could pull it off. But it was what Sarah wanted! And the whole point of a wedding was giving the bride everything she wanted, right?

It's impossible.

That was Quinn's verdict when she saw my first practice attempt in my kitchen.

Nothing is impossible with God and fondant, Quinn.

That better be holy fondant then, Poppy, because anything short of divine power isn't going to hold that monstrosity together.

She was wrong, I'd made it work. But I was more than a little worried about it all working out upon assembly in a totally different environment and with an audience.

A watched cake was a much more finicky beast than one that would be seen by no one but the baker, in my experience.

But I had to manage my anxiety around that because this was supposed to be my shift.

I worked in my grandmother's bakery from the time I was a sophomore in high school, until she'd died just six months earlier. It had been the most terrible dark time of my life. I still felt the ache, sharp and hard every time I took a breath.

At first I tried to run the bakery just like she had. But I came to the conclusion pretty quickly that what worked for her wasn't working quite as well for me. So I took a leap.

I was still falling.

I wasn't quite sure if I was going to land in a decent spot. I hired extra people to help cover shifts at the bakery, so that I could invest in wedding cakes. Because I liked the fussy, decorating part of working in a bakery.

I liked the mass production and early mornings a lot less.

You don't have to keep the bakery open. You used to want to be a wedding planner, why are you limiting yourself?

Quinn was my ally in all things, and she'd been concerned about my ambitions getting lost.

Limiting myself would be just doing the bakery. I'm expanding. Halfway.

I felt like it was a reasonable compromise. Yes, I'd gone to school for business management with the hope of starting my own event planning company, but life changed. And I was changing with it.

It felt like a gamble, spending all that money to try to keep the bakery going while I tried to invest in this new business. But so far it was . . . well, I was surviving, anyway.

And working my very first wedding after building a portfolio of cakes for birthday parties, baby showers and bridal showers.

I wanted to be sure I was ready for the main event before I attempted to make a wedding cake.

Last month I'd gone to a convention in LA to get ideas and to talk to experts in the wedding industry. I'd met up with my mom, who'd I'd seen just six months prior at the funeral. If it could be called a funeral.

Gran had been a complicated woman. The people who'd loved her had done so mostly in spite of her. I'd just loved her. But I think she was softer with me than anyone else. Out of guilt, I sometimes thought.

My mom had come and stood by me, large sunglasses on her face to disguise her identity, even though everyone knew who she was.

In Pineville, they just didn't care.

I'd always wondered if that was the real reason she hated it.

Either way it had been a lot of loss and a lot of my mom in the past few months and I still felt raw with it.

This felt like the first step to something new. Something healing.

When I pulled up to the wedding venue, I was astonished by the natural beauty. The trees looked like something from an alien planet. Like palm trees that had grown twisted and bent trying to avoid the harsh sunlight. The sky was a gloriously bleached blue over the round sand-colored rocks and boulders, broad expanses of dirt punctuated by scrubby green plants. It was entirely different to the scenery I was used to.

The lush green and towering pines of Oregon. I would've said that I didn't like the desert.

But this felt magical. Even more so as I took the cake layers out of the back of my car and brought them into the white stucco building that had been allocated as a staging area for the different wedding cast members.

Privately, I thought of us as cast members. All preparing for this big show.

Bits and pieces of it were of course Derek and Sarah. But so much of it was how Derek and Sarah wanted everybody else to see them. A production.

One that was going to be beautiful.

I loved the whole scope of weddings. If I really dreamed big, I would want to help plan the whole wedding, from beginning to end. But baking was my special skill, so it had made the most sense to handle cakes, rather than trying to get into planning.

It connected to the bakery. And I needed to keep the bakery going.

The cake was going to be glorious with this scenery as a backdrop. I had seen pictures, and I had listened as Sarah had described her vision, but until I actually got there, I didn't fully appreciate how spectacular the design was.

The feeling of satisfaction that I got as I looked at the flowers I had selected to go on the cake, the rust colors in context with the desert surroundings, told me that I was in the right place.

That I had made the right decision.

I was so settled in that, that when I turned around and nearly ran smack into the broad, unwelcome chest of Ryan Clark, I couldn't formulate a sentence for a full fifteen seconds. Which doesn't sound like that long, but when you're standing there, looking up at a man who hates you in utter, shocked silence, believe me when I tell you it's an eternity.

"I didn't know that you would be here."

That wasn't what I meant to say. I had no idea what I actually meant to say, but there was no way that it was that. Because that was stupid.

"Why would you?"

He didn't smile. I studied his face for a hint of welcome.

No. And honestly, *why* would I expect a welcome from him? He didn't like me. He never had. And maybe it was because we had a long history of unfortunate incidents, but in my opinion most of it was petty kid stuff.

Things that a person should have gotten over by now.

Things he definitely had not gotten over.

Which might be less of a problem if he wasn't friends with my boyfriend Josh. They were a package deal. They'd hooked up in high school. Josh and I hadn't hooked up until after college.

That meant that whether I wanted to or not, I occasionally found myself in Ryan's surly company.

Though this was the first time I had ever encountered him . . . *in the wild.*

Sure, sometimes I saw him walking down the street in town, but that was different.

He was in context.

This was . . . bizarre.

He had only been around town intermittently for the past few years. His work as a photographer took him around the world. He was a beloved credit to the town of Pineville. A success story. You kind of had to be made of stone to not be somewhat impressed by him, and I was not in any way stony. But that didn't mean that I . . . liked him.

He had done an exhibition of the faces of Pineville, a portrait of the small-town Main St. in America, a stirring collection that showed it wasn't a myth, or a bygone era, but demonstrated the change and diversity that had come to those spaces. The old colliding with the new, the occasional tensions, the acceptance of new ideas and new people – even if it was sometimes met with resistance.

It had been brilliant. And honest. Nothing glossed over or painted with romanticized brushstrokes. Portraits of people and their businesses, captioned by their own words. Comments about the changes that had come to town. Stirring speeches about how wonderful it was that there was a new bookstore, and pride displays in the window. And also laments about the very same.

That display had traveled around exhibitions and galleries for two years before ultimately being installed in the Chamber of Commerce in town. Pineville, warts and all. And while certainly some people were unhappy about it – apparently not everybody liked to see their own bigotry reflected back at them in black-and-white – for the most part, it was roundly praised by the populace.

Too bad he was such a jerk.

It isn't like I meant to break his solar system five minutes before our sixth-grade science fair.

I was carrying a bowling ball.

My project was on inertia.

So it was successful at least.

It had also made me an enemy for life.

It was just that things always seemed to happen with him. And maybe it wasn't even that he held a grudge against me for all of that. Maybe it was just that . . . every time we were near each other it was difficult.

That was what made me so wary about him. And it definitely put a dampener on my joy regarding my very first wedding.

"Why exactly are you here?" I did not recall his name being in the credits. Or, the wedding program, whatever you wanted to call it.

"Last-minute replacement. The photographer they originally hired couldn't make it."

Ryan Clark photographing a wedding. That seemed . . . unexpected.

If asked, I would have said that he would find photographing the wedding a bit too pedestrian for his lofty photography aims.

After all, he'd had a major global exhibition.

"Oh," I said. "I . . . I paid Melissa extra money."

"Okay," he said, looking at me like I was an intrusive jackrabbit that had wandered in from the outdoors, rather than as a human being.

"Melissa, the original photographer."

"I do know who Melissa is. Thank you. I'm unclear as to why you paid her extra money?"

"To photograph the cake. Once I'm done with it. I have to assemble it. But, she was supposed to take some extra pictures for my website."

"Right. Well, I will do that. Everything got forwarded to me. Except for instructions. So."

"Great," I chirped.

It was not great. Really not, that somehow Ryan Clark was going to end up photographing my first wedding cake for my website. It just felt portentous. And I hadn't really been in the market for important.

One thing I've learned is that life doesn't exactly ask you about these things.

So, I determinedly went into the kitchen area and began working to assemble my cake layers. It was a huge cake, enough to feed the three hundred guests they had coming all the way out here to their magnificent venue. I had never served that many people before, but I was pretty confident that everything would go fine. I told myself that, repeatedly, as I assembled the vanilla and spice cake layers, in alternating order and with the largest layer on top and the smallest on the bottom.

Each cake layer sat on its own platform that hung suspended from a special stand designed to let the cake hang in space like a frosted chandelier. Cascading coral and cream-colored roses helped hide the structural elements and support the magic of the illusion.

The hours flew by, and when I was finished, my heart was pounding.

Because it was beautiful. It was exactly what I had promised that it would be. And I just had to get it down to the table at the venue.

The only problem was, as I began to lift the whole cake platform from the counter, I realized it was heavier than I thought, and each layer swung with more force than I wanted. I wasn't an idiot, I had brought a cart to wheel out to my car, which I was going to pull up to the door, but what I hadn't realized was that lifting it off the counter was going to be a physical impossibility for me. And then, of course, that followed that it was going to be impossible to get it into the car.

Great. It was blazing hot outside, so there was no way that I could have decorated it out there. I was finished just in time. I had everything planned down to the minute. Except this. I didn't realize that I was going to have to pump iron too . . .

The door opened again, and in walked Ryan.

"Are you ready for pictures?"

"I don't want you to take pictures on this random counter. I want to take pictures down at the reception venue before the ceremony finishes." That seemed obvious to me. And he was supposed to be an artist. He should know that.

I didn't say that to him though. Which felt like a feat.

"The ceremony doesn't start for twenty minutes. I just finished all the before photography."

"Well, I need to get the cake down there."

"Okay. I probably won't be able to take a picture until just before you cut it."

"That's fine. But I need . . . I need your muscles." I grimaced. He lifted a dark brow. And I hated him right then for being as handsome as he was irritating.

"I told you," he said slowly, his blue eyes never leaving mine. "I only have twenty minutes."

I couldn't explain what those words did to me. It was like the dry desert air suddenly flooded my nose and mouth and left them indescribably dry. While *dryness* wasn't exactly the effect anywhere else.

And I suddenly wished that the floor would open up and swallow me whole. Not even just so I wasn't standing in front of him, but so I didn't have to unpack the implications of that.

"No," I said, rather than putting my head in the oven, "I need help getting the cake off the counter. It's a lot heavier than I anticipated."

"Right," he said.

"Will you help me?"

"Sure."

He crossed the space and I moved back, maybe a little bit further than necessary. And suddenly, I remembered the bowling ball. The science fair.

"Please don't . . . hurt my cake?"

"I'm not going to hurt your cake," he said.

And I realize that the comment had been a miscalculation on my part, because where he had been neutral before, he was irritated now.

And about to touch my cake.

"This is my first wedding," I said.

"Congratulations."

"I just mean, this is what I want to do, because my grandmother died. You know. And I want to expand the business. And I want this to be my focus. And it's really important to me. The cake was . . . well you can see this is an elaborate cake and it was a last-minute change from the bride and I've never done it before but it needs to be perfect." I was breathing hard when I finished my speech.

He looked at me, his expression dispassionate.

"You'll get over it, trust me."

"What does that mean?" I asked.

"It means, that eventually, you will see that weddings are a farcical exercise that do nothing but waste people's time and money."

"Excuse me. You're here photographing it."

"Yes. For money. I wouldn't be here for any other reason."

"Well, I'm here because I like it. I like decorating wedding cakes.

I like finding out what somebody wants and helping make their dreams come true."

"That's what I don't get. How your dreams can revolve around a day. It's unrealistic. As is demanding your baker do a cake that defies the laws of gravity, by the way."

"You are . . . *wow.*"

He ignored me, and slid the cake off of the counter, holding it firmly, his large hands curled around the edges of the big tray. And my heart stopped. He was lifting it effortlessly, no strain whatsoever, but still, I was more than a little bit nervous, watching him hold that cake. I might as well have been watching him hold my baby.

At least, I assumed, that's what it would feel like.

He set the cake on the cart, and my breath exited my body.

Then I gripped the cart. "Thank you." Then I began to wheel it toward the door. "I'm going to need help again, getting it into the car."

"You can't roll it down there?" he asked.

"No. I have to drive it. But there's a paved road to the edge of the venue, and then there's another sidewalk."

"This feels unnecessarily extreme."

"Well. This is what you do when you make people's dreams come true. For love."

"Great."

I led the way with the cart, and he followed me. I rolled the cart carefully down the sidewalk, and right to the edge, where I had parked my car with the hatchback facing toward where I rolled the cake.

I opened the hatchback, the seats were all laid flat, there was a vast field of space, and I had done some testing on birthday parties and the like with driving large cakes short distances. It could be done.

He picked the cake up again. "Okay," I said. "Just follow my instructions. Because you have to kind of lower it to get it underneath the tailgate but you don't want it to swing."

"I've got it," he said.

"No!" I said, as he listed a little bit too close to the edge of the car. And my exclamation may or may not have startled him slightly. Which made his movement a little too big, and made the cake swing, as I'd been afraid it would, and caused the widest layer to hit the side of the car. Leaving a big gouge in the side.

He set it down on the back of the car.

"Oh no," I said.

"You can fix that," he said.

"Oh. Great. I can fix that. Just that simple, right?"

"It's just frosting."

"Maybe you should give me your camera and see if I can make a little disaster that you can fix."

"Should I give you a bowling ball?"

"I knew it. I knew you were going to ruin my cake because I ruined your solar system. That is so petty. And it is childish. You are a small," I said, looking up at him, "petty man."

He wasn't small. I was small. He was six and a half feet tall, built like a brick house and far too imposing and masculine to ever be called anything like childish. But I said it anyway. Because I was furious. An accident would've been one thing. I knew that he had been hanging onto that. I just did.

"You honestly think that I decided to get revenge on you for a sixth-grade science project by scarring your cake?"

"You're the one that mentioned it."

The corner of his mouth lifted upward. "I guess I did."

"So it seems plausible."

"To *you*," he said. "Not to a rational person."

"Well. Well. I . . . You don't even like weddings. You don't care. That's the thing. At the very least, you just don't care about love.

And now you have gone and destroyed this symbol of Derek and Sarah's love."

"Get some extra frosting and slap it on the side once you get down there."

"Are you physically incapable of apologizing?"

"You created the situation, Poppy. I don't know that an apology is warranted."

I was incandescent. I knew that my rage didn't exactly match the drama of the moment. Because the fact was, he was right. It was repairable.

I could fix it. No structural damage had been done.

But for some reason everything felt like it had come to a head. Maybe it was standing there in the hot sun. That I had been in for five minutes. But still.

"You know, you've just always been a dick."

He nodded slowly. "You've always thought so."

I stormed back into the venue building and grabbed different things for serving, and for emergency repairs. And when I went back outside he was gone. Belatedly, I realized my mistake of completely alienating him, since I was going to need help getting the cake out of the car.

I wasn't sure why I had combusted like that. Why the whole thing had combusted like that.

I didn't have the kind of grandmother who would have told me to be nice, or that everybody was fighting a secret battle that we didn't know about. She would have said that Ryan was a Clark, even though he had been adopted into the family late, and wasn't genetically related, he was tainted by association.

She would have said that we were cursed to be at odds, and I had to honor said curse.

My grandma hadn't been a sweet old lady. I loved that about her.

Because if she was nice to you, then you knew that she really cared about you.

She had really cared about me.

My grandma would've hexed Ryan Clark.

She'd have told him to fuck off into the sea.

And I really wished that she was here to do it.

I tried to muster up an incantation.

To wish that his hair would fall out, or that his muscles would atrophy. Except as much as I disliked him, it felt like it would be such a waste that I couldn't bring myself to seriously hope such a thing happened.

So instead, I drove as carefully as possible down the road and toward the isolated spot where the wedding reception was being held. There was a large metal frame with lights strung up and over it, that I knew would look stunning once darkness fell. Tables and chairs were set up beneath a canopy, and that was where the cake table was.

Thankfully, the catering team was down there, and I was able to get help moving it from the car to the table, though it took two men, whereas Ryan had done it by himself.

But that was only because it was a longer walk. I wasn't going to exalt Ryan and his muscles to quite that degree.

I got the cake repaired just in time. Guests began to filter over the rise and down toward the reception area, coming from a trail that was nowhere near the highway.

It took an additional twenty-five minutes for the bride, groom and bridal party to arrive, since they had been getting their pictures taken.

And that was when Ryan appeared. Wordlessly, without speaking to me or making eye contact, he took pictures of the cake.

"Stand beside it," he said, addressing me for the first time.

"What?"

"The cake looks great. You should stand beside it and be in the picture."

"Oh I don't need that."

"Trust me. That's what you should have on your website."

Normally, I would've argued, but there were people watching. So instead, I did what he asked.

I stood behind the cake and smiled, he snapped the picture, and lowered his camera, and that was how I found myself smiling at Ryan Clark. He didn't smile back.

CHAPTER 3

Present Day

"*P*oppy." I turned and looked at Quinn, who was holding up a smudge stick and looking at me accusingly. "Did you try to hex Ryan?"

"No," I said. "I was cleansing."

The house was old and my grandma had always said it needed the occasional smudging to ward off ghosts and bad luck drifting over from the Clarks.

The family feud was a storied one. The Loves and the Clarks had been in Pineville since the gold rush, and they were predisposed to hate one another. It was said to have begun due to an alleged affair between Ezekiel Clark and Madeline Love on the Oregon Trail. True story. There was a near duel and everything.

After the affair, Madeline and Ezekiel had gone back to their respective spouses, who had then opened businesses on the main streets of Pineville. In buildings that had been in our families for all the generations since – the general store eventually becoming a restaurant still run by the Clarks, the old saloon eventually becoming my gran's bakery.

But the feud didn't die with Madeline and Ezekiel.

In the early 1900s the Loves and Clarks had opened competing restaurants. There had been wild accusations of sabotage and even one instance of accused intentional food poisoning.

In the Depression era, businesses on Main Street closed and there had been a desperate attempt at reviving some of the old gold mines in the hills and the Clarks and Loves had competed bitterly over a claim that both felt they had rights to.

The Clarks had won. And the Love family had maintained that the Clarks' superior financial success in generations since had come from that mine, stolen from the Loves.

The feud might have evolved through the years, but it never ended.

In the eighties, my gran opened up her bakery around the time Hamish Clark opened his restaurant. Right across the street, in the same buildings our ancestors had occupied once upon a time.

When Hamish launched breakfast, with pastries, Gran had taken it as a direct attack on her business. She'd started offering pancakes and waffles. When she'd added bacon, Hamish had taken it as shots fired.

I knew all about it, even though I wasn't born then, because my gran didn't forgive or forget. Ever.

Maybe Ryan and I were fated to be enemies.

It had all started with my attempts at being friends with him when he'd first come to town. There were no Clarks in my age group, so the feud had never been a reality to me.

Though funnily enough, it was the feud that first brought us into contact.

When the Clarks adopted Ryan, we were in sixth grade. And Gran and Hamish Clark might have businesses across the street from each other, but they were not on speaking terms.

So when mail arrived at the bakery addressed to Hamish Clark, I was tasked with walking it over to the restaurant.

When I walked in, there was a boy sitting on a shiny red stool at the lunch counter, his dark hair in his face. He turned to look at me and I was struck by the intensity of his blue eyes. And the anger in them.

It felt like the anger was directed at me.

I couldn't quite muster up the courage to say hi to him, but I couldn't forget him either. So when he came to school that first day I decided, feud or no feud, that boy was going to be my friend.

I would make him like me.

That had gone down like an absolute lead balloon. For months I tried. And then . . . there was the science fair.

Which had been the moment that cemented Ryan and me as victims of the family feud, no matter how hard I'd tried to make it otherwise.

I'd been so proud of my inertia project, with a massive bowling ball and a big ramp to roll it down. It had been the first time I'd really been brave enough to ask my gran to help me with something. I was always so afraid of being too big of a burden that usually I just tried to do things myself.

But not that time, and Gran had even come to the science fair to watch my demonstration.

Ryan Clark was next to me. The new boy who'd only been in town for a few months, a former foster child who'd been adopted into the Clark family. I'd tried befriending him but he'd been . . . standoffish. And every attempt at being nice to him had gone awry. He'd always acted like he wanted to get away from me as quickly as possible and I just couldn't stand that.

We'd had one nice interaction. *One.* And I'd taken it as a personal victory. I had been hungry for another one.

He'd made a solar system which was really, really good and I'd gone over to tell him I thought so, but then tripped and launched my bowling ball right into all his planets, which were sitting on the floor waiting to be suspended from a rafter he'd constructed in his booth.

What the fuck is wrong with you?

He'd growled that at me with all the deep anger that lived inside abandoned kids – I knew because I felt the same anger but I never let it out.

It was an accident . . .

You're always trying to get my attention like a sad puppy, but I don't want you around me. Leave me the hell alone!

That was the end of any possibility of us ever being friends.

Or maybe it just confirmed what he'd been trying to tell me all along: he didn't like me.

And at first he might not have had a reason to, but then I gave him one and he'd held onto it like a talisman all these years.

In the two months since we'd been jointly asked to be maid of honor and best man, nothing had risen up to change our personal status quo.

Nothing good could happen between us without something enormously shitty to balance it out.

This was the way.

He'd been Josh's best friend for years, Ryan and I had some nice moments during that time. When he was in town, sometimes we all went out for a drink and it was good. He'd joined a D&D campaign I was in once and he had not tried to kill me. So there was that.

And then there had been the weddings.

Two and three had almost been nice.

We'd almost been friends for a minute.

But just a minute. Because we were us.

Contact since the maid of honor/best man titles had been bestowed had been minimal, but we were involved in planning a big going away party at Quinn's parents' house for all the locals who weren't making the trek to NZ to see the happy couple tie the knot which meant Ryan Clark was *in my texts*.

An irritating development. But not a hexing offense.

"Grandma was the one who hexed. I would never try anything that intense. I'd end up deflating my own boobs or something."

"I can't argue with that," Quinn said.

"Your lack of faith in my witchcraft is disturbing."

"I just know you too well. In hand-to-hand combat defending a friend using nothing but your determination and berserker rage, I would bet on you. For skilled spell work? Not so much."

And I couldn't disagree. I had a sporadic set of skills. Team sports? No. Wild summer camp games that relied on grit and an inability to give up? Yes. Sewing? No. Cake decorating. Yes.

"Speaking of your berserker rage," Quinn said. "Have you forgiven me for deciding to move away or are you going to sabotage my cake and never speak to me again?"

I felt myself wither. I leaned over the counter and rested my forearms against the cool white surface. "First of all, you know I could never sustain not speaking to you again. Second of all, New Zealand still has internet and phone service, I hear. So it's not like we'll never speak." I was trying to be brave even thought I felt gouged.

But the problem was me, and I knew it. People moved away and it wasn't personal. They moved away and it wasn't going to sever relational ties entirely. I knew that.

My specific wounds weren't for Quinn to manage for the rest of her natural life. But it felt like . . . a lot.

I'd come to terms with my mom. More or less. I'd also come to terms with the fact that – much like putting sprinkles straight into cake batter – if you experience something while you're still raw, it ends up baked in.

I was a funfetti cake of abandonment issues.

Gran's death, the out-of-the-blue-no-fault-no-reason breakup with Josh, were sprinkles on the cake. They weren't foundational in the same way, but they were there.

They'd changed me.

I wouldn't have said I was a romantic, even then. I felt like I'd had a practical outlook on romance. I had never wanted extraordinary sums of butterflies. Just stability.

I used to think if I found the right man and I found love and I got married, I wouldn't have to worry about being left. Not because marriage as an institution is so sacred and stable, but because I was sure I could find the *right* one. I was sure Josh was the right one. Seven years and I thought I couldn't be more certain.

I'd been wrong.

My phone flashed and Josh's name popped up on the screen. Another testament to my abandonment issues, after he'd come to pick his stuff up that night two months ago, we'd slid back into texting each other. Not romantically. And I never instigated it. But it was like I was on his friend list again.

There was something comforting about it. It made me feel less abandoned. Like I could still keep one grip on a person who felt foundational to my life rather than losing them entirely.

This is very you.

And under it was a picture of a mug with a raccoon holding a cupcake.

LOL I said, my mouth barely twitching.

Was this . . . him trying to be friends? Did I want to be friends?

Well. It seemed churlish to not attempt it.

See you at Quinn's party tonight?

It stood to reason Josh would be there. And it was another chance to . . . be friendly.

I sent a thumbs up emoji and put my phone down.

I was very aware Quinn was staring at me. "I know we'll speak," she said. "But I also know . . ."

"That I am a shattered feeble mess when it comes to anything that feels like change and people leaving? Yes. True. But that's not your problem."

I was torn. Because I wanted my feelings catered to — who didn't? But I also didn't want to feel burdensome during the happiest time of Quinn's life.

"You're not a problem, Poppy. You're my best friend. I'm scared to move away, to be honest. This whole thing has been . . . very not me. But Noah is something I could never have planned for. I thought I'd end up married to one of the hometown guys when they came breezing back in after failing out in the big city. I figured I would work for my dad's accounting business until I took it over after he retired. I just . . . I didn't think I'd ever be the one to change this much. But he makes me want adventure."

I said nothing about the very short nature of their relationship and how little I trusted such things because my issues were mine and some thoughts were inside thoughts.

"You don't have to justify yourself to me." For a second, though, I was envious. Because my last relationship had made me want to close myself up in my grandma's house and never leave it and never risk myself again.

It had made me want to make cakes for other people's weddings forever, and never think of my own again. Because there wouldn't be one.

I'd wanted love.

I'd been convinced I had it.

And maybe if he'd cheated or he'd transformed into a monster I could have dealt with it. Maybe I could have recategorized it all, because if he'd been lying about who he was the whole time, then I could have pretended I never knew him, and therefore never loved him.

The whimper it went out with had been worse than any bang.

This isn't going anywhere.

He'd just said it, like that, on our couch two weeks before Christmas. While I was looking at the Christmas tree.

Wouldn't we have gotten married by now if it was supposed to be forever?

It isn't that what he said wasn't wildly hurtful. It was. It still was.

But it was the fact that all that had been swirling around inside that man's brain while we went to bed together every night and I'd had no idea. And I couldn't even be outraged because people were allowed to change their minds. Because he'd been honest with me.

He hadn't been cruel, he hadn't blamed me, he hadn't betrayed me. He wanted a different life, he thought we could both have more.

But I didn't want more.

I'd wanted exactly what we'd had. Nights at home and toothbrushes in the same cup. Comingled coffee mugs. Of course, we'd had issues. Everyone did. But we'd compromised on them. I'd found it easy.

The biggest point of contention had been my traveling for weddings, but we'd . . . worked it out kind of. It had been a big deal for me to do it even knowing it bothered Josh, and I had.

I was especially grateful for that since the relationship had ended.

Now I understood I couldn't pin my security on another person.

Quinn leaving was a great example of why I couldn't.

She'd been my best friend since second grade.

"Well, I'm sad," Quinn said. "Sad to leave you and to leave my parents and to leave here. I'm just doing it anyway."

I couldn't really understand that. All I'd ever wanted was security and safety and permanence. Leaving that behind and betting it all on a guy I'd known for less than a year, moving to a foreign country . . .

Could. Not. Be. Me.

"I appreciate your sadness on my behalf, Quinn."

"And I appreciate you providing goodies for tonight."

"I would literally be offended if anyone else baked them. It would be a sugar-based infidelity and our relationship can stand distance, but I don't know if it could weather that."

"Hate to break it to you but I may have to eat cakes baked by other people when I live on the other side of the world."

I pretended to consider that. "You can have a get out of jail free card in New Zealand. I won't ask about your buttercream affairs as long as they occur over the date line."

I congratulated myself internally for my maturity and magnanimity.

"You could move to New Zealand," Quinn pointed out.

She was smiling like she knew it was silly. But I heard the hopeful note in her voice, and honestly . . . I felt a little bubble of *what if* rise up inside me. I could. Gran was gone and my mom coming to visit was a blue moon event that I could and would never array my life around.

But this house was a tether. This town was part of me.

Gran's legacy with the bakery. My place here. It all meant too much to me.

The security and familiarity meant too much to me.

"I just feel guilty that I'm leaving and you're staying in a town that contains Ryan Clark."

I laughed. A hoot, really. "You're making me co . . . whatever this wedding with him."

Quinn pressed her hand to her chest. "*I* don't hate Ryan. He's the reason Noah and I are together. The author of my fate."

"He's not Jesus, Quinn." I went to my fridge and opened it aggressively, revealing the trays of goodies I'd made for tonight. Cupcakes, tiny pies – savory and sweet – and little petit fours.

Quinn gasped in appropriate excitement over everything and I took that as the offramp from this very sad and difficult conversation to something lighter and more casual.

We would have two weeks in New Zealand before the wedding to spend time together. And I would be able to imagine my friend in her new home. Yes, it was a long flight and I wasn't a huge fan of planes, but it was just . . . a pill and a long night over the Pacific Ocean. I could visit.

Quinn would visit me.

It would be okay.

I ignored the weird panicky sensation that made me feel like I wanted to peel my own skin off and escape the discomfort filling my body.

It just happened when I felt life shift and change. It didn't mean things were really that bad, it just meant that I was dealing with normal things that were especially hard for me, but I had practice with it and I would be fine.

Quinn hung out and we got ready for the party together. The rest of the bridal party pulled into my driveway about forty minutes before show time.

Hannah, Caitlin and Sierra filled my tiny living room with enthusiastic chatter and balloons.

I batted a balloon to the side and tried to smile. The truth was, I wasn't being left in Pineville with only Ryan for company. I'd known all of these women since at least middle school and they were all good friends. Though not my *best* friends.

Only Quinn was my best friend.

Noah and Quinn had met at Caitlin's wedding, so she took partial credit for the relationship. Fair, I thought, but I'd still known Quinn longer so deserved my maid of honor positioning.

Hannah had married her high school sweetheart when she was twenty, so they were a decade into marriage with three kids who were all in elementary school. She was great, but living a totally different life than I was.

Sierra had gotten married right before I started my cake business and had two kids who were still toddling around in diapers. Hannah and Sierra weren't coming as early to the wedding because of the logistics of children.

I was trying to be buoyed by this atmosphere of friendship and not depressed by being the odd one out.

I was, at this point, opting to be the odd one.

I was consciously objecting to the institution of marriage.

Even if it made my heart feel like it was being twisted at the center because I really did love weddings. I really believed in soulmates.

At least, I'd always wanted to. Deeply and desperately.

I wasn't mourning Josh so much really. I was mourning a belief system.

Because, in spite of it all, I'd believed in love.

I still did, really. I couldn't look at my friends and their lives and convince myself love wasn't real. But how I saw myself experiencing it had changed completely.

That was a little bit sad. But nothing about tonight was supposed to be sad. We were celebrating Quinn. Celebrating that she had found love.

That she was brave. That she was going on an adventure.

I absolutely could be happy for her for that.

It wasn't a struggle.

We all gathered the goodies and headed to the party earlier than it started so that we could help get things set up and I was overcome by a weird nostalgia. Like this was every slumber party I'd been to in middle and high school and not a goodbye party for my friend getting married and moving across the world.

But soon people began to pull into the driveway and it was time.

Quinn's parents' house was a far cry from the modest place that I had grown up in with my grandmother. It was built into the side of a mountain just on the outskirts of town, with a large expansive deck overlooking the town below. There was a massive pool, and a huge courtyard area where we'd had innumerable parties.

It was so strange to see it like this now.

With her parents, and other people from that generation, plus everyone we knew from high school. A blend of those two parts of our lives. A lot of our old friends had kids, while many didn't. Another little clash.

Different pieces of life all present and accounted for.

Including Josh, who was standing by a table with chips and dip looking familiar and alien to me at the same time. It was weird that you could see someone more days than you didn't, for years, and then suddenly not see them at all.

"It was nice of you to come," I said, smiling so that even I believed I meant it.

"Yeah. I couldn't let Quinn leave the country without saying goodbye."

Of course, he didn't know or love Quinn well enough to go all the way across the world to see her get married. But who wouldn't want to come to her parents' awesome house to say goodbye?

"You made all of the desserts?"

That was such an odd question. He knew that was what I did. He'd lived with me for years while I did it.

"Yeah," I said. "I did."

"Hi."

I looked up and saw Ryan standing behind Josh. He was addressing Josh, but there was a strange edge to his demeanor, probably just exposure to me. Josh turned around. "Hey man. I haven't seen you much recently."

"No," Ryan said, an agreement, but it didn't necessarily sound easy.

"Well, when you guys get back from the wedding, we should get another campaign together."

Ryan shrugged. "I'm not coming back here after the wedding. I'm taking an assignment overseas."

That was the first I'd heard of it. But then, why would Ryan tell me anything.

"Oh wow," said Josh. "That's . . . awesome for you."

"Yeah. It'll be interesting."

So, I wasn't going to be stuck here with Ryan Clark. How . . . how interesting.

"Where are you going?" I asked.

"Croatia. The Czech Republic. Switzerland."

"That's really interesting," I parroted his own words back to him without meaning it and felt stupid. "I mean . . . good for you."

There was a glint in his eye that I couldn't read, and I suddenly felt all the discomfort that had been mitigated by my shock.

Because for five seconds, things had been okay between myself and Ryan. And then it had been ruined.

Then all the ease had been sucked straight out of the vicinity.

And there was none left to be had.

I should have been happy to hear that he was leaving. Or at the very least I should have been neutral about it. But I didn't feel neutral, as I stood there, looking around the courtyard, and the evidence of how much time had passed, how much everything was changing, at this one last moment where I was going to have my friend here in town with me.

Now even my nemesis was moving away.

And I had found out while I was standing there talking to my ex-boyfriend, trying as hard as I could to be friendly and neutral and not . . . remember that I had spent seven years chucking his dirty underwear into the hamper.

Not that I had always had to do that. And not that he had never done it for me.

It was just . . . It was weird. That was all.

It was like someone had gripped the pavement beneath my feet and pulled it right out from under me. I couldn't find my footing. I couldn't find my breath.

I didn't want Josh and Ryan to see me struggling for either one. What a nightmare.

"Well great. Everything is going great for everybody. Everybody is doing life." I grinned, and then I went straight to where the margaritas were being served out of a little portable trailer. It was some trendy pop-up drink bar, and under normal circumstances I would pause and ponder how cute it was. But in this present circumstance,

I was just pondering my need to drink something that might dull the edge of this discomfort.

This wasn't like a wedding. I didn't have a giant cake to serve.

I didn't have to stay sober.

And that was my justification as the night wore on and my drink consumption increased.

I wasn't the only one, so it wasn't especially notable. Except, to my horror, the drinks were not making me feel giddy at a certain point. Instead, the drinks were making me feel maudlin. I was battling crushing, intense feelings of loneliness and the most appalling self-pity I'd ever experienced, and I was trying to keep a smile on my face with diminished control of my faculties.

Apparently, some people got sexy the more margaritas they consumed. And I got weepy. Fantastic.

I wasn't a big drinker, so it wasn't a theory that I had tested to its limits. Or even part way to its limits.

"You look like you need to go home and get tucked into bed."

That voice, gravelly and familiar and suggesting I get tucked into bed, created an avalanche of reaction inside me that I wished I could ignore. But everything felt sharp, like I'd been running with emotional scissors and fallen right on the point.

His voice also felt too sharp.

I turned and then instinctively stepped away, because he was too close and tall and I just *couldn't* with him. "I don't have any idea what you're talking about, Ryan."

"You look upset. You don't need to . . . you don't need to do that here."

I was mad. Because I felt like it was another scolding from him. Another slap on the wrist about me having emotions because everything in my life was changing dramatically. That it wasn't his right to go ahead and scold me. To try and tell me what I was allowed to feel, or make me feel like those feelings weren't in position. "Fuck off," I said.

"I could do that, or I can give you a ride home, Poppy. It's really up to you."

"I don't need you to give me a ride home."

"You look like a lost lamb. One that's about to burst into tears."

"I am not . . . I am not *a lost lamb*. What the hell does that even mean?"

"If you could see your face right now you would know exactly what it meant."

"Well I can't see my face. So there."

"You don't want Josh to see you this upset, do you?"

I frowned. "Josh?" I laughed. "Josh doesn't have anything to do with this."

"He doesn't?"

"No. I don't give a fuck about him. It's Quinn. It's just everything. It's all the changing. It's all that . . . and you're leaving too?"

"You're mad that I'm leaving?"

"I don't want things to change anymore. I don't like it. I want to stay in my grandmother's house forever. And I wish she was still there in her bedroom. I want the bakery to always be there. I want your parents' restaurant to always be there. I even want your god-awful photography exhibition to always be there in the Chamber of Commerce where everybody talks about how amazing you are and I scoffed because I think you're a dick. And I want *you* to be there. Being . . . grumpy and unknowable and my nemesis."

I could hear myself, I just couldn't really stop myself. He was staring at me like I was insane or maybe just sad and I still couldn't stop the word vomit.

"I just want to grab onto this moment and hang onto it. So that it doesn't pass. Because next week we are going to be in New Zealand. And Quinn is going to marry Noah. And she's going to stay there. And she is my beautiful unicorn of a best friend. Before her I didn't have any friends."

"You're going to be fine," he said.

"Well. I feel awful. *Disgusting.*"

And a little bit like I was going to be sick. So that was great.

"Excuse me," I said and then I dashed into the bathroom in the pool house and cast up my accounts.

I stayed in there for a long moment, hating everything. But I just hope that Ryan and his misguided attempt at . . . saving me from myself? Saving everybody else from me? Was over.

I stepped outside, and nearly ran into him.

"I'm happy to give you a ride home," he said.

"I'm with the bridal party. I don't need a ride home."

He stared at me, and I ignored my irritation. I ignored everything else. "You were just sick," he said.

Humiliation washed through me. I didn't know why it felt so awful. Only that I felt the worst and saddest and more embarrassed I could ever remember feeling. Perhaps that was the tequila. But maybe everything was hopeless.

You could never discount that as a possibility.

"I don't need anything from you," I said, shoving past him.

"I thought you needed me to stay," he said. "And be your nemesis."

That stopped me in my tracks. "Well, I'm drunk, and I am being an idiot. I don't care what you do or where you go. It won't make any difference to me."

And with that parting shot, I went and rejoined the rest of the party.

CHAPTER 4

$\mathcal{T}$he day we were set to leave for New Zealand, I was still mired in my embarrassment from Quinn's going away party. The only thing that I could be grateful for was that I hadn't made an ass of myself on a grand stage. It had just been with Ryan.

And I could handle that. Because that was basically the story of my life. Whether I wanted it to be or not. There was always something with him. Always.

Of course, the infamous science fair incident, but also the time that our ninth-grade class went to the coast in vans, and I happened to slam his hand in the van door when we got out — which was a total accident. And there were things that weren't individually notable. Just the way that we could never manage to communicate without offending each other. It was years of it. Of speaking at cross purposes and generally misunderstanding one another. And then at a certain point, I'd just decided not to bother.

There was no fixing something like that once it was broken.

Of course, me drunkenly telling him I didn't care about him or what he did was probably not a great thing either.

It was always something.

Fated enemies. That was the thing.

I had decided to take the earliest flight possible from our small-town airport down to LA for the evening flight to New Zealand. Because I was paranoid about something happening.

Every time I traveled, whether it was a road trip or air travel, I had to make peace with my death.

I wish I was kidding. But there was something about leaving my comfort zone that did that to me. I was all kinds of rattled as it was, so I wasn't in the best frame of mind when I boarded the overly small plane at six a.m.

The problem with short flights was they were a little bit too short to medicate through.

I traveled with a small pharmacy to help me manage the symptoms of my travel anxiety.

I opted for one that my doctor had given me because it literally kept my heart from racing.

It didn't really affect your brain, but it mitigated panic symptoms.

Basically by calming your body down and theoretically tricking your brain into thinking you were fine. I'd had mixed success with it.

I traveled a lot for work. I appreciated that there was a certain level of irony in that.

Because I also could have just run the bakery. But I didn't. It was like I was always fighting with my neuroses.

Trying to push myself past them. Trying to . . . learn to live with them, I guess.

I questioned my own sanity and decision-making on that two-hour flight to LA.

And then I questioned it again as I rattled around the international terminal for ten hours.

I could have gone somewhere else, but then I would've had to come back, and that would've meant dealing with airport security again, which was one of my least favorite things in the entire world. Really, everything about airports stress me out. Not just the flying. There have always been a whole lot of factors to my travel anxiety.

With driving, I was usually fine the morning I actually left. It was a brief night before panic, about all the dangers that would befall me on the road, and then by the time I actually got on the road, I didn't think of them at all.

With flying, though, it was everything. What if I didn't catch my flight? What if it got canceled? Or then there was the awful what if it didn't get canceled? And I actually had to get on the plane. If I was running late, or having difficulty getting through security, and in danger of missing my flight, should I push to try to make that flight, or should I accept it as fate trying to keep me off the flight?

There was so much magical thinking involved in an air trip.

It just about sent me over the edge every time.

But I had managed to reduce myself to a little zombie rattling around the different stores, eating, sitting in corners and disassociating.

I did prefer that to trying to race to my gate.

But perhaps *prefer* was overstating it. Honestly.

My heart lifted when I saw a group of familiar people walking toward the gate.

Quinn.

I stood up and met her part way to our gate. "I'm so glad you're here," I said.

"I really can't believe you took the earliest flight."

"I can't believe you took the latest one. What if something was canceled? Delayed?"

"On second thought it's probably for the best that you took your own flight," Quinn said, patting me on the shoulder.

I didn't see Ryan, but decided against asking.

Because I didn't need to know his whereabouts. So much as I just wanted to avoid him after the party.

He knew I'd vomited. That was the thing. He hadn't seen it but he knew.

It was a horror.

I hadn't told Quinn about that, and I didn't want her asking.

Because my little meltdown at her party wasn't her problem, it was mine. I should be grateful that Ryan had been there for me to make an ass of myself at, because the alternative was potentially me finding Quinn and vomiting my sadness on her and I would have really hated myself for that.

Soon, the whole area was filled up as we got prepared for boarding and I turned my focus to my boarding pass, and making sure I had my passport open to the right page.

I had used my passport to go to Canada once. That was it.

So this was very outside my comfort zone.

But it was too late. Too late to make a different decision. I was in this for Quinn.

I waited in the massive line of people for my boarding group to get called. Quinn and Noah were flying business class, with lie flat beds – must be nice – and the rest of us were interspersed throughout economy class.

My seat was by the window, which had been a devil's bargain. Did I want ease getting out and using the bathroom, or did I want to be able to curl up and lean against the plane wall, and also have control over whether or not I had to look out and see the ground below. I had opted for window control. Because it was what made me feel the most secure.

I slipped into my seat and shoved my overstuffed bag beneath it, and a few moments later, a child that couldn't be any more than seven years old plopped into the chair beside me. He elbowed me, and then grabbed an iPad out of his bag and started to play a game without headphones in.

I really did wonder what I had done to anger God recently. Because it was starting to feel pointed.

A man slid into the aisle seats, his legs spread wide as he sat splayed, looking at his phone. Then the woman leaned over our seats. "Excuse me."

The man didn't look up. Neither did the kid.

"Yes?" I asked.

"Would you be willing to trade seats with me?"

"What?"

"This is my son," she said. "I have a window seat."

The man kept ignoring her. As if he could not have also traded and put her next to her child. Though, I guess in fairness, she had a window seat. Why the hell hadn't she booked it with her kid?

I was anxious, and experiencing what I affectionately referred to as *airport stomach*, which was when I began to feel like I was in urgent need of a bathroom, and that I might not make it to take off, and the blessed moment when the seatbelt sign went off. And mostly, I didn't want to be talked to or messed with.

"I . . . sure."

"Oh thank you. Thank you. We were in row 54. Back there."

I looked back where she was gesturing.

"Ah." Well, that just sucked. But I was going to hate this flight either way.

"Right," I said.

I stood, and the kid pulled his legs up in the seat. The man acted like nothing was happening.

"Excuse me," I said to him.

He looked up at me, unconcerned. And he didn't move.

Frankly, this lady could have her kid *and* that guy. I did not want them as seatmates anyway.

I grabbed my bag, and then slipped past Mr. Manspread, though I did whack him with the corner of my bag. Normally I'd have apologized but he'd put himself in my bag's path.

I just wanted to sit down and take a lorazepam.

I worked my way down the narrow aisle, heading even deeper into the recesses of the massive aircraft. But I didn't care where I sat, honestly, because I'd be out of it for as much of the flight as I could manage anyway.

People were still in the aisles taking items out of bags in the

overhead bins and generally getting situated. I kept my eyes on the
row numbers and a woman moved into the aisle followed by a man
who was facing away from me. The woman gestured up toward
the overhead bin. She was much shorter than the man and didn't
seem like she could reach her belongings. He took the bag out – a
heavy looking bag – with one arm.

I couldn't help but admire the masculine physicality because I
was only human after all. And who didn't enjoy watching a tall
muscular man handle things?

Then he turned sideways and my heart launched itself into my
throat.

Oh no.

No.

I had just paused to check out Ryan Clark because of course I had.

The woman was looking at him like he was savior of the world
and after she was done with her bag he hefted it easily back into the
overhead bin, and both filed back into their seat. I continued to
walk toward them with ever growing trepidation because it had
almost looked like . . .

Like maybe it was possible that was my new row.

Dread crept over me as I continued on.

And there it was. Row 54.

And just *of course.*

There he was.

The man, the myth, the pain in my fucking ass.

In a middle seat. With an empty one right next to the window
which was absolutely, surely mine.

My mouth went dry.

"Excuse me," I said.

Both the woman in the aisle seat and Ryan looked up.

His expression shifted, his brow lifting.

"I just traded places with someone who wanted to sit with her
child."

The aisle woman smiled wordlessly like she wasn't sure why I was sharing that level of detail, because of course why would she assume I knew Ryan.

"How nice of you," Ryan said.

It didn't actually sound like he thought it was especially nice of me, but I was too busy trying to do math on what the odds were that my seat switch had landed me next to him.

I had a wild mental image of him deciding not to move, and forcing me to shimmy over him like I was giving him a lap dance. The very idea sent a streak of erotic panic through me. I was loath to call it that, but I couldn't deny it, since a sensation stabbed me through the stomach, but it didn't stop there.

No. It managed to find itself between my legs. And I could only give thanks when he got up out of his seat, following the woman who vacated.

"Thank you," I said, slipping in and taking my window seat.

"Middle seat, huh?" I said, looking at him sideways. Because it was weird. He was very tall. And this was a very cramped seat to choose.

"Airline miles," he said.

"I don't think that means you have to book a middle seat."

"I booked what was left."

"Right."

I started to arrange myself in the seat. Taking everything that I needed out of my shoulder bag, from my noise canceling headphones to my various pills, and a bottle of water.

Ryan moved beside me, and pulled out the white airsick bag, gesturing toward me. "Did you need an extra?"

I narrowed my eyes. "No."

"Just making sure. These are the only shoes I have on the plane."

"A gentleman wouldn't mention that," I said.

"I felt like we had a long-standing understanding between the two of us that I am not a gentleman in any capacity."

I thought about New Orleans.

"True. You are not."

"You don't like flying?" he asked, looking pointedly at my prescription pill bottle. I took one of the small white tablets and slipped it into my mouth, swallowing a mouthful of water and the pill down quickly. "No. I don't."

"It's—"

"Safer than driving," I finished his cliché for him. "I know. Driving also scares me. So."

"Why?"

"You know what I like to do when I get on a plane? I like to put on my noise canceling headphones and my sleep mask and completely block out the world. With that and the power of pharmaceuticals I'm able to manage this without having a panic attack."

"Okay. Far be it for me to interrupt your routine. But, it's a very long flight. And we're going to land at about five-thirty in the morning New Zealand time. So it's better if you can stay awake for a little bit. Eat some food."

"Thanks. Really."

"Why don't you like traveling?"

I turned my head, still rested against the head rest. "The variables," I said. "And why are you asking?"

"I'm distracting you."

"Why?"

"Because believe it or not, I'm not a monster."

I knew that, that was the problem.

"You travel a lot for someone who doesn't like it," he said. "So I'm curious."

"Yes I do. And I don't like it because I like being home. I don't know. I like being at another place, but I don't like getting there. And pretty much I like knowing that my home is there waiting for me, and there is always a little bit of fear that I won't make it back there."

"I think that's the beauty of having a home you can count on. Knowing that it will be there."

"The world is perilous," I said.

"Sure. Crossing the street is perilous."

I frowned. "Don't give me a new anxiety."

"No one can give you a new anxiety without your permission. I'm pretty sure Eleanor Roosevelt said that."

"She didn't," I said.

I looked at him out of the corner of my eye and saw that he was . . . it wasn't quite a smile, but there was a softening around the corners of his mouth, and I didn't quite know what to do with that. He was maybe trying to make me feel better. He had kind of tried to do that at Quinn's parents' last week, and I had been entirely unreceptive to it.

It made me feel guilty.

I didn't like having any guilt associated with my Ryan Clark experience because the thing about having a lifelong nemesis was that of all the people in Pineville, I never felt obligated to try to please him. Because I couldn't. There was no way. No matter what I did everything went wrong. So I embraced it. And just let it be like that.

I didn't like it when things upset the balance.

Things like the camaraderie of the second and third wedding. And then the discomfort at the end of that third wedding.

And, of course, the fifth wedding.

I didn't even let myself think about the fifth wedding.

"Maybe I can never really trust life on that level."

"Yeah I can understand that."

The instructional video for the flight started, and I reflexively took out my noise canceling headphones and put them on.

He lifted up the left side. "You're supposed to listen to the instructions from the crew," he said.

I pressed the ear piece back over my ear. "I don't."

"Why is that?"

I lifted a shoulder. "If we have a disaster I am simply going to expire from fear."

"That doesn't seem like a great plan."

"It's not a plan. It's a fact. If we have a catastrophic situation, I'm done. I'm not even going to try to live through that level of terror."

"Come on, you're a fiercer fighter than that. Remember the great bear war."

Classic second wedding reference. We hadn't done references in a long time because they were dangerous now.

I huffed a laugh. "That was different. I'm not a fighter of any kind in these sorts of situations."

And I meant it. I never listened to those instructions because I knew there was no way I was going to be any help to anybody in heaven in error emergency. Not only that, my anxiety couldn't even allow for a situation where life vests might prove useful if our plane were to end up in the Pacific.

No thanks.

He lifted up my headphone here a second later. "It's over."

"I require complete silence and isolation for takeoff."

My sleep mask velcroed at the back, and I put it on over the top of my headphones, squishing them to my ears.

I closed my eyes and laid my head back against the seat, and waited.

When the plane started to move, I knew that familiar sweep of panic, even as my muscles began to relax thanks to the pill. It wasn't quite doing enough to cancel out the panic. Because my panic was fierce. He was right about one thing, parts of me were fiercer than others. And my anxiety was a real contender.

"Do you know how to use your seat as a flotation device in the event of a water landing?"

His mouth was too close to my ear and I shivered.

I dramatically unstuck my face mask, which made a loud ripping sound, and took off my headphones. "What?"

"Since you didn't listen . . ."

"Okay. So let's say I did know and we managed to make a water
landing. We would be little *floating pieces of chum*."

"Chum?" he asked, lifting his brows.

"Yes. And if there were great whites they would come up from
underneath us and take one big bite, which just leaves you to bleed
out. The tigers and hammerheads would simply savage us."

"You're an expert on shark hunting behavior?"

"Yes. Shark Week."

Ryan shifted in his seat and I was suddenly very aware his shoulder was touching mine. "You . . . watch Shark Week?"

"Yes, Ryan."

"I've never understood Shark Week."

I blinked. "It's a week of quality shark programming." I had
watched it ever since I was a child. Every summer the week of
shark-themed nature shows on TV had been a highlight for me.

It was comforting. I'd watched it in LA in the apartment I
shared with my mom, and it continued on when I was sent to
Pineville with Gran. Shark Week was a constant.

"But I don't get it," he said.

"There's nothing to get!"

"Why would anyone *want* a week of shark programming?"

"Because sharks are scary!" I said.

"You think airplanes are scary too, do you also watch plane
week?"

"There is no such thing as *plane week*, Ryan, and I think you
know that."

There was a dinging sound and then a voice came over the
speaker announcing that we could now take out our larger elec-
tronic devices.

"Hey look at that, champ. You made it through takeoff."

The plane wasn't climbing and I didn't have that sick, dizzy feeling coursing through me anymore. Of course, the pill was taking effect and I had to ask myself why I had now – two times – put myself in a position where I was at diminished capacity with Ryan.

My muscles were beginning to relax, which was an incredibly weird sensation. I realized that I never relaxed next to him. Ever. It was a weird, out-of-body sensation.

"Just eleven more hours to go," I said.

"You'll sleep through most of them."

"My seatmate won't stop talking to me." I gave him a squinty-eyed look and sat back.

I spared the woman in the aisle seat a glance and saw she had headphones firmly in place.

"People are so rude," he said.

"So rude," I agreed.

It felt easy sitting with him. I felt floaty.

I was drugged.

Not magically getting along with Ryan. I had to remember that.

Because when I started believing Ryan and I were friends, things got difficult.

And with Quinn moving away and all my issues rising up to the surface to swallow me whole, I did not need difficult.

CHAPTER 5

The Second Wedding
Yellowstone
Four Years Ago

I stepped outside the cabin that had been rented out for me as part of my compensation for this wedding.

It was beautiful.

I hadn't realized just how many women in my hometown liked to have destination weddings until I started specializing in wedding cakes.

It stood to reason. If you got married in Pineville, there were only so many venues. I had done several of those since the wedding in Joshua Tree last year, but when Lydia, a vague acquaintance from high school, had asked me to do the cake for her wedding near Yellowstone, I was thrilled.

She didn't have the budget for a cake really, not when she had to rent a whole block of cabins, but I'd agreed to do the cake just for the cabin, with no compensation because she'd really wanted one of my cakes and I'd felt flattered, and also driven to not disappoint her.

I had never been to Wyoming before, and it was a great chance to visit a state I hadn't seen.

I had come a couple of days early, with the cake already baked and the icing made, and I was really enjoying being out in nature like this. My porch overlooked woods and mountains, towering pine trees and lush greenery. I inhaled the scent of the forest. And went back inside to look at my cake which was sitting in the middle of the counter, disassembled, because I had learned a few things from last time. It really was better to try and get it all together on site. But everything was as frosted and decorated as it could be, and ready to be shifted into the back of the car.

The only issue . . . and really, it wasn't an issue. Because I didn't need to be like that, was my neighbor, in the cabin next door.

The photographer.

Yes. Because of course Ryan Clark had been hired to be the photographer at this wedding. Apparently, I was becoming the go-to baker, and he was the premier photographer. Which he hated. It didn't really seem fair. If he hated weddings, why was he involved with them at all?

And definitely, *why was he in the cabin next to mine?*

I grumbled as I took my cake layers out to the back of the car.

At least he hadn't come out to the porch this morning at the same time I had to drink coffee. That had been a little gift from yesterday. We had both opened our doors at the same time, and stepped out onto the deck. He had been wearing plaid, of the very red and lumberjack variety that made me wonder if he chopped his own wood. Which had given me that same dry-as-a-desert feeling in my mouth I had experienced during the wedding in Joshua Tree last year.

It was *this*. This seeing him out of context. Seeing him without any buffers.

He didn't like me, that was the thing. And it bothered me.

It really did. Because everybody liked me. I worked so hard to make sure that was the case.

I knew it came from unhealthy coping strategies. But I also knew my fear of flying wasn't logical. It didn't make it go away.

Because my mother left me when I was a child and abandoned me to be raised by my grandmother, so consequently I'd always behaved in ways designed to keep people with me so that I wouldn't experience that level of abandonment again. I knew that. But it was a pattern. Ingrained and well-worn. And knowing that the man was wandering around on the streets just disliking me for no real credible reason was extremely irritating.

That was all.

But I did my best to ignore him, diligently. Because he ignored me. Like I wasn't even there. Sipping his coffee and taking in the scene like I wasn't fifty feet from him on my deck.

I whistled. Because I knew it would bother him. And that if it did, I could pretend I didn't know he was there.

I hadn't seen him yet today, though. I did wonder sometimes if I took a little bit of pleasure in disliking him because there were so few people that I openly disliked. And who openly disliked me. It was a paradox. I hated it, but there was also some freedom in it. I was always working so hard to get people to see me in the most positive light. I was relentlessly cheerful in the bakery, relentlessly giving and understanding with all of my clients, I was always doing extra work that I didn't quite bid on, and doing people favors around town.

I knew that if Gran were alive to see it, she would scoff and tell me to grow some spite.

That was why my grandma had always been such a gift. Because she didn't perform for people. Of course, her husband had left her, and her daughter had abandoned her, so it wasn't like it had gone great for her. But she had been exactly what I needed. Whatever her issues had been when she was younger, they had toned down enough by the time I came to live with her. She was a crotchety old lady. But again, I was a people pleaser. So we had gotten along fine.

She had been salt and steel to my sugar and everything nice.

The sweetest thing about my grandmother was her baked goods.

We'd bonded over them. For my grandma, cake had been more than a treat, it had been a way for her to survive when she'd ended up a single mom looking for a way to survive.

And baking had been a way for me to connect with her.

To feel secure.

It had been survival for me too.

I packed my cake up into the back of the car and closed the hatch back. I didn't need any insects flying in there and getting stuck in the butter cream.

Then I went back into the house to make sure that I had all the necessary accoutrements that I would need. Knives, serving utensils, extra frosting; everything that I would need to assemble the cakes.

I had it all, and I began to put them in tote bags. Then I decided to make myself an extra coffee for the road because it was going to be a long day; delightful, but long.

The wedding was in three hours. And it would probably be an hour until cake service after that. I really had plenty of time. Getting up here early had made it so easy and delightful.

I slung the tote bags over my arm and grabbed my travel coffee mug. Which was incidentally lumberjack plaid.

I chose to ignore that.

I went outside and stopped when I saw a flurry of movement. I froze. There was a dark black shape rumbling up next to my car and for a moment I couldn't believe what I was seeing.

When I entered the park I was given a handout with information on wildlife. What species you could find in the park and how to be safe around them.

But when I'd thought about seeing wildlife, I'd thought . . . maybe a bison.

Perhaps a pika.

I was ready to be charmed by a pika.

I was not prepared for a bear.

A black bear and not a grizzly bear, which I knew to be a crucial difference in terms of my odds of being eaten alive. So there was that.

There were black bears in Oregon. One time, in fifth grade, we'd been barred from recess for a day because one had been seen in the woods around the school. But I had never personally seen one alive. Stuffed and fashioned into rugs, and once hit by a car, yes.

But never living, powerful and this close to me.

Still, I stood frozen, unable to access any of the information given about what a person was supposed to do when there was a *goddamned bear* in front of them.

If I ran from it, it would probably just come after me. And I wasn't faster than a bear.

I loved a good Animal Planet marathon. I knew a lot about wildlife.

I knew enough to know bears were fast. But not enough to know what the hell I was supposed to do to come out of this ungnawed on.

The door to Ryan's cabin opened, and he stepped out onto the porch. For one moment I debated running straight to him.

But that would take me past the bear.

That was a big no.

"*Bear*," I whispered, because my throat was tight and my voice refused to go any higher. Maybe yelling would make the bear mad anyway. "*B-bear.*"

It was no louder or clearer the second time I said it.

"What?" He looked across the expanse, and his eyes collided with mine. The first time we had made eye contact since he'd checked into the cabin.

"Bear." I gestured wildly toward my car. But realized that he couldn't see what was happening on the driver's side of it.

"*Bear?*" he repeated.

"*Yes*," I said, in that same strangled whisper.

I couldn't take my eyes off the bear, who was shuffling and snuffling by my car and in general acting like we weren't there. Maybe I could just back away.

Then it stopped, and raised its head, its eyes connecting with mine.

My mouth went totally dry, my whole body drawing tight like a bowstring.

I was prey.

I had never been more aware of that in my life.

Humans had front facing eyes. Which was nature's way of lying to us and convincing us that we were the predators. Right then, I knew what a lie that was.

Without a gun, a bow and arrow, a knife, *something*, I was nothing but soft, pink dinner to a bear. An antelope without the ability to outrun my quarry.

But I refused to simply lay down on the ground like a picnic.

In the back of my mind, I remembered seeing something on an outdoor survival show. People yelling something like . . . *hey bear*?

I decided to give it a try.

"*Hey bear*," I shouted. "*Hey bear!*"

The bear did not respond in kind. I'm not sure what I expected. A wave and a good old: *Hey, Poppy!*

Certainly not.

"Why are you saying that?" Ryan asked, moving to the edge of the porch like he was ready to race down the stairs and . . .

What was he going to do? *Fight* the bear?

My heart was pounding so hard I thought I was going to pass out.

"You're supposed to," I said.

The bear turned its focus back to the car, sniffing at the door. Relief crowded my chest, making my heart slow down just a little.

I took a step back and the bear didn't look at me. "I'm going to try to get back inside," I said, taking another step backward.

Then the bear stood up. On its hind legs. And that was when I got a real sense for the size of it. That was also when Ryan saw it.

His eyes went wide and I was very nearly satisfied by the shock I saw there.

"See!?" I hissed. "It's a whole ass bear!"

"I didn't doubt you," he said, his voice more of a hushed shout now that he'd seen it. "Well, don't just stand there . . . keep backing up!"

The bear sniffed the air and then went back down on all fours, snuffling at the tire on the front driver's side.

I stepped back and then the bear partly launched himself upward again, his paw on my door handle. I heard the claws scrape the paint and winced.

"My car . . ."

But then he moved his paw over the handle. *Scrape. Scrape. Scrape.*

"No no," I said.

"What's it doing?"

"It's . . . it is trying to get in my car."

"Is it locked?"

"*No.* I was loading it and it isn't like a bear can open—" But then it did. It full on opened my car door. "*Holy shit.*"

"What—"

And then the bear slipped into the car, and the door snapped closed behind it.

And I was momentarily gratified to see Ryan Clark's eyes go wide. "Holy fuck."

He could clearly see the bear now, just as I could, perched in my driver's seat.

But my satisfaction was very, very momentary because the issue of there being a bear in my car was not a small one.

"*Holy fuck,*" I repeated.

"You have a bear in your car," he said.

The one good thing was that now I had a vehicle separating me from the bear. But there was also one very, very bad thing.

"Yes. I have a bear in the front seat of my car. And I have a wedding cake in the backseat."

Normally, before a trip, I had a lot of anxiety and my end conclusion — every time — had been that I'd panicked too much beforehand.

Not this time.

I hadn't panicked enough.

"Well, that's why the bear got in your car," he said.

I wanted to kill him. As if that was some normal thing any old person would have thought of.

"I wasn't *storing* it in there, I just went inside to get some supplies. And some coffee."

The bear was now rummaging around my car. Bumping about like a furry bumblebee, without a care in the world.

It was so damned cute. And so horrifying.

And then, the cute little bear turned in my seat, and its claws dug into the headrest, and it knocked it off. Beheaded it. Like it was nothing.

The bear's claws sheared off pieces of the car like it was made of butter and I was jolted by the realization that it could have been me.

My hands were shaking and I still couldn't move as I watched it dismantle the whole dash.

Then the bear rambled toward the back of the car, right to the cake.

The cake.

The representation of love that I had created for this couple in exchange for staying here. The very place that was now responsible for the death of the cake.

It was devouring it, moving its devastating paws through the soft sponge, its gaping maw powering through my perfectly frosted layers like they were nothing.

Ryan took his phone out of his pocket. "I'm going to call . . . animal control or something."

I didn't answer. I didn't have an answer. I was mesmerized by the power of this predator unleashing its fury on . . . my cake.

Anyway, it hadn't really occurred to me to do anything other than let the bear do what it was going to do, because what was the point? The bear was in the car. Could anybody even get a bear out of the car?

I blinked, like I was coming out of a haze and I realized what he'd just said.

Animal control.

"I don't want them to *kill* it," I said.

I was surprised that I meant that, considering what the bear had done to my car and cake, but I was staying in a cabin plopped in the middle of his woods, so it really didn't feel like he should suffer the consequences for that.

"They're not going to kill it," he said.

But then I saw a piece of the cake that I had made fly up and hit one of the interior windows.

My benevolence wilted.

"Maybe they could kill it a little bit," I said.

I had no idea what I was going to do. I was going to have to drive down to a grocery store and try to find a sheet cake.

Honestly. What the hell were you supposed to do with the bear who had got into your car and consumed your wedding cake? He wasn't even eating it, actually. He was just flinging it around. It was the flagrant disregard for the cake really. And . . . my car.

He made the interior of that car look like it was made of soft butter. His claws cut through everything, door panels pulled off like they were nothing.

And I had worried that if I left the back of the car open some insects might fly in. Much like an insect, the bear seemed to know only how to get into the car. And not back out.

And all I could do was stand there on the deck and stare.

The utility vehicle that pulled up ten minutes later, courtesy of Ryan, had two park rangers inside. They had tranquilizer guns, and a couple of real guns.

"What are the real guns for?" I asked.

"In case the tranqs don't work," said the female ranger, nodding.

"Is that . . . a genuine risk?"

But she didn't answer me.

She was busy, understandably.

The man lunged forward and opened up the back passenger door. Then stepped back, his gun aimed at the bear. But the bear tumbled out and started to run. Up the street, past Ryan's cabin, and away.

No shooting required.

The interior panel on that open door slid off and landed on the ground; the sound loud in the silent, still forest.

"You gotta leave your cars locked," the man said.

"Thanks," I said. "I didn't realize that there was a break-in risk around here."

I realized that I didn't feel like pleasing this man at all.

So that was kind of nice.

"Bears are attracted to food." He leaned into the car. "The cake back here is toast."

Great.

My cake.

My cake.

After giving me a couple of unhelpful tips like I should report the damage to my insurance, the rangers left. And I simply stood there and looked at my rack of a vehicle, and my wreck of a cake.

At my wreck of a car.

I wanted . . . to curl up on the ground – in the house not outside, because there were bears out there apparently – and cry. I wanted to fall apart and scream and freak out.

But people were counting on me. I couldn't fall apart.

"My cake is dead."

"But you aren't," Ryan said. "And I'm pretty sure no one can get mad at you for a bear destroying your cake."

"Maybe not, but they still won't have a cake. They were so excited and I . . . I needed two ovens and four hours for that cake, plus time to cool and I . . . I don't even know what the ovens are like here or if I'm at an altitude that will make this difficult and . . . but if I don't do something they just won't have a cake on their wedding day."

The idea of letting them down like that . . . it killed me.

And if that wasn't enough impetus to hold my shit together, then Ryan standing there was certainly added fuel.

I took a breath and I tried to imagine what Gran would do.

Spite and steel.

I needed some steel.

"Okay," I said. "I have two hours and thirty minutes to make a new cake. In a cabin without any of my specialty equipment."

"We better get started."

I looked up at Ryan. There was no way that he was offering to help me.

"Are you serious?"

"The carnage that I just saw . . . I wouldn't wish on my worst enemy."

Why did I have a feeling he actually meant me? And that while he wouldn't wish it on me, he had enjoyed it a little bit. But he was also offering to help me.

So. *So.*

"Are you going to sneeze into my cake batter?" I asked.

"You've had enough for one day. Let's go inside and bake. I'll have to leave a little bit before you, but you can use my oven. I'll even run the stuff over there. And babysit it. Whatever you need."

I was stunned. Not only did he rarely say this many words to me, he was never, ever nice.

But then, I supposed being mean to me right now would be the equivalent of kicking the Little Match Girl into a snowdrift. And Ryan wasn't cruel. That was the thing. We didn't mesh. But it wasn't like he was a bully.

Still, where I grabbed an apron and put it on, and tossed him the other, which he took wordlessly, and then stood there, awaiting orders, I was shocked.

I looked up at his stern face. It wasn't like there was a hint of softening or kindness there, nothing quite so extravagant.

But maybe . . . maybe after this he wouldn't hate me so much. Maybe what he needed to do was pity me.

"Okay," I said. "I need to start getting ingredients out. I also need cake pans. I brought a bunch of specialty items in those bins. So, if you can get out every square cake pan that you see, that's what I need. And I've got enough ingredients to basically feed a village. So."

I knew my recipe by heart, and it was easy to get everything out and start measuring.

We had to get baking as quickly as possible, and he ran over to preheat his oven, as I preheated the one in the cabin we were working in.

We didn't make conversation. But it surprised me how easy I found it to work in tandem with him.

Soon, I had new, freshly baked cake layers. I stuck them in the freezer immediately, doing my best to get them cooled down so that I could start decorating and frosting.

While that was happening, I mixed up new batches of buttercream, and cut new lengths of ribbon, rolled new fondant pine trees. And I had to give credit where credit was due, because if Ryan hadn't been there assisting, it never would have gotten done.

As he helped me with the frosting, I watched him. His hands were so sure and certain, like he'd done this before.

"You aren't a novice at this," I said.

"I've made cakes before."

I laughed. "Why?"

"Why not?"

"Because men usually . . . don't."

"I didn't realize you were so married to traditional gender roles."

I huffed. "I'm not, Ryan, the world is."

He slowly moved his knife over the buttercream and I stared a little bit. Because watching him in my environment like this, watching him be so comfortable with it, was doing things to me I couldn't explain.

And I didn't want to explain them.

"My mom made me my very first birthday cake when I was thirteen."

"What?" I asked, my heart going still.

"Yeah, I . . . you know I moved from home to home a lot when I was younger and I never really had a birthday or anything. She made me a birthday cake and it was the nicest thing anyone ever did for me. I asked her who made her birthday cakes and she told me she always did." He smiled just slightly. "I told her fuck that. She told me to watch my language. But I make a cake for her every year."

I was stunned by that revelation. Both that he hadn't had a birthday cake prior to being thirteen and that he'd made it his mission to ensure his mom never had to make her own cake again.

It was a level of care and thoughtfulness I'd never ascribed to the boy who'd been so mean to me when I'd accidentally damaged his solar system. The boy who'd scowled at me all the time after.

"I . . ."

He checked his watch.

"I have to go." He tossed me the keys to his truck, and I just stood, staring at them and him.

"What's this for?" I asked.

"You can't drive your car. So, you can take mine."

"Oh. Thank you."

I stood there for a second and looked at him, and I had to wonder if I had been wrong about him. From every angle. All this time. I had to wonder if maybe some of what had gone wrong really was me, and I hadn't fully appreciated it until now. Because this was just nice. He was being nice. And I would've said that Ryan Clark was incapable of being nice.

"Did you need a ride down . . . ?"

"No," he said. "I'll walk."

"But . . . there are bears out there."

I might not like him, but I didn't *dis*like him enough to let a bear eat him.

Chew on him for a minute maybe. But not *eat* him.

"Just one. A small one. And I think he's full."

I huffed a laugh. "If you got eaten I wouldn't be able to forgive myself."

"Nice of you."

I looked at my cake, which still needed to be assembled, and quickly.

"How about I do all of this down at the venue." I tossed the keys back at him.

"If you insist."

We loaded everything up as quickly as possible, and I climbed into the passenger seat of his truck. "You know, this kind of vehicle really isn't convenient when you have short legs."

"I wouldn't know," he said.

I looked at him, and he was smiling.

Reluctantly, I felt my mouth twitch.

We drove down winding roads, until we arrived at the venue. A gorgeous cedar gazebo next to the creek, the brilliant mountains as a backdrop. He went to go and take pictures, and I unloaded the truck.

Whenever I looked over at him, it was like I was staring at someone entirely new. Like I had never really known him until today, even though I'd known him since the sixth grade.

The legend of the bear eating the cake traveled like wildfire through the wedding and since I had a cake to present in the end, the story was funny and not tragic at all.

"What happened exactly?" the groom asked Ryan, his eyes wide.

Ryan recounted the story, smiling. Laughing. I wanted to memorize the way his face looked when he did that because I saw it so rarely.

It felt almost like my car had died for a good cause.

I finally cut the cake and I looked up, right at Ryan.

I smiled, and he took a picture. I knew that was going on my website.

CHAPTER 6

Present Day

*W*e stumbled off the flight, gritty-eyed and crispy. I had managed to sleep thanks to the pills, but it had been an uncomfortable sleep. I'd been curled ferociously against the hard plastic window cover because I didn't want to accidentally shift my weight and find myself snuggling with Ryan.

No.

Noah was sent off into his own lane for citizens reentering the country while the Americans were funneled into a much more crowded customs line. I didn't have any experience with this kind of thing so I watched Ryan closely, as he handled every stage with ease.

I didn't have contraband in my suitcase, but I did know a sudden fear that I could be an unknowing drug mule.

Or that I'd brought a suspicious amount of aspirin.

But when we finally got through, and into the domestic terminal of the Auckland airport, I could breathe again. Except then we were getting on another plane, and it was too short of a flight for me to take pills. Plus, I had just slept for about ten hours.

Ryan and I were not seated together on that flight. He was in the row behind me, praise be.

Noah had warned all of us that flying into Queenstown could be rough and bumpy, since you came in over a significant mountain range.

I found that helped. If I could expect rough air, then I at least knew it wasn't some anomaly, or an impending accident.

I felt cocooned by my jetlag. By the sense of floating I had felt since I got off the last plane.

And when we landed, I actually opened my window shade and watched as we descended with snowy mountains all around us.

It was too beautiful for my anxiety to ruin.

It was a miracle.

As we got off the plane, we walked down the stairs onto the tarmac. It was cold outside, jarring considering we had just left the intensity of summer back in Oregon.

The wind was blowing, with a biting chill, and I reflexively reached for my phone to snap a picture of the mountains around us.

"No photos on the tarmac," a flight attendant shouted at me as I raised my phone.

I stuffed it in my pocket, feeling like an idiot. Doing the wrong thing and getting scolded like that was the kind of thing that had the power to ruin my day.

"Don't worry about it," said Ryan.

I hadn't realized that he was standing so close to me.

"I wasn't worried about it." A lie.

I would be worried about it all day. I'd broken a rule. Even if on accident. I would replay that moment over and over for nights to come. It might even join my *All Time Greatest Hits of Times I Did the Wrong Thing*. A favorite slide show of mine to run before I went to sleep.

"You worry about everything," he said.

"Not sharks, Ryan," I replied. "Because I know exactly how they attack."

Then Quinn caught up with me and grabbed my arm, pulling

me away from Ryan. "How were you? That flight from LA was so long!"

"Oh fine. Did you enjoy your pasta and lobster up in the front of the plane?"

Quinn laughed. "We had venison. And it was delicious. Thanks."

"We got suspicious eggs and a granola bar. But I'm happy for you." I really was.

About all the things. *All of them.*

The airport in Queenstown was much smaller than the giant hub in Auckland, and we quickly got our bags, and linked up with two of Noah's other groomsmen who had flown in from Auckland. Then we ended up in an endless line at the rental car counter.

Quinn had insisted that we have a couple of cars between us. Though, I knew that I was not driving on the wrong side of the road. No thank you.

Ryan clearly had no such issues, as he was named one of the drivers, with Noah acting as another – for now. He and Quinn didn't have their own house or car yet – they would move into a place they'd already secured and sort out all the permanent living issues after their honeymoon.

Ryan ended up chauffeuring the groomsmen, with Noah driving me and Quinn.

I was annoyed to realize that some tension in my chest seized without Ryan in proximity.

Annoyed that he affected me at all.

We had a large vacation rental on Lake Wakatipu, and I had of course done my due diligence on that. Meaning that I had looked at all the photographs and done a mental walk-through.

I wouldn't be sharing a bedroom because the other bridesmaids weren't arriving until later, but the groomsmen were going to be stacked two to a bedroom. According to the itinerary that Quinn had presented us all with, that wouldn't matter, because we were going to be falling onto our mattresses completely exhausted, and the guys probably wouldn't even notice that they had a roommate.

I was excited about it.

I felt completely disoriented sitting in the backseat of the car, with the driver on the wrong side, and the turns taking us across lanes when I didn't expect them to.

But that was only a distraction for a moment, because soon the scenery took over completely.

It wasn't completely unlike Oregon, and yet it was.

The snowcapped Remarkables truly lived up to their name, tall and imposing on the other side of the lake. When the wind whipped up, the waves in the water looked like an ocean, rather than the contained body of water that it was.

We bypassed town, going straight to the vacation rental, which was on the outskirts, an easy walking path promising a fifteen-minute walk down to all of the restaurants and shopping.

The house was positioned on a hill, with three floors, each with balconies that made the most of the stunning view.

We pulled in at the same time as Ryan and the car that contained two other groomsmen. They'd flown in from Auckland, and there was one other groomsman who lived in Queenstown and would be hooking up with us for other wedding festivities.

I could see why Quinn wanted to move here.

I could see why she was embracing the adventure.

And while part of me – the bitter, broken-hearted part of me – had wanted to be bitter that she was doing it for a man, or at least afraid that she was doing it for a man, I realized then that she wasn't.

Yes, he was part of it. Loving him was part of it, but this would be an adventure regardless.

And no matter what happened, Quinn would never regret she'd tried this.

"Okay," I said. "I get it."

Quinn turned from the passenger seat and looked at me. "It's really different."

"But it's beautiful."

"I never thought that I would move so far away," Quinn said. "But everything about it feels right."

Noah smiled. "Glad to be one of the things that feel right."

"You most of all," she said.

My eyes felt extra gritty then, and I tried to ignore that.

They pulled the car into the garage, and I got out. "It was very clear on the instructions for the vacation rental that we are to take our shoes off," Quinn said, in a very stern and maternal voice.

"Oh good," one of the guys said, as he crowded into the garage. "I love house rules."

He turned to me, and grinned. "I'm Trev. What's your name?"

"If you fuckin' hit on my future wife's friends I'll kill you, mate," Noah said.

I was about to say something that I'm sure would've been super witty. What else could it have been, when I was jetlagged and exhausted? But then Ryan walked forward, all of us bottlenecking in the door between the house and the garage, and I raced forward, kicking my shoes off as quickly as possible.

The entryway was small, with just a staircase leading up to the main part of the house.

I raced up the stairs, making exclamations about the view and the beauty of the house.

Quinn came up behind me. "He's harmless," she whispered.

"Who?"

"Trev."

Oh right. Trev. She didn't know that Trev wasn't the source of my reaction. It was just the idea of getting stuck in that tight space with Ryan.

I took a circuit through the living room, looking out the window at the lake below, and at the glorious view of the mountains.

"I thought maybe we could go to town and do some shopping," asked Quinn.

"I thought we were doing all nature adventures," I said.

Quinn wrinkled her nose. "Well. We will be doing some of that. I know Ryan has a bunch of photography spots he wants to hit, and Noah of course wants to accommodate our matchmaker."

I made a growling sound in the back of my throat. "You give him way too much credit."

"If not for him we would never have met."

"If not for a moldy petri dish we wouldn't have penicillin."

Quinn snorted. "I'm actually not sure if that's supposed to be insulting or . . ."

Ryan appeared then on the landing. "Was it about me? Because if so then it was meant to be insulting."

I flashed him a wide, fake smile.

"You two have to get along," she said. "This is our wedding."

"The whole two weeks isn't your wedding," I said.

"Yes it is. It's the sacred bubble of my wedding. All of Queenstown is the sacred bubble of my wedding. Indeed, the entire South Island."

"I like that about you," said Noah.

The men brought all the suitcases upstairs, and then I dragged mine up another flight of stairs to the small bedroom at the top.

I heard the door close in the hall across from me, but didn't see who had occupied the space.

Instead, I decided to get dressed and head to town with Quinn. If I sat down for too long then I was going to fall asleep, and I was determined to make sure that I didn't let jetlag win.

We decided to walk along the lake, past other vacation rentals, and through a park, down a winding path that led into town. Queenstown was filled with lovely stone buildings, delicious restaurants and adorable boutiques, and I played my favorite game where I imagined what my life would be like here.

I thought about having a bakery wedged in between the Irish pub and the coffee house.

We got ice cream at a place that made their own treats, and made our way to a shop with massive sculptures made of Greenstone, then on to look at lovely wool products, which were an essential New Zealand item.

It was a country known for its sheep, and therefore its exquisitely lovely yarn and sweaters.

"So," said Quinn. "Are you going to hook up with Trev?"

I blinked. "I'm sorry?"

"He's clearly interested."

"And I believe your fiancée told him not to touch me."

"Sure. But . . . Trev is hot, and he also doesn't listen. At least, if I'm going off of every story that Noah has ever told me about him."

"No," I said. "I wasn't considering that."

I felt extremely uncomfortable, and I shouldn't. Quinn was my best friend, we talked about sex. We talked about men.

But there was something extraordinarily uncomfortable about the conversation given some of the context.

The context about Ryan. And the fifth wedding.

Which I had no desire to relive. Thank you.

There's a reason I haven't spoken about it out loud ever to anyone. Not even Quinn. A reason it lives behind a blockade in my brain so that I don't even think about it.

"You need to get back out there," she said.

"Counterpoint: why?"

"Because I'm worried about you, because I selfishly want to know that you're going to be okay?"

"And fucking your groomsman who lives in another country is going to make you feel better?"

"No. Okay. He isn't specifically going to solve that, I guess. Though, you could marry him and move to New Zealand."

"I'm not leaving Pineville," I said. "My grandma's house is

there. My grandma is buried there. The bakery is there. My business . . ."

"My family is there. But I'm leaving. For love."

"That's great. And you're right, Trev is hot. But I don't think he's the love of my life. And anyway, I'm not looking for the love of my life."

"Why not?"

"Because . . . I don't need it to be happy. I have enough. Because . . . Quinn, *you're* one of the loves of my life. And I'm going to have to deal with the fact that you're moving away. I can't replace you with some guy."

Quinn wrinkled her nose. "I know. You're one of the loves of my life too. That's why this sucks so much. If I hate it here, he will move to the States for me."

"Oh hell no. Stay in New Zealand. I'll visit. Please don't change anything because of me."

"Why should I not change something because of you?"

"Because . . . because this is your real life, with your husband. And I'm . . ."

"It isn't ridiculous to think that people might make different decisions because of you, Poppy. You're *that* important to me."

"Thank you," I said, feeling my chest get tight. I believed her. I did, and that was a really difficult thing for me in most cases. But even though I believed her, I also knew that you didn't up and change your plans for your married life because of your best friend. You had to marry and make your spouse the person that you made decisions around. Not the sad girl that you adopted like a stray animal when you were in second grade. It was fair. And it was fine.

I understood.

But it hurt.

"Anyway," I said. "A man is going to cause me more problems than he's going to solve. So you can't try and mitigate my sadness by hooking me up with somebody."

"I'm just still mad that Josh broke up with you."

"*Are* you?" I'd never had the impression Quinn was all that attached to Josh.

Quinn's forehead wrinkled. "I'm mad that you don't have a built-in family back in Pineville. I guess you could . . . visit your mother?"

"Do you know what my mom's Wikipedia page says?"

"No. Weirdly, I have not googled your mom recently."

I had. But that was because my relationship with her was mostly confined to what different gossip sites said about her.

"It doesn't even say that she has a child. You know, normally it's in the little table of stats on the side. Or at least down under *personal life*. I'm not even mentioned. There are a couple of lovers, a marriage or three. But no child."

I had thought often that it would've been more hurtful if she would've gone off and had other children, or some otherwise totally stable personal life. So, I did feel that perhaps I should be grateful that at the very least she had proven to be entirely uninterested in motherhood regardless of what stage of life she was in. It wasn't personal, in other words. Which was good to know.

"That really sucks," she said.

"It only sucks because Gran is gone. Because now I feel . . . I don't know. Like I'm missing something, and I didn't for a really long time. Because of Gran. It sucks, but what can you even do about it?"

"I guess if you really want to, you try to see about building a relationship."

"And get rejected."

"Maybe she wouldn't reject you."

"I feel like if she was in a space to be accepting of me, I would at least appear on her Wikipedia page, and I am quite certain that she sees to the edits on there personally."

I reached out and squeezed her arm. "Quinn," I said. "All the other bridesmaids that are coming here are my friends too. I work at the bakery, I make cakes. I am not going to be by myself. Just because I'm not looking for the same thing that you have, doesn't mean that I'm sad."

"But you wanted it for a long time. You used to have bridal magazines hidden under your bed."

"Yeah. But that was back when I imagined that things were different when you were in a relationship, and now I know they aren't. Now I know that it isn't all about a fantasy wedding. It's about spending your life with somebody, and that somebody could change their mind. I just don't want to do it again. I don't want to invest all that time and have somebody walk out the door. I have worked way too damned hard at being a little bit more stable with my abandonment issues."

"And now I'm leaving you. I really feel like an asshole."

"Please don't. Please. Because I can't bear it. I honestly can't. If you feel bad about making this amazing leap because of me, then I really am going to feel like an inconvenience. I mean, miss me, please, but don't feel bad."

"Well, how about I feel bad, but I do it anyway. Because I love him. And I'm actually looking forward to a little bit of a fresh start. I love Pineville too, don't get me wrong. But you live somewhere all of your life and you have such a prescribed role that you fill. I am the accountant's daughter. And I myself am an accountant. And not in a sexy, euphemistic way. Just an accountant. And people don't understand . . . they think that I'm boring. And no, I didn't think that I was boring. Noah met me, and he didn't have all these years of assumptions about me. He didn't see me and think of me as Roger's daughter."

It was to me funny that it bothered her. Because I love nothing more than being Rose's granddaughter. I love having ties. Links. I loved being known. Because I knew what it was like to bounce around, to know nobody. To have no friends. To feel like you were invisible to your own mother.

To have a father that you didn't even . . .

"There's no real happy medium, is there?" I asked. "I don't even know who my dad is."

"Have you ever thought about looking for him? DNA testing or . . . door knocking around Hollywood?"

"Yes. I have. Or at least trying to ask my mom again, but . . . I don't know. It's another person to be disappointed by, and should I not be doing like, shadow work on myself, to make it so that I'm not so dependent on people?"

She laughed. "We're all kind of dependent on people."

"Well, I don't like it. It's shitty."

"No argument from me."

"Except all the people that you love stay with you," I said. I meant to say it light. But it came out a little bit heavier than I intended it to.

"Oh, Poppy."

"Don't. Don't make the Sad Poppy face at me. I'm not sad. I'm not." I grimaced. "Okay, I'm a little bit sad."

"Your mom literally plays a mom on TV, but never parented you."

I couldn't help it, I laughed. It was absurd. Painful too, of course, but everything with my mother was. She couldn't have just abandoned me, oh no. She had to abandon me in a way that meant I'd see her on billboards everywhere.

"I know. She's ridiculous. Everything is ridiculous." I shook my head. "But I have an excuse to come to New Zealand now."

"And you hate flying."

"I know. I do. So maybe that's the growth that I'm making. Trust me. I'm fine."

If I kept saying it, then it would be true. Except really, it was. I needed to be fine because my life was mine. Nobody could live it for me. Nobody could physically fill that yawning void inside of me that had been placed there by my mother when I was seven years old.

It was just work that I had to do. I understood that. It was on me. On me to sort out all of it.

"Let's head back," I said.

"Yeah. Sounds good. We want to go to the ice bar tonight."

"That sounds freezing. I think I'll stay behind."

"It'll be fun."

"You're just trying to matchmake me with Trev."

She snorted. "You know, there is a difference between a relationship and sex. Maybe I'm just looking out for your orgasm tally."

"No offense, but I don't think a guy named *Trev* is going to help with my orgasm tally."

"Way harsh, Poppy."

I grinned. "A little bit. Anyway. I'm not concerned about it. I am much more interested in the mountains than in men. Right now."

I felt guilty. Because I had never told her . . .

But there were just some things that had to stay private.

There were just some things you needed to keep to yourself.

What happened at the fifth wedding was one of them.

CHAPTER 7

The Third Wedding
New Orleans
Three Years Ago

After the wedding in Yellowstone, there was something of an uneasy truce between Ryan and myself. A cease-fire, if you will. Nothing dramatic. It wasn't like I stamped into the local coffee shop waving a white flag and marching around him in a circle while he tried to drink his latte, it was just that . . . things felt different. There was some ease there that I hadn't experienced before. When he came over to play D&D with Josh and a few of the other guys, I didn't even feel tense about it. It was fine. Totally fine.

I could even almost see why my boyfriend was friends with him. Because if Ryan decided to do something nice for you, it felt like the sun had come out from behind the clouds. A smile from Ryan was like a rare thing. A gold coin. Or something.

It was good that we were fine because not only was he part of Josh's life, he was a persistent part of my professional life. He was the photographer at the next wedding I was doing too.

I had never met the bride in this wedding, not until she had come to town with her fiancé – who I did know vaguely from high school – to meet his family, and had swung by the bakery, and seen photographs of the cakes. They were moving to Pineville after the wedding, even though the bride's whole family lived in Louisiana. But because she would be opening her own small business on Main Street, she wanted to use local businesses for the wedding. But, of course, that meant traveling to New Orleans.

I was personally thrilled about that, because I had never been there, and it seemed like an amazing place to visit. I didn't even have to ask though. As far as who the photographer would be. I just knew.

But I wasn't even mad about it. Because we had a cease-fire. He had helped me. After the whole bear incident.

My poor car. There had been no fixing it. I got a new one, covered by insurance thankfully.

Even bigger, so that I could fit bigger cakes in the back. Though I didn't need my car for this wedding.

I had flown in early – with the aid of lorazepam – to do a little bit of sightseeing, and was staying at a boutique hotel in the French Quarter where the wedding would be based out of. It was the humidity that surprised me. Yes, I'd been warned about it, but I hadn't adequately appreciated that my feet might actually swell up to two times their normal size, rendering the shoes that I brought entirely useless.

I was so inspired by the city itself and I felt . . . transported in a way I often didn't because my anxiety could be such an anchor, dragging me down, making sure I was never really away from Pineville and all the worries about the bakery, or Gran's house, or the vague feeling that I was failing.

I didn't panic about my feet. I bought new shoes, and I wasn't deflated, because it was the most magical place I had ever been to.

I listened to music on the street corners, went on ghost tours at night, ate beignets at Café Du Monde, and tried not to die of powdered sugar inhalation as I did.

I went to a restaurant rumored to be haunted, the table set every night for a temperamental ghost who didn't like to be left out of dinner service.

I had seen all of the decorations for the wedding and they were beautiful, but I found myself wishing I could have helped with the details. The city was so inspiring to me. It would have been amazing to design a whole wedding around it.

A couple of days later, the wedding party arrived, and the boutique hotel was filled with the flurry of pre-wedding activity. I was so entranced by the magic of the city, by my own growing confidence. The one thing about a bear destroying your car and wedding cake was that after that nothing seemed like a super big deal. I asked the bride if she was open to a few changes with the cake. I pitched the idea of making some layers white with bold black designs, and others purple with gold leaf over the top.

She was excited about my changes and it felt good to follow my creative impulses. To actually do something that felt a little bit like me. I was allowed the use of the professional kitchen to make the cake, which was a luxury compared to trying to bake a cake in two hours after a bear attack.

Though, many things were.

The cake itself was a gorgeous, aromatic affair with marzipan and a hint of rose, and some almond buttercream. I was so involved in my love affair with the cake that when he walked through the kitchen I was momentarily stunned.

Like I'd forgotten he was coming at all.

Ryan was wearing a tan button up shirt with the sleeves rolled up past his elbows, and pants that looked like they were made for a hike, along with boots. Sort of an odd ensemble in the current weather.

Normally, I wouldn't ask, but I was intrigued, and he and I were actually speaking to each other.

"Where have you been?"

"Do I look like I've been somewhere?" He pushed his dark hair off of his forehead, and I ignored the corresponding movement in my stomach.

"Yes. You do. You don't look like you were out wandering Bourbon Street, anyway."

"I went on a river expedition. In the swamp. A good place to take pictures."

I thought of everything that was probably hiding in the murky swamp water and shivered.

"If you say so."

"Well, I thought it might be a little less dangerous than staying in and trying to navigate the list of rules associated with Denise's grandmother."

He did have a point. One thing we had all been made aware of during the planning of this wedding was that Denise's grandmother was extremely traditional, and nobody was to do anything to upset her. There wasn't going to be any alcohol present at the wedding – at a wedding in New Orleans – because her grandmother felt like alcohol went against Jesus.

I assumed that pointing out that Jesus made wine for a wedding one time was probably going to fall under the header of *upsetting grandma*, so I kept that comment to myself.

But the big one was that grandma thought her granddaughter and future husband were saving themselves for marriage. So nobody was supposed to mention that they in fact lived together.

It was an interesting contrast. It actually reminded me of the Jesus statue that was visible when you stood in a certain spot in Bourbon Street. The holy mixed with the profane. An extremely New Orleans experience.

I had no doubt that many in the wedding party were going to find their way to sin and vice even if it wasn't present at the wedding.

The preponderance of hurricanes – the beverage not the

storm – made it easy to get drunk. I had been wandering around by myself, so I had kept my consumption to a minimum.

New Orleans was amazing, but I also often had the sensation that if I turned down the wrong street I might find myself stepping through a portal into another world. And I wanted to make sure that I had my wits about me so that I could avoid portals.

Grandma wasn't coming in until the day of the wedding, though, which meant that the bridesmaids and groomsmen were gearing up for their respective bachelor and bachelorette parties which included some extreme partying in the French Quarter.

I couldn't help but wonder what kind of bachelorette party I would end up with.

Josh and I had been together for years. And known each other even before that.

Everyone I knew was getting married. And I . . . I just believed so firmly in the institution.

Or rather, I wanted to.

My grandmother's marriage hadn't lasted. I had never even met my grandfather.

I didn't know who my father was. Though, my mother had endless stories about it. Implications that he was a well-known leading man, or maybe even an Oscar-winning director had been common staples of her visits.

I didn't believe it, because I thought if either of those things were true my mom would have used them to parlay herself into greater success. Or at least greater riches.

Maybe that was a cynical view to have on my own mother. But if you knew her, I don't even think you would find it unkind.

She was an ambitious woman. She had returned to Pineville and had me in secret, leaving me with my grandmother because she knew that it would put a damper on her career. She had wanted that.

She didn't want a traditional family. She didn't want a traditional life.

But I did.

I actually wanted it.

I wanted a simple life.

I wanted to come home every day to somebody who loved me.

If I had children, then I wanted to raise them. I wanted to give them everything I never had.

Maybe it was that generational thing. Where it was so easy to see the mistakes of those who came before you, and you felt the urge to overcorrect.

My mom hadn't wanted small town life because she had watched her own mother struggle with it. Had watched her own mother grind through, raising her alone because she hadn't had a career before her husband had left her.

So she had fled for the city, for glory of her own.

I didn't want that kind of glory, because I saw the loneliness that you could leave in its wake.

I wanted connection. Those same things that my mother had spent her life running from, I wanted them.

So yes, I thought about my wedding.

I was chronically monogamous. I'd had one boyfriend before Josh, who I dated all through college, and then when I had come back to town, I had met Josh and decided that was more reasonable than trying to maintain a long-distance relationship.

And we'd been together for years. The proposal couldn't be far off.

We'd had our share of adjustment issues – who didn't?

I smiled as I began decorating the cake.

Domestic.

Yeah. I wouldn't be having a Bourbon Street bachelorette party. It just wasn't me.

I wasn't wild or spontaneous. I didn't want to go out on the town and blow off steam before I made my commitment.

Because my commitment was made.

That was just who I was.

I finished up the cake, and put it in the industrial refrigerator; I really was so excited to have that for my use, and then wandered out into the hotel lobby, where I encountered Ryan, and five members of the bridal party – the groom and his men – soaking wet and looking frantic.

"It's gone," the group was saying.

"What is?" Ryan pressed.

"Her ring," the groom said. "And we are all supposed to meet soon. I am too fucking drunk to figure out where the fuck . . ."

"I'm sorry what?" I asked.

"He lost her ring," Ryan said, looking at me.

"Where?"

"Somewhere on Bourbon Street."

I imagined that Street, teeming with people, the ground sticky from hurricanes and vomit, and I couldn't imagine a world where that ring hadn't been either picked up, crushed, or kicked somewhere entirely off the beaten path.

"Are you kidding me?" I asked.

"No," the group said, looking miserable. "She's going to kill me. Because we went to—"

One of the groomsmen practically slapped his hand over his friend's mouth.

"You guys are drunk," Ryan said. "And if you want help finding it, you're going to have to tell me where it was."

"One of the strip clubs," the groomsmen said.

"Are you fucking kidding me," I said.

And then I felt bad, because they were drunk, and they needed help.

But I was shocked that Ryan was trying to offer help, because that didn't seem in his wheelhouse. And anyway, he was the one that said he didn't care about weddings.

But then, he had known the groom in high school, so maybe that was why it mattered.

They were friends, more or less.

And I had seen that Ryan could be loyal when things were upside down.

"You guys go sober up," I said. "Ryan and I will go look. Give us a list of the places that you went to." I shook my head. "Why the hell did you have the ring with you?"

"That was my fault," said the best man. "I've been hanging onto it in my pocket, and then I let the stripper try it on . . ."

"Do not tell me that," I said. "Don't tell me that. Because I just can't. I can't know it."

Thank God it wasn't the groom who had done that, because that would've been instant divorce. Instant wedding cancellation. But still. There were things that I just needed to not have in my head, because if I did, I would never be able to look the bride in the face and not wear it right there in my expression.

"Why is there always a disaster?" I asked, as Ryan and I exited the revolving door of the hotel, and found ourselves out on the street.

"At least it isn't a bear," he said.

"I'm not sure if this is better."

We stood under the awning for a second, rain sprinkling onto the canvas. It was dark out on the streets, other than the light from the gas lamps. On Bourbon Street, it would be brighter, even in this weather. Because while many of the revelers would have gone into the bars, they definitely wouldn't have gone back to their rooms. People came to New Orleans to party.

I braced myself. "Are we really going out in that?"

It had clearly been raining harder earlier, but it was still sprinkling, and mist was rising up from the ground, adding to the soupy consistency of the air.

"I thought you were bound by honor to do anything for love?"

I looked up at him. "Yes, although, it is a little bit difficult to muster up enthusiasm for it when we have to do more than the groom."

"Well, we could let the wedding fall apart."

He sounded like he didn't care either way.

"True," I said. "We definitely could let the wedding fall apart. I also feel like perhaps that would be a poor showing for us."

"After you," he said.

I ran into the rain, bracing myself for the cold to hit me, even as the air around me remained warm and wet.

I heard Ryan's footsteps moving quickly behind me, and we dashed around the corner, to Bourbon Street.

It was still filled with people, who didn't seem to mind over much that it was sprinkling, or that they were now walking through puddles that were a cocktail of rainwater, alcohol and sick.

We stood there for a moment, and I laughed. Because it was just so absurd. Here I was, standing half a country away with Ryan Clark, in the damp.

"I'll go across the street to the first bar they went to, you can go to that one."

"Right. Where am I going to meet you?"

I looked around. "Over there," I said, gesturing toward a street preacher. "Maybe he'll save our souls."

"Great. Meet you there for the sermon."

I dashed over to the bar, and the first thing I did was ask at the counter if anyone had turned in a ring. The bartender laughed at me.

Then I began to search the floor, and didn't see anything.

I had a feeling we were going to find it at the strip club. I just did. But it was best to check everywhere.

I walked out of the bar, and onto the busy street. There were people up on balconies above the bars, shouting and waving beads.

A woman next to me put her arm up, and some beads came

sailing down toward her. I was under the impression that a person had to flash their tits to get beads. But if that wasn't the case . . . I put my arm up and caught a bundle of red, green and gold beads myself.

I put them on, and continued on down the street. Because the whole thing was just . . . absurd. It felt like I had stepped into another dimension. Another time.

I scurried back across the street, over to where I had told Ryan I would meet him, and he came jogging up at nearly the same moment. He looked at me, his eyebrow raised.

"Oh," I said, gesturing to my beads. "You want to know how I got them?"

Suddenly, the look on his face changed. "The usual way, I suppose."

Well, I had just learned that the usual way was actually a lot less costly than I had been led to believe, but I wondered what he thought.

There was an intensity to his gaze, and it made me feel . . . something that I wasn't familiar with at all. It wasn't domestic. And it wasn't . . .

I turned away from him. "No. Sadly. I'm very boring."

"You're not," he said.

That was strange. Because I couldn't think of anyone else who could stand there and look at me seriously and say that I wasn't boring.

I was out on Bourbon Street in a rainstorm, so that wasn't all that boring.

"Let's just go to the strip club," I said. "I have a feeling . . ."

"Yeah," he said, his expression grim.

"You don't have to go in," I said.

He lifted a brow. "I'm okay to go in."

Something about that made me feel uncomfortable. This acknowledgment of him as a man. That he might have, like, a sex drive and things.

But then, I didn't tend to think over much about my own sex drive, so I didn't exactly go around pondering the sex drive of others.

I was fine with sex.

But I was more interested in the other trappings of a relationship. The sex was sort of an incidental. Something nice, that kept me feeling connected to my significant other, sure. But my sex drive wasn't a free roaming, disconnected entity. It existed in context with Josh. And that was it.

I told myself that aggressively as we carried on toward the club. The club itself was spilling out into the streets, with male and female revelers alike lifting their tops up in the rain and dancing outside.

The party atmosphere was decidedly electric tonight, and it was a lot different to experience it standing there with him versus when I had been wandering around on the outskirts of it by myself, barely dipping in it at all, not . . . in the thick of it as we were trying to get into the club.

Ryan and I soon were inside a darkened room with the well-lit stage, where women were . . . well, it was naked. It was fully naked. I clamped my knees together reflexively, and stole a look at him out of the corner of my eye.

He wasn't looking. He seemed at ease. It gave me follow-up questions.

I wasn't going to ask them right then.

We paid a cover charge at the door and we walked in further, and Ryan approached a waitress who was dressed in a black bra and short shorts. "This is kind of a strange question, and I'm sure that you've had a lot of bachelor parties in here tonight, but there was a group of men in here earlier who apparently let one of the dancers try on a wedding ring."

The woman laughed. "Oh. No, I know exactly who you're talking about. Those guys were very drunk."

"Yeah."

She shook her head. "We put the ring behind the bar. They dropped it."

"Oh. Great. We need that."

She looked at us. "Well, you weren't with the group."

"No," I said. "We weren't. I made the wedding cake. He's the photographer. They were so drunk they couldn't figure it out by themselves."

"Yeah. That tracks." She shook her head. "Well. If they come back and complain because I let you guys steal it . . . nothing. They were the dumbasses that lost their ring on Bourbon Street."

"That's kind of my feeling," said Ryan.

She went behind the bar and produced a ring with a glinting diamond on it.

"Lord," I said, the deep horror the whole situation left in the pit of my stomach overwhelming me then.

The only good thing was that the bride never had to know. Well, at least not until it was safely in the rearview mirror. We had headed the disaster off.

"Let's get this back," he said.

I nodded.

"You don't want to stay for a dance?" the woman asked.

"I'm good," I said.

We stepped out of the club, and it was pouring rain again. Like the sky had opened up and decided to dump everything down right here. Ryan gripped my hand, and started to run, my stomach getting left behind somewhere back at the club, the feeling of his strong hand around mine, and the odd exhilaration of everything that had just happened making me feel dizzy and fizzy.

We reached an awning just off the main drag, where it was quieter. And I looked up at him, his face half lit by the streetlamps.

He was beautiful.

My breath stopped for a moment, then my heartrate sped up.

He was *beautiful*.

I hadn't really noticed that before. Yes, that he was good-looking. In an objective sense. But not in a way that was personal to me. It was that compartmentalizing thing that I was so good at. That was a survival skill I was pretty sure.

Right then, it wasn't functioning. And I didn't know if it was New Orleans, and the magic of it, dark or otherwise. If it was that we had just been in a strip club, where sexuality was unapologetically on display. Or even worse, if it was me.

If it was me, that was terrifying. If it was me . . . I had no idea what I was supposed to do with that.

He looked at me. But it was different. Different than every other way he'd ever looked at me before.

And I felt like I was standing suspended at the edge of something.

Time slowed. My body felt electric.

He moved, just slightly.

"Let's go," I said.

And I ran.

From underneath the awning, into the rain. I didn't hold onto him anymore. I ran straight to the hotel. I didn't look back.

I couldn't.

We returned the ring. I hoped that I had imagined the tension that had just swelled up between us in the humid air. In the thunderstorm.

Because none of this was my life. Our lives. This was . . .

We had walked into a portal. That was all. I had let my guard down, and had found myself in a different reality.

But it wasn't my world. It wasn't us.

I repeated that to myself as I walked back to my room. We intersected each other in the hallway. We had come up in different elevators.

"Thank you," I said. "For helping with that." I was determined to be friendly. I was determined to keep us both on neutral ground.

"No problem," he said.

"I just have to go call Josh," I said.

It was a reminder. To him, and to me. And I was angry at myself for making it so clear that I wanted that reminder. That I needed it. Because maybe he hadn't been in the same portal that I was in. Maybe I was experiencing all this alone.

It was possible.

He was back to being unreadable, and so I just went into my room and closed the door behind me.

I didn't even call Josh. I just changed and went to bed.

The next morning, I pushed everything aside. Nothing had happened. And it didn't mean anything.

I simply set to work on the cake, and then enjoyed the beautiful wedding, where none of the aftereffects of what happened the night before were on display. Where the bride and groom could pretend to be sober and chaste for her grandmother. Where there were rings for all, and no one had to know how fraught the night before had been. And I certainly didn't have to think about it.

It was a genuinely beautiful wedding. And the cake had turned out amazing.

I watched Ryan take pictures, we were closer together in this indoor venue than we had been in some of the other weddings. I wondered how he had ended up neck deep in weddings when he just didn't like them.

I was curious what pictures he had taken on his swamp trip. Did he photograph wildlife? Or scenery. Did he do all of it?

I had never really thought much about it. I knew he had traveled around. Of course I knew about the exhibition in Pineville, and had seen it, because everybody had.

Yet again, it had me asking myself whether or not I was the one who was the problem when it came to interactions between the two of us.

I wanted to thank him. I was weird last night, and that was

really my issue. He didn't need to suffer because I was being a head case about realizing he was handsome.

He didn't deserve my standoffishness, or to be on the receiving end of weirdness when he hadn't done anything.

So I just felt like I needed to thank him for the last two weddings.

For the fact that even though this wasn't his thing, he was . . . he was the kind of guy that you really wanted to have on your side.

That was just true.

I watched him work with all the other people, and I saw an ease that I just never saw when he was with me. I wasn't even sure that I saw that ease when he was with Josh.

I felt . . . strange about it. But again, I wasn't going to project my weird feelings onto him. Or at least, I was going to do my best not to.

I finished serving the cake, and noticed that Ryan had slipped out of the reception hall.

I went out, and wandered through a couple of the other event rooms, which were empty.

And then I pushed open one of the doors, and there was Ryan. With one of the bridesmaids, pinned up against the wall. He was kissing her, and she had her leg up over his hip.

I had definitely never seen him in a moment like this before. And it scalded me.

I felt like somebody had reached inside of me and grabbed a hold of my guts and flung them out onto the ground.

I felt burned by it. I couldn't even say why. But I couldn't quite define the sensation that I was experiencing. Just rampant discomfort over watching my boyfriend's best friend, who I had known since middle school in a sexual moment, or was it . . . was it about last night?

Suddenly, the bridesmaid realized that I was standing there.

"Oh," she said.

And I turned and ran. As quickly as I possibly could. I didn't want to see him see me, I didn't want to make eye contact with him in that moment.

I . . . he was hooking up with the bridesmaid at a wedding. He was so condescending of all of this, and he was using it to get laid. And how many weddings had that been true of?

It just . . . it made me angry. And it made me feel like maybe my feelings about him had been right on the whole time.

I felt justified then. For judging him a long time ago, because I'd known.

A tragic backstory didn't make him sympathetic.

He was just . . . the kind of man who was so cynical about love and life that with few exceptions every connection was about satisfying himself.

It's why he was so bitter at me all the damned time.

I wasn't a woman he could fuck so why bother to be nice? I wasn't useful.

The words made my stomach ache, they made my ears ring, even though they'd only been in my head and no one had said them out loud.

I didn't say good night to anyone. My job was done and I slipped out, went back to my room.

I took a shower and tried to wash the night off. But it clung to my skin like the humidity.

I slept like shit. When I got up in the morning, I didn't see Ryan.

I didn't want to see him anyway.

CHAPTER 8

Present Day

W̲e were up bright and early to head to Milford Sound. We were caravanning in a couple of different vehicles, and I was riding with Quinn and Noah, and Trev. I felt a little bit railroaded. And as we got started on the road, I was beginning to feel more than railroaded. I felt sick. Extremely sick.

The road was so winding, completely ghastly, with sharp gouges taken out of the pavement, and turns that set my teeth on edge.

I hadn't anticipated the amount of snow. There were practically glaciers rising up at the base of the mountains that we were driving around, and I felt like my heart was up in my throat.

It was a very long drive, and I had thought rather foolishly that I was going to be immune to the windy roads because these sorts of drives were common in rural Oregon, but this was another level, and I was in the backseat.

"You're very quiet," said Quinn.

Because I was trying to keep my breakfast firmly down in my stomach.

"I'm fine," I said.

I didn't want to slow us down. We were trying to make a boat tour that lifted at a specific time. I had heard nothing for days about how Milford Sound was one of the most beautiful places in the world, and I was amped to see it. I didn't need to derail us with my vomit.

Really, vomit had been too big of a factor in my life lately.

Thankfully, though it took three hours, we made it relatively without incident to the harbor.

When we got out of the car, I felt instantly dwarfed by our surroundings. They defied photographs. The scale could never be readily translated. You really had to be there. I looked up, through the low hanging misty clouds, at the sheer rock cliffs that rose up out of the water. There were waterfalls trickling down the side of the mountains, in thin streams, pouring into the gunmetal ocean below.

And we were going to take a boat out in it.

It was freezing, but thankfully, I had come prepared. And staring at all this natural wonder, I didn't feel quite so cold.

I felt small. Which normally made me feel afraid. Because it made me feel unimportant, which was potentially my most leading phobia. Being immaterial. Not mattering. But that wasn't the small sensation I had standing there.

It felt like me and my problems weren't quite so big. Like the world was wide enough to carry all of my concerns. Like my fears about losing Quinn, about love, about flying, were all petty in comparison to the stone that had seen millions of years.

It was just a moment. A blink and you miss it event. Yes, my problems were everything to me, but in the context of time, they were nothing.

I found that oddly cheering.

"It's time to board the boat," Trev said, putting his hand on my elbow. I looked up at him. He actually was hitting on me. He was cute. With a round, boyish face and dimples. Floppy blond hair and blue eyes. But I still didn't want to sleep with him. I was very clear on that.

Still, though, I might accept the attention. Because who didn't like to feel like they were beautiful?

I hadn't felt beautiful in a long time. Well. I could remember the last time. Far too clearly.

"It's like an airport," he said.

"Have you been here before?" I asked.

"Ages ago," he said. "I moved to Auckland for uni, but I grew up here. My dad took us down here a couple of times."

"This must have been an amazing place to grow up."

I realized how unusual it was for me to talk to a man who was completely disconnected from Pineville. Who didn't know me at all.

I understood then, what Quinn had meant. Because he didn't look at me and see years and years of history.

Solar systems and bowling balls.

Yeah. There was something slightly comforting about that.

A comfort that I hadn't fully realized I wanted.

"Yeah, of course you don't realize you're living in one of the most beautiful places on earth when you're a kid, you just want to get out and go somewhere bigger. So first it was Auckland, then I lived in London for a while. I came back a few years ago."

"I went to college three hours from home. That felt pretty adventurous," I said.

"What did you major in?"

"Business," I said. "I . . . I have a bakery. And I make wedding cakes."

"I thought you seemed sweet." He wiggled his eyebrows, in case I'd missed the double meaning in his words.

I laughed. "Does that work?"

"You're going to have to tell me."

I felt warm. Not aroused really, but complimented, happy. I felt seen. And it was nice.

Just then, the hair on the back of my neck prickled, and I turned. Speaking of being seen.

Ryan was staring at us.

It wasn't an angry stare, but there was an intensity there that jolted me.

I turned back to Trev. "Well, let's get in this line."

It was like an airport. We were moved through in boarding groups, and got onto the boat, which wasn't massive, but had an inside area on the lower deck, and the middle deck, with outside railings, and then a full top deck outside.

The rain was beginning to come down, and the wind was intense.

"I brought ponchos," said Trev, opening up his backpack.

"Oh," I said. "That's amazing. Great."

It really was, because while I had clothing that would insulate me from the cold, the wet was another matter.

They were green with Bunnings Warehouse emblazoned on them.

"What's Bunnings Warehouse?" I asked, looking down at the logo.

"It's a home and garden store."

"I'll file that away in my New Zealand Lore folder. Along with the phrases 'hard case' and 'good value'."

"Very good," Trev said.

"Don't ask me to define them though."

"Oh I would never. Same as I'd never ask you to try a Kiwi accent."

"Why not?"

"Americans can't do them. Don't feel bad actually, no one can."

"Choice as, bro," I said.

"Yeah nah," he said, laughing good naturedly at my terrible attempt.

I slipped a plastic poncho over my head as we boarded the boat. We entered at a lower-level deck, the interior old and covered in red carpet, with wooden benches and tables all throughout the space. There were windows to the outside, but the view wasn't as good as I'd have liked inside.

There were other, larger boats that apparently did tours, but ours was a bit wee.

We were given a ticket for a drink and a sack lunch that we had prepaid for when we bought the tickets.

I stuffed mine in my pocket, and went upstairs to the top deck. I watched as the ship pulled away from shore, and we began to pitch and roll in the waves.

"It gets rougher when you get out toward the open water," Trev said. "But if you keep your eye out, you might see fur seals, and maybe some keas."

"What's a kea?"

"It's a parrot, actually. A big green one."

Well, I was charmed by that.

Even though it was raining, I found myself completely captivated by the view. The walls of the sound were sheer rock, and the rain, as it increased, created even more waterfalls streaming down the side, joining in waterfalls that were more permanent, that roared loudly three quarters of a mile down those impossibly large cliffs.

Everything was great, and shrouded in mist. I could see why they filmed *The Lord of the Rings* here. It was truly otherworldly.

Normally, I would take my phone out. Normally I would try to capture it, but there was no point in trying.

I turned and saw that Ryan, of course, did not agree.

His camera was covered by part of a poncho, and he was carefully snapping photos even as the ship pitched and rolled, his feet braced on the deck, as he angled to get a good shot.

"Do you think those are going to turn out?" I called across the wind.

He turned to me. "I know they will."

Trev was talking about wildlife, and about the history of the area, and I found myself drifting slightly away from him and the rest of the group, to where Ryan was. I wanted to know what he was seeing. What he was seeing that was so interesting it was worth looking through a lens. It seemed like a distancing thing, and I had never really thought about that before. If he put a camera between himself and everything else for a reason.

"Do you see anything other than waterfalls?"

He looked at me. "Not yet."

I wondered if things were actually healing. If maybe we would be able to go back to town after this and . . .

No. Because he was leaving. Because he wasn't going back to town. I had forgotten that.

"Trev said that there might be fur seals."

"There are sometimes. I've been out here before."

I hadn't even thought to ask him that. "How long were you in New Zealand doing photography when you met Noah?"

"Six months. I left and came back. I spent quite a bit of time here."

"Is this your favorite place that you've been?"

"One of them."

"Why did you come back to Pineville?"

"My dad. When he got cancer seven years ago, it just seemed like the right thing."

I had vaguely heard that his dad had cancer, but he had seemed to get through it fine, so I hadn't really thought about it recently.

"Is he doing well?"

"Yeah," he said. "Just like it never happened. But then, even if he did have some after-effects from it, he would never admit it."

I tried to imagine his dad, who was fairly taciturn, acknowledging anything like the kind of trauma that came after an illness. I hadn't experienced it personally, but my gran had suffered some strokes, and the aftermath, all the changes, the hospitals, the doctors, they took their toll.

"Yeah. I can see that."

He lifted his camera again, and took some more pictures. The water was starting to pitch and roll even more. But I was captivated by our surroundings. Every so often there would be a cloud break, and sun would pour through the holes in the mist, like a waterfall of light. I found myself leaning against the railing, looking at the scenery, ignoring my hunger, ignoring the cold. The wet.

And I didn't worry. Not about anything. It was the strangest thing.

I wasn't even aware that my stomach had been queasy on the drive over.

And it would've been reasonable for me to have my sickness compounded by the waves.

"There," said Ryan, pointing off to the right. "Fur seal."

I looked, and saw a brown animal draped over a rock, his head lifted toward the rain, toward the sky.

I laughed. "Incredible."

"Better than a bear."

I laughed. "Yes. Better than a bear."

I looked up at him as the rain poured down on us, and I was instantly transported back to New Orleans. To that third wedding. To that first time I . . .

And then I remembered everything else. I turned away from him. "I'm just going to go . . . Check out the other side."

I moved to the other side of the boat, grateful for the distance, a little bit irritated at myself for being so painfully obvious.

I forgot to grab my sack lunch, and by the time the boat ride ended, I was starving, and we still had a long drive back to Queenstown.

"You should ride with Ryan," said Quinn. "So you don't get sick."

"What?"

"I could tell that you weren't well on the way. And I would let you have the front seat, but I will throw up. So, I just think maybe we should be in different cars."

That was how I found myself sitting in the front seat of Ryan's rental SUV, with just him and me. I had been on the verge of begging Trev to come with us, but I really didn't want him to get the wrong idea.

"I'm a vomit hazard," I said, as we got back on the road.

"I'm actually aware of that," he said. "Though I didn't bring any airsick bags from the plane."

"Wow."

I realized that this was the first time we'd been alone since the fifth wedding. We'd talked, but there had always been people around and within reach. Now it was just the two of us in his car and that felt different.

It felt dangerous.

It shouldn't. I'd known Ryan for a million years. And there had been one . . . thing. Just the one and otherwise we'd been fine. Infinite disaster defined our relationship far more than that ever could.

"Did you enjoy the tour?" he asked.

"Oh, yeah it was amazing."

We were doing small talk apparently. Maybe next we could talk about how cold it was.

"Oh look." He suddenly slowed the car to a near stop and pointed out his window.

"What?"

He pulled off onto the side, which felt risky given how narrow the shoulder was and how icy it was.

"*What?*" I pressed.

"Kea."

I straightened in my seat and he rolled the window down with his camera pointed out. I could see them then, two of them. Round birds perched on the rocks, walking around and picking at something in the cracks there.

"They're so funny," I said.

I watched, captivated, while he took pictures. But as the wonder of the birds wore off, I started to feel awareness. Of how close I was to him. Of his body heat. He smelled like soap and spice, even though we'd been out getting rained on all day. It was a scent that felt familiar even though I was sure I'd only been close enough to him to smell it one other time.

The strangest urge to move closer gripped me, right at the base of my throat.

It was so visceral, so unexpected, that I had to stop myself from gasping out loud.

I didn't, thankfully.

I was already in a charity car ride due to my delicate stomach, so I didn't need to go giving such clear signals regarding what was happening inside my body thanks to this man's scent.

Slowly, he pulled back onto the road, and we left the little birds behind.

"Maybe we'll see a kiwi," I said.

"Not likely. They are very shy, and nocturnal. Though there is an aviary, if you really want to see a kiwi."

"I'd like that. Where is it?"

"In town. I'm sure that Quinn's itinerary isn't quite so punishing that you can't squeeze in a trip."

"I'll keep that in mind. Did you go to the ice bar last night?"

He shook his head. "No. I went up to the ski fields at the Remarkables to take some pictures."

"Oh."

"I would have thought that you'd have gone."

I shook my head. "No. I . . . I was just feeling tired." Except maybe there was more to it than that. I was having a hard time saying for sure. If it was grief over Quinn leaving, then I needed to get it together. Though, rather than accepting that, I latched onto something else. "We really are the only members of the bridal party that have jobs."

"True."

"I have to bake a cake, you have to take the pictures. How are you even going to do that? You're the best man, and you're not going to be in any of the pictures?"

"Tripods and timers exist."

"Sure. But that means you won't be in most of them."

He shrugged. "I prefer it that way actually."

"Why?"

He shook my head. "I don't know. I have never liked having my picture taken."

I puzzled at that. "That seems . . . strange."

"Why? I managed to get myself into a position where I'm rarely the one that has to have their picture taken. And so many people enjoy it."

"Take the pictures so that you don't have to be in them?"

"Something like that."

"Pictures are such a weird thing." I looked out the window. I felt . . . a little bit silly taking the conversation this direction, but also, it was either that, or we sit and marinate in silence, and the fact that he smelled good, and I didn't want him to know that I thought so. "I mean, they're such a common thing. Now. Now that everybody has cell phones. But they used to be a lot more work. And . . . it is weird, when you go to somebody else's house, and there are all these family photos, but you don't have anything like that." I squeezed my face up just slightly, trying to mitigate the pressure building behind my eyes. Why was this making me emotional? Maybe it came back to the same question that I had been circling regarding not going to the ice bar.

"I don't have any pictures of myself before I was seven. I don't even really remember what I looked like. I remember I had very blunt bangs and a bob. But I feel like that was sort of a standard issue childhood haircut. I think my hair was lighter then. I remember I had a t-shirt with a smiley face and daisies on it. But I have trouble remembering some of the other things. And when you have friends who have baby pictures . . ."

"Yeah," he said.

I'd had the thought that we had things in common before. But this very concrete thing, it was a strange realization. Neither of us had pictures from our early childhood. And I knew there had to be something tangled up in that for him. In the way that he captured everything now.

"Do you have any?" I asked.

"No. I can't even remember . . . all the schools that I went to. The names of all the families I lived with. It's strange. To not remember those things. I used to. I don't remember quite when it all started to fade. It doesn't really matter. I moved in with the Clarks, and that was my home. And I think maybe that was when all the other things started to fade away. But now . . . I wish I had a stronger hold on it, I guess. Or at least some fixed memories. Maybe I'm always trying to take all the photos I didn't have of all the places that I go, because in my past, I didn't have those. And there are all these places that don't even make sense to me anymore. Like I remember going shopping at certain stores, but I don't know what they are, and I can't ask anybody. So I can't go back to them. And I can't . . ."

He couldn't make sense of his past. I'd had just a piece of that, half of it, compared to him. And even though I'd lived with a certain level of instability, there had been one caregiver.

"When did you get taken away from your biological parents?" I realized I didn't know that.

"I don't remember them," he said. "I think I got put into foster care before I was one. So . . . I moved all the time, starting from then. Sometimes more and sometimes less."

"I'm sorry. You don't have to . . . talk about it."

"It's just the way that it was. It's not really good or bad. It just is."

I sort of understood that too, because sometimes I felt that way about my own life. I did my best not to hold onto bitterness about it. It was the trauma responses to all the little things in life, that was much harder. Harder to banish, harder to cope with.

"I saw my file once," he said. "I know that I got taken away from my mom because she was a drug addict, and she neglected her kids."

"Kids?"

He nodded. "I have half siblings, somewhere."

"Any interest in doing a DNA test of finding them?"

He shook his head. "No. I have a family. And they're a good family, whatever your grandmother used to say about them."

He was the one person who had been bold enough since my grandmother's death to acknowledge the fact that she was a spiteful crone. I appreciated that. More than I could even say, because it was one of the things that I loved about her. Even if that didn't make sense to anybody else.

"Yeah, she wasn't a fan. But the great lettuce heist of 1980 . . ."

"That's made up," he said. "Why would anybody steal lettuce?"

"Apparently she caught it on the security camera. That was back when she served sandwiches at the bakery, and your grandfather's restaurant was in a rough patch, and somebody was stealing the produce that got left outside during delivery time. He was stealing two heads of lettuce every week."

"Two heads of lettuce. In the eighties, what did that even cost?"

"It's the principle of the thing, and anyway, it would've been commensurate cost wise to prices of other things. And wages. So anyway, that doesn't matter."

"Is that why the Loves hate the Clarks?"

"Oh no. It goes back to the Oregon Trail. Surely you know that."

"I don't know that, Poppy. You're going to have to explain it to me."

"You mean like I had to explain Shark Week?"

"Yes. Slowly, using small words."

I felt a little bit better now that the conversation had moved away from trauma. "Apparently, there was a grand affair back on the Prairie, and it caused a degradation in the relations between the two families."

"What?"

"Yes. Madeline Love had an affair with Ezekiel Clark. Brief, but passionate, and it nearly ruined their marriages, though in the end, the families decided to stay intact for practicality. After all, they had already uprooted their entire lives and moved across the country."

"How do you know this?"

"My grandma had a bunch of old journals. She liked family history, because then you can keep track of grudges. And she loved a grudge. She maintained that Madeline was nefariously seduced."

"Oh really?"

"Yes. Though I have to say, in my opinion, the journals make it pretty clear that she was a very enthusiastic participant in the affair. So, it's difficult to try to pin the blame on Ezekiel entirely."

"Well, if anybody would've tried."

"Gran would have. Yes. She wasn't a soft woman. But I didn't need softness. I just needed somebody stubborn enough to see everything through."

He nodded slowly. "I know your mom is Caroline Love."

"Yes. *Everybody* knows that. I mean, around town. No one outside of town is aware my mom has a daughter."

"You don't talk about it."

"No. Because she doesn't talk about me." I cleared my throat. "I'm not trying to be bitter or petty about it." Here we were, childhood trauma. How did that happen? "But, she doesn't even acknowledge that she has a daughter, not at all. And . . . I don't know who my father is. She was trying so hard to make it when I was little. We moved all around California, and she would try to get auditions and go for acting jobs. And I think mostly there was a lot of exploitative stuff happening. A lot of modeling gigs that turned out to be more than she bargained for. And I don't know if what she did was right or wrong. Because she achieved her dreams, didn't she? And now she's in charge of her own life. So maybe it was worth it. All of it."

"Except there was a casualty."

I looked at him, at his strong profile. It wasn't really fair of him to try and compare our wounds. Because his mom had been a victim of her own addiction. Mine had made choices, and yes, there had been a cost, but there had also been real results. Maybe his mother wasn't even alive anymore. That thought made me horribly sad. There were a lot of unknowns in my life, but . . .

Well, I guess with my dad it was like that. Whoever he was. Wherever he was.

"Yes. There was a cost. To her and to me. But life is like that. We can't escape generational trauma, I don't think. Because every single generation reacts to the trauma that they were given by the one before, but they have their own blind spots. And oftentimes that hits even if they don't intend it to."

"Explain."

"I don't know why my grandmother was the way she was. I mean, going back to her childhood. Because she didn't talk about it. Which tells me enough. I do know that she married a man who abandoned her and her daughter. I know that it played a part in her bitterness. In her wariness. She scraped by, she was stubborn and prideful. She worked her fingers to the bone. And I know my mother didn't want that. She felt like her own mother had trapped them both in this small-town existence. She felt like she hadn't given them . . . enough, because she hadn't been willing to leave her comfort zone. Because her loss of her husband made her contract in on herself, and all my mom wanted to do was expand. Dream. And her mother couldn't do that. I am a product of both of those women's successes and failures. The way that my mom raised her daughter . . . well, it landed me in the position that I was in. But then, she made it right by raising me. And I have my own baggage."

"I don't know. We all have a responsibility to try to do better than those people, I agree with that. But I don't think it leaves us exempt from owning the consequences of our actions. Your mom is famous, what has she done for you?"

"Nothing. But she doesn't have to."

"She fucking does. You're her daughter. I'm sorry. She chose to have you."

"I'm happy to be alive. I don't know that she owes me beyond that. Yes, we hope for more from our mothers. But we don't all get it. So . . ."

How weird that bickering with Ryan Clark about my mother could make me defensive of her.

"I don't even have enough of a concept of my mom to feel like she owed me."

"How old was she? Do you know?"

"I think sixteen. It's hard to hold a sixteen-year-old accountable."

I nodded. "That's a little bit how I see my mom. She was eighteen when she had me. And she didn't want it to define her life. Everything I've heard about motherhood suggests that it does define your life. So, I guess I can't really judge her, for trying to make it work differently, and when she couldn't . . . I have to believe that she did it a little bit for me. Even though I suspect it was mostly for her. But, it doesn't help me to think that way."

I cleared my throat. "I do think that I would have ended up in foster care if not for my grandmother. We were probably on the verge of it. We moved all the time."

"Is that why you were so nice to me when I moved to Pineville?"

I was startled by that. Because I thought that his memory of our interaction was entirely colored by the disasters that had occurred in the intervening years. I had been nice to him. And he had been mean to me. Cold and abrasive and standoffish. It had made me so nervous around him that . . . well, bowling balls.

"Kind of. Even though I moved to Pineville when I was in second grade, I know what it's like to be the new kid. I know what it's like to be the outsider. I really do."

"I couldn't be nice to you, because I didn't think that it was going to last. If you thought I was a dick to you, you should've seen how I was to Mary and Michael. They were trying to prove to me that they meant it, that adoption was forever. That it was different than what I had experienced before, but I couldn't take that on board. I couldn't see . . . I couldn't see a way that things were going to be secure. So, when you walked up to me, and you were friendly, friendlier than anybody else in the whole school, I decided that you were part of the scam."

I didn't know what to do with that. Because so much of our relationship was rooted in those difficult first interactions. Yes, we were adults now. There was no reason for me to hang onto irritation about that on the level that I had. But that wasn't really the point. I had thought that Ryan had hated me on sight. But in reality, it was a lot more complicated than that. And I had allowed my simple, middle school take on him to continue to be the level of understanding that I had. When actually, he and I had more in common than anybody else that I knew in town.

This conversation had driven that home.

"I just thought you didn't like my face."

The only sound then was the tires on the road.

"I liked your face a lot, actually."

I didn't know how to respond to that. So I didn't say anything. And he turned the radio on, for which I was grateful, because apparently we had gone from having nothing but shallow conversations that consisted mainly of us sniping at each other, to this. This deep uncovering of old wounds. This excessively difficult bracketing with the truth about what we were and why.

Things that I didn't even like to think about when I was alone.

We stopped in a very small town and bought some coffee at a place that also had an outdoor store attached, and I was bemused to find elk mounts and rifles on sale in small town New Zealand, when my perception had been that this place would be entirely different to my experience of rural Oregon. When I could have been convinced that I was back home in that moment. Except that in the pastry case at the coffee shop side, they had something called a sausage roll, which we absolutely did not have in Oregon.

I bought one, and we spent the rest of the drive making small talk about sausage rolls, meat pies, and other foods that he thought I needed to try while I was in the country.

"We can find out if everybody wants to go to FergBurger or Ferg-Baker tonight?"

"What is that?"

"Very famous hamburgers and meat pies."

"Well, I'm interested in that. Which is funny, because a lot of times famous things just trigger my fight or flight."

He smiled at me, and I realize that we had just gotten perilously close to making a date.

Well, a date by the standards of the middle schooler, since we were going to be with the whole group, from the sounds of it.

It was dark by the time we pulled back into the vacation rental, and when we went upstairs, the group was laying down on couches, arrayed about the living room.

"Is anybody interested in heading to town for meat pie?" Ryan asked.

"I think we're going to order UberEats," said Quinn. "Exhausted."

I was starving. Because I had not eaten the sack lunch on the boat, and it had really caught up with me.

"Do you still want to go to town, or do you want to do delivery?"

"I want the famous meat pie. And a burger."

"All right. Let's go."

Well. That was a plot twist.

It was entirely possible that I had a date with Ryan.

CHAPTER 9

*W*e decided to walk to town, even though it would take about fifteen minutes to get there. The parking in Queenstown proper was so difficult, that it just didn't seem worth it. There was a parking garage, but according to Ryan, it was a far enough walk away from FergBurger and FergBaker, that we might as well just walk and save ourselves the trouble. I stuffed my hands in my pockets, and tried to buffer myself against the wind blowing across the lake, as we walked along the sidewalk.

"Trust me, this is worth it. It's better than anything you can get delivered here."

"I am trusting you. Because I'm starving. I didn't eat on the boat."

He shook his head. "Me neither. But I've been on that tour before. And let me tell you, it's not worth it. There are carrots on that sandwich."

I wrinkled my nose. "Why would someone do that?"

"It's weird."

I was suddenly even more curious about him. About what had brought him to New Zealand in the first place, and how exactly he had met Noah. I was pretty sure that I had heard the story, but I filtered all these things about Ryan. So, even though I had hung out with Quinn and Noah, and he undoubtedly had been mentioned, it was like I did my very best to not claim details regarding Ryan.

"When exactly did you come to New Zealand?"

"I went to the University of Auckland for a couple of years. I was really interested in traveling around and taking pictures. So I did that. And that's where I met Noah. During break I came back home with him and met his family. Saw the North Island for the first time. And how can you not love it here?"

"Wow. I mean, I can definitely see loving it here."

"Then Noah came to the States to live for a couple of years, so we saw each other a lot during that time. Then obviously he was living in Tahoe when he met Quinn."

"Oh."

"So, of everywhere that I've traveled, this is more a second home to me than anything."

"What brought you back to Pineville?"

"It's hard work making money the way that I do. Possible. I'm fine. I bought a house." He said that casually, but I wondered what it meant to him. To have a permanent base. And right there, I think I grasped the crux of why he was back in Pineville.

It had become home when nothing else had. It was the same reason that I stayed.

But it must be hard, when you wanted to do the kind of job he seemed to love. When your ambition asked you to travel.

I could feel how those things must feel like they were pulling him in different directions. I felt that sometimes. I loved this. Being in this new place. But there was always this underlying feeling of being untethered that made me feel precarious.

I knew it was childhood issues. It was just knowing that didn't make it go away.

"I wanted to be closer to my dad. Especially after the cancer. I was worried . . . I was worried that we'd have limited time. And even though he's in remission, the truth is, it makes you realize that you *do* have limited time. I lived twelve years in foster homes. Moving from house to house. I had parents for six years. Six years of childhood. It wasn't enough. Nothing is ever really going to make that enough. But it made me feel like I needed to be home. Once I felt that, the time slipping away, I couldn't make that feeling go away."

"I get that. And having lost my grandmother, I know that you won't regret the choice."

He made a musing sound in the back of his throat. We crossed through the park, down past a lit sculpture of a fern on the edge of town. I stopped and looked at it. And then at the lights sparkling across the lake. There was a bar on a boat, lively and packed full of people. The town had a party atmosphere in the dark, but it felt joyful. There was nothing like the edge of chaos or violence that I had felt in some party cities. And it was a different vibe still to New Orleans, which had a darkness underlying all that glitter.

But being with Ryan felt the same, and that made my whole body go tight.

We walked away from the lake, headed toward a more central part of town, when we saw a massive line extending down the sidewalk.

"This is it," he said.

FergBurger and FergBaker were right next to each other, and they were clearly very popular. Because it was like lining up for a Disney ride.

"I promise it's not as bad as it looks."

There were heaters above, providing warmth while people stood out there, and that sort of joyous, excited atmosphere I had first felt when we came into town continued even to the queue with people bundled up and waiting for food.

"The question is: bakery or burgers?"

"I really want a meat pie first," I said.

"All right. Bakery it is."

The bakery did have the shorter line, so given that I was desperate for food, it definitely seemed like the more excellent choice.

What amazed me was how easy Ryan struck up conversations with the people around us. Everybody was a tourist, though many were from the North Island. Apparently, town was extra busy because the ski fields on the North Island hadn't gotten enough snow, which meant that all of the enthusiasts had taken their gear to Queenstown for the skiing. It was school holidays, and this was the only place to get any winter weather this year.

We chatted all the way to the front of the line, where I saw an array of pies and pastries behind the case. With great difficulty, I narrowed it down to two pies, which I knew I couldn't finish, especially not when I intended to get a burger, but I was bound and determined to try a variety of things. I got a classic pie, with mince and cheddar, and a chili pie, which just sounded too good to pass up.

Ryan got a chicken curry pie.

"I'll split the chili pie with you," I said. "That one feels like a risk."

We bought bottles of Coke, and then went outside with our spoils, wrapped in paper. Thankfully very easy to eat standing, so we immediately got into the hamburger queue, and I pulled out the mince and cheddar pie and tucked into it with relish. It was so good. I couldn't even imagine wanting anything as ordinary as a hamburger after exposing myself to the glory of a meat pie.

"I ruined myself for America," I said.

"It's pretty good," he agreed.

"Life changing," I said.

There was an ease between us that I really wasn't used to. That made me feel a little bit lightheaded.

The burger line was definitely longer, but I was warmed and cheered by the pies, and no longer hungry by the time we got to the front. I didn't care.

I ordered the FergBurger and then we went outside to wait until our number was called.

"Thank you," I said.

"Well, you might want to try your hamburger first."

"I mean, this is amazing, even if I hate the hamburger. Much more my speed than the ice bar."

"Must be the company," he said.

My heart did something weird when he said that. I knew he was kidding. Because of course he was.

The burger was as delicious as everything else had been, and we took our food off to some benches on the sidewalk. I sat down, and tucked one of my legs underneath me, and realized a bit late that it put my knee in extremely close proximity to his thigh. I chose to ignore that, I chose not to make a big issue out of it. Just like I had done earlier in the car.

I took a bite of my burger, which had to be one of the more unsexy things to take a bite of, and happened to look up at him right when he was looking at me.

My breath froze solid in my lungs, and so did my hands, my shoulders, my heart.

It was too easy. To try and look back on every interaction we had and recast it, based on the conversations we'd had earlier today.

It was too easy, and too tempting.

He'd said he liked my face.

It was tempting, also, to weave webs out of the connections that we found earlier. To apply significance to them.

Why?

Even if we *could* have a friendship, he was leaving. For how long, I didn't know, and I hadn't asked, because I didn't want him to think that I was curious about it.

Though that was old stuff. Old wounds when it came to him, old habits.

Here, it had been like being friends. A little bit.

Except there would always be something else there. An undercurrent that I didn't want to deal with.

That truth that had hit first in New Orleans, in a sultry roll of warm air, and then like a bolt of lightning in Tahoe.

I was attracted to him.

Undeniable, and harsh. Terrifying.

The fact that it lingered still, after everything. After all of our history, and the fifth wedding. After all the changes that had happened inside of me . . . well, it was a lot. Foolish, even. And yet, if I had ever been in control of that, I would have changed it a long time ago. I never would have opted to remain attracted to Ryan Clark.

I definitely would not have chosen to feel struck by lightning mid bite of a hamburger.

I forced myself to start chewing. To stop being weird.

I looked away.

Suddenly the silence between us wasn't comfortable. And I had to move my knee, because I couldn't handle the near touch. The closeness.

I sat down firmly, straight on the bench, and ate half of the hamburger, and about half of the fries. The meat pie was entirely consumed.

It felt like such a strange, domestic moment, or had, here in this place across the world from where we normally were.

But that was sort of us.

Us.

There wasn't an us. It wasn't like that. There was baggage, and weird stuff. There was a preponderance of charged moments and mistakes. Of both of us interpreting the other's actions in the meanest possible way. "Ready to walk back?"

I nodded. "Yeah."

I stuffed all of my leftovers into a large brown bag, determined to eat them at some point the next day. They were too good to sacrifice.

The walk home felt more awkward. It was crazy to me that I

was so affected by a little bit of unexpected eye contact. A rogue glance that had connected the two of us for a moment, and hadn't quite let me go.

I knew what it was. I wasn't an idiot.

It was the intensity of it, the profoundness of it, that was what surprised me. Every damned time. It just didn't feel like it should be like that. Honestly.

It didn't feel like it should be that intense.

Because if there was one thing I knew, it was that . . .

It couldn't go anywhere. For so many reasons, and the biggest one was ourselves and our traumas.

We were such spiky disasters with each other.

And, while I didn't know for certain, I suspected Ryan wasn't hunting for permanence.

You're not either. Not anymore.

Which left me with a question I'd never especially wanted to ask myself, but that Quinn's teasing me about Trev had promoted. At what point was I going to rip the Band-Aid off and have sex for fun? Not to try to keep somebody with me. Not to try to build a relationship that would last . . .

I looked at Ryan out of the corner of my eye. Because honestly, he would be the one.

That thought slammed into me with all the force of a freight train.

Hadn't I learned anything?

No. I really should hook up with Trev. That was the smarter thing. That would be the more sensible thing. Not to make Quinn feel better about moving to New Zealand, but because I would probably never see him again.

Or maybe I would. Sometime when I came to visit Quinn and Noah for the holidays. And what if he was married, and had children? That would be weird. Still less weird than having to deal with that in your hometown. That was . . . not on my list of ideal things.

I would have to deal with it with Josh.

Someday.

I didn't feel singed by that, though. Not that.

He stopped walking, and it seemed natural for me to do the same. "I just want to snap a couple of pictures. You can go on if you want. The rental house is just three places up."

"I'm not in a hurry."

"Just go," he said.

I looked up at him, and my stomach twisted. "Ryan . . ."

"We both know you don't have any intention of following through with this. So stop."

That was so unfair. That was so deeply unfair.

"I am not the one—"

But it died on my lips, because I couldn't . . . I couldn't deal with the truth of it. I didn't want to rehash what had happened a year and a half ago. The reason that I didn't think of it now, ever, was because it was just too hard.

Because I felt too damned guilty.

And somehow angry at the same time because it wasn't all my fault. It wasn't all one moment. It was years.

But instead of saying that, I turned away from him and made a dash across the street for the vacation rental.

And when I got inside, I greeted everyone with a smile and acted like nothing had happened.

When it came to Ryan, I'd gotten good at that.

He came in about a half hour later, and I ignored him, choosing instead to bustle around the kitchen that overlooked the living area, but made it easy enough to never make eye contact with anyone down below.

"Everything okay?" Quinn asked.

"Totally fine."

"You had a lot of Ryan today."

"Everything was awesome. This is the best trip ever," I said. "Thank you."

Quinn crossed to me and pulled me in for a hug. "I'm glad you're here. I'm glad you came to Pineville. I know the circumstances sucked. But, from the minute I met you, I knew you were going to be my best friend. I knew you'd be in my wedding. I knew I needed you."

All the difficult, sharp things from today were dulled by that.

She needed me.

Maybe my mom never had, but there were people who did. That mattered.

I looked at Quinn and considered telling the truth. But I wasn't sure what the truth was, so it died somewhere in my throat.

As far as my feelings for Ryan were concerned . . .

I had no idea how to talk about them, because I had never been able to decide exactly what they were.

CHAPTER 10

The Fourth Wedding
South Lake Tahoe
Eighteen Months Ago

The cease-fire Ryan and I had enjoyed after the great bear war was compromised after New Orleans. I'd seen him, of course. I'd gone out for drinks with Josh and we'd ended up with Ryan because we'd run into him at the bar. He'd come over to game a few times. I'd felt like he was firmly back in the category of Josh's friend, and definitely not mine.

Which was fine.

And nothing I was worrying about as I drove to Lake Tahoe, because I had more pressing concerns.

This was a loaded location for me, and I'd been nervous leading up to it because I didn't know if I'd have intense flashbacks to my childhood or anything. To the moment my mom had decided she was going to leave me with Gran so she could pursue her acting dreams without me hanging around.

I didn't think I was sentimental about that moment in quite that way. I'd made peace with not spending my childhood with my mom, in the way that you could. I had issues from it, sure. But I wasn't . . . sad about it. I loved Gran.

I was more worried about Gran memories feeling more heavy,

more painful. The loss feeling more pronounced in this place where she'd first become my primary caregiver.

Josh was meeting me in Tahoe the day of the wedding – he couldn't get time off to go early – and I decided to combat my road trip nerves with a loud playlist and my even louder singing, followed by a phone call to Josh once he was off work.

As soon as the clock rolled over to five, I pushed the phone button on my steering wheel and asked it to call him.

"Hey," I said when he picked up.

"Hi. I miss you."

That made my whole face warm. It didn't matter how many years we were together, the way he needed me made me feel so . . .

Well, it made me feel good. Especially as I drove to the site of my parental abandonment for the first time as an adult.

"I miss you too," I said, as I looked around the beautiful scenery, the last song on my personal playlist still lingering in my memory. The joy of solitude, I realized then. Choosing your own playlist.

"You doing okay? With the whole Tahoe thing?"

"Oh. Yeah." I scrunched up my nose. "I'm just going to focus on the wedding. It isn't like I have time to sightsee beforehand. But we can do a little of that in the couple days after the wedding."

"I never get to travel with you. This will be fun."

For some reason his words tangled up with a memory from New Orleans and it made my stomach go tight. It wasn't a full memory. It was like a sensory feeling. A thunderstorm and heavy air and my breath being frozen in my lungs.

"Yeah," I said, overly bright. "And this time I won't be left alone with Ryan." I hated myself for saying that. It was weird and not the kind of girlfriend energy I was trying to bring to the table. I did my best not to telegraph that Ryan and I had a weird and difficult relationship because why? He and Josh were friends. Best friends, even. Why would I make that weird?

There was a slight pause. "Yeah. I mean. I know it's weird because he doesn't like you."

He. Didn't. Like. Me.

You know that, why are you shocked?

Because it hadn't felt like that. For a couple of years, it really hadn't. I thought, for a while, that I'd won. That I'd convinced him I wasn't so bad.

Even weirder, I'd assumed his dislike of me was so buried, so unspoken, that Josh – who was sweet but not an emotional mastermind – hadn't noticed.

"Poppy?"

"Yes!" I said, smiling aggressively at my windshield.

"I'm sorry you know he doesn't—"

"Totally," I said, keeping the smile in place, because I would be damned if I sounded shocked or saddened by that statement.

"I just meant it must be weird having to work with him all the time."

"Not weird," I said. "He's been not liking me since sixth grade."

That was true. I let myself marinate on that. Sit with it. Let myself fully remember how – after obsessing about him when I'd first seen him in the restaurant – the first day he'd been at school, I'd bounded up to him with a bright smile and full of enthusiasm. He'd been so much taller than me, even then, and he'd looked at me with that same anger I'd seen the first time I'd encountered him.

But I was determined to blast through it with my cheerfulness.

Hi! You're the new kid, Ryan, right? I'm Poppy.

He'd looked at me like I was a slug that had crawled out from under a rock and up onto his shoe, leaving a slime trail behind. Like I was a horror. Or worse, like he hated me.

Did you think I'd beg you to be my friend or something?

His question had shocked me.

No. I didn't . . . I'm just saying hi. I'm being nice.

Oh, because it's a nice thing to do? To talk to the foster kid?
N-no.

I'd wanted to tell him that I was like him. My mom didn't want me either. But it was like he could see something in me I had always been afraid everyone would see someday. That my friendliness was fake. That it was just a desperate bid to get people to like me.

I don't need a friend.

I'd left him alone that day, but it had been like a festering wound. A fear that if I couldn't get that boy to like me, he'd eventually make everyone see I wasn't likeable. That I didn't belong.

So I'd tried. Over and over again.

Until the bowling ball.

Until I'd ruined it for good.

Until I'd started to accept that I couldn't overcome a multi-generational feud.

And then it had been like freedom. Once there was a reason for him to dislike me, however stupid, I'd felt like it was okay. He could dislike me. And I never had to try to make him like me again.

So it had gone on for years.

Then I'd been stupid enough to think things had changed.

"He's a good guy," Josh said, suddenly sounding defensive. "It's just . . . you know. His past kind of messed him up in some ways."

So say we all.

An ironic conversation to have as I rolled into Tahoe, the site of much of my own childhood trauma.

Feeling all upset about a guy not liking me, when I didn't need him to like me. Behold, my own *messed up*.

"You're coming in at around three on Saturday?" I asked, eager to change the subject.

We finished the phone call right as I pulled up to the vacation block that had been rented out for the bridal party and wedding crew.

I made sure to bring all of my food ingredients into the cabin before anything else, because I did not truck with bears. And never would again.

Then I grabbed my overnight bag, and walked up the steps into the quaint little cabin. It was markedly different to the one I'd stayed at in Yellowstone. Newer, more modern. I liked both.

I did my best to not ruminate on the conversation I'd just had with Josh. I was a champion ruminator. My mind ping ponged to my mom, my grandma, as I explored the cabin and started organizing my baking supplies.

All those things were connected. Why it made me feel sick to my stomach that Ryan didn't like me, and my mom taking me on vacation in Lake Tahoe to meet Gran, buying me ice cream, and telling me I wasn't going home with her. I was going with Gran.

I stood in the middle of the kitchen for a moment, frozen in place.

I had been better off with Gran.

Gran had been a great maternal figure to me.

And my mom had been successful. Though only after she'd given me up.

Had she been wrong? If she'd needed to not have me to live her dreams, was that a worthy sacrifice?

It was just that it meant I didn't have my mom. It was just that it meant my mom was better off without me, and I very likely was better off without her. It was a difficult pill to swallow and always had been.

Because everybody wanted to have a mom, I supposed. The kind that you are supposed to have. The kind that mine played on TV.

But never in real life.

And I'd been left to feel like there was something wrong with me. Something that had made me fundamentally not enough. Which was the full circle that brought me back to Ryan, and his instant dislike of me, and why it haunted me this many years later.

I let out a hard breath that sounded a lot like a dying wildebeest and decided to do something to stop the endless thought churn

I was trapped in. I found a restaurant on UberEats and ordered myself a burger and fries and while I waited I started plotting out my baking plan.

I was excited because it was a pink cake, that was going to be strawberry flavored, and it was one of my favorite things to make. Because it was bursting with flavor, and provided all the natural pink color that you could want.

There. Just like that, I was back in the present where there were plenty of good things to focus on, and I didn't have to wrestle with existential questions about my childhood.

My food arrived and when I poked my head out the door to grab the bag, I saw Ryan's truck parked in the driveway next to mine.

How did this keep happening? I was haunted by this man and his disdain.

But then it was like New Orleans inside me again. Like a thunderstorm and nothing quite as simple as dislike.

I took a shower, and changed into sweats, because I was in for the night, and then started getting out all of the ingredients for my cake.

I began cutting the tops off the strawberries, putting them into a pot with sugar to mash and reduce them, so that they could flavor the cake without adding a surplus of extra liquid. I had always found baking to be therapeutic. Distracting.

I put the butter and sugar into the mixing bowl and turned it on, the whir of the motor steady. When I was a kid, I'd like to sneak a taste of the creamed butter and sugar. Better still if the eggs had been added. I laughed to myself as I added the eggs and vanilla.

It had horrified Gran that I'd liked to taste the batter at that stage. She'd told me off every time I sneaked a fingerful, tutting about e coli and other dangers.

I whisked together the dry ingredients. I knew cakes by heart. Cake flour, salt, baking soda, baking powder.

It grounded me in the moment.

The smell, the textures of everything, the opportunity to taste different stages of batter and frosting and filling.

I had just gotten my cake layers into the oven when I looked up out the window of the cabin and saw Ryan. It was dark outside, and with the lights on over in his cabin, the view was a glorious beacon that I couldn't ignore.

He was walking through the kitchen and living area of that cabin, shirtless. I felt my jaw go slack. I couldn't look away. My heart started to beat faster, at first from the visual, but then from panic.

His chest was broad and well defined, with a smattering of dark hair over his pecs, going down his washboard abs, which I could see from the next cabin over, which meant they must be absolutely insane close up.

But the panic wasn't from that. It was from the physical reaction that it created in my body that I could no longer ignore, mislabel or deny.

I was attracted to Ryan Clark.

It was why I was so angry about what had happened in New Orleans.

It was why I had stopped breathing when we were underneath that awning in the French Quarter.

It was why I felt betrayed.

By him kissing that other woman. By him acting like we hadn't fought a bear war, or run in the rainy French Quarter streets every time we saw each other this part year.

I was stunned by this realization that couldn't matter. How long had I felt like this?

It couldn't matter because I had Josh.

I had Josh and I loved him, and he was the one I was planning on spending the rest of my life with.

But I was attracted to Ryan.

"No," I said.

I said it out loud even, because it was just too much, as I stood there still, frozen and looking at his body.

Then he looked up, and his eyes met mine. Through the glass, across the expanse outside. I felt it. I felt it hit me straight in the chest like a freight train.

I turned away from the window, my heart pounding so hard I could barely breathe. My movements so obvious that there was no way he couldn't know exactly why I'd turned so sharply.

I moved around the corner of the kitchen and leaned against the wall, my hand pressed to my rapidly beating heart.

And I worked to untangle the horror inside of me.

Of course, I lived in the world, I was realistic. There were other attractive men besides my boyfriend. Who I thought was cute. Thank you.

But it wasn't *this*.

This had teeth. Teeth that had been sunk into me for I didn't know how long.

Okay. This was the problem. I had accepted that there would be other men in this world that I would find attractive. But there was a line between attractive . . . and attracted to. Because of the incident in New Orleans I couldn't pretend it wasn't the latter.

And that was terrifying. Because that went against everything that I wanted, everything that I was.

It felt like danger.

Danger in the streets of my hometown. Danger here, away from everyone and everything.

Good thing he doesn't like me.

Right.

He didn't like me. He didn't suffer from the same affliction. That much was clear. He had been up that bridesmaid's skirt two hours after I had experienced a breathless meltdown in the streets of New Orleans. And every day since he'd acted like nothing had ever happened at all.

It didn't have to mean anything.

It wasn't going to mean anything.

I would never do anything, act on, linger on, these feelings.

It wasn't healthy, it wasn't sane.

And I was going to pretend that I hadn't seen him like that, and that I hadn't felt what I did.

I waited until I absolutely had to go check on my cake layers in the oven. And when I dashed out into the kitchen, I was relieved to see that his curtains were closed downstairs, and the lights were off.

But then I wondered if he was upstairs. If he was going to bed. If he had taken off any more clothes . . .

I stopped that train of thought. Hard.

I wasn't going to think about Ryan Clark or what state of undress he might be in.

I had a cake to bake. I had a life back home.

I had never understood the concept of enemies to lovers. Because for me, a relationship had always come with feelings first. A sense of safety.

I had never been able to understand how animosity could be a thinly veiled cloak hiding attraction between two people. The worst thing was, I still didn't understand it. I could only marinate in the realization that for me, it was apparently a thing. And I hadn't known it until it had gotten obvious and half-dressed.

It explained the horrible, sick feeling that I'd had when I had seen him kissing that other woman. Because then I had known what he looked like when he was kissing. When he wanted somebody.

And it was in my head.

It wasn't as simple as wanting to be in her place. I didn't think I wanted to be in her place.

Even knowing that I was attracted to him, I didn't think that's what I had been responding to. Or why I had reacted that way.

It was . . .

It could never be jealousy. Because I wanted what I had. I didn't want him.

Maybe that was part of the tangled, nuanced aspects of physical attraction that I had never had to parse before.

I was attracted to him. It was specific. Not theoretical. That was bad.

But I didn't want him.

Because we didn't mesh. Because he was the opposite of safe.

Because he was difficult.

That wasn't what I wanted my life to be.

There was another sort of person who might blow up all of their safety, all of their security, for that level of intensity. But it wasn't me.

Because I had experienced too many explosions in my life when I was younger to ever willfully cause one as an adult.

I finished the cake, continually repeating these new truths in my head, because when I saw Orion tomorrow I couldn't be stammering or blindsided. Because I needed to accept it so that I could process it and move on. Like this was a trauma I had experienced that I needed to apply therapy to it.

Well. It was a trauma that I had experienced.

But I could get over it.

It wasn't maternal abandonment.

It wasn't the death of my grandmother.

It was just an inconvenient heart flutter.

I slept fitfully, and when I got up in the morning, ready to get the cake loaded up and put into the car, I ended up stopping mid-motion.

I'm attracted to Ryan.

"Okay," I said. "Get it out of your system, Poppy."

I put it in the back of my car, and did not leave it unattended, as I drove to the wedding venue.

And I asked for a sign from my grandmother. To sort me out.

To let me know that she was there. To make me feel something other than turmoil.

She had always told me that I could ask for a sign after she left.

I hadn't done it, because I didn't want to bother her. Because she said that, but I could also see her being as cranky in the afterlife as she had been in this one.

But I asked.

I pulled up to the wedding venue just as somebody picked up a long folding table and swung it around, moving it abruptly. My eye went straight to the table, and I continued to ease forward a few feet. Until I saw movement out the driver side window. And heard a harsh curse.

It was Ryan. Right there, next to my driver side window.

I rolled the window down in a panic. "Did I run over your foot?"

"No," he said, his face like granite. "Just my camera lens."

"*Oh.*"

My first thought was Gran moved quickly.

Fuck this man and his abs, she'd said, and struck his camera lens dead.

I didn't know why she had chosen to act in the form of re-creating the sixth-grade science fair, but it definitely seemed like a reminder.

Of who we were.

Of why it was never going to be anything but this.

"Why was it on the ground?" I asked. I practically wailed because I hadn't wanted for things to go like this.

He leaned in just slightly, and I felt the air exit my lungs. "It wasn't. It was on that table. Because I was changing lenses, and then they moved it. And it fell on the ground."

"I didn't do it on purpose," I said.

"Do you really think I'm immature enough to think that you did?"

I had thought that he had mangled my cake on purpose.

But I realize that's what he was referring to.

That I was immature, and he wasn't.

"No. Of course not."

That was all the reminder I needed.

This was who we were. This mess of crushed camera lenses, ruined solar systems, and irritation.

We were not a rainy night in New Orleans. We were not whatever had happened to me last night.

"Do you need help with . . .?"

"No. I don't need your help with anything."

He picked up the shattered camera lens, and I rolled up my window.

"Thanks for the help, Gran."

I meant it.

After that I set up, while trying to keep myself from having a breakdown about everything that had just happened. From last night to that moment. Josh was actually coming to this wedding because he knew the groom from high school. Quinn was in the wedding, and I needed to keep everything together.

I saw Quinn dash by at some point.

"How did everything go with the pictures?"

"Fine. Why?"

I shook my head. "As long as it was fine. It's not important."

Then I worked at getting everything set and ready for when it was time for me to cut the cake.

At that point, Josh appeared, while the bridal party was still off getting photos taken.

He kissed my cheek, and I felt my stomach twist with guilt.

I shouldn't feel guilty. I hadn't done anything wrong.

I had just . . . noticed Ryan when he was shirtless. And grappled with some unflattering truths about myself. But it was just . . . it was what it was.

"I'm excited that I finally get to see you do your thing," he said.

I felt something in me soften. He was supportive. He was a good boyfriend. And feelings were just feelings. Looking at a man who was aesthetically pleasing was just that.

And so was running over his camera lens.

I had Josh. And that was what mattered.

Everything went smoothly after that. Serving the cake, the reception. Ryan was taking photos on the periphery, but I felt like he kept more of a distance during cake photography than normal.

He was mad at me.

I couldn't really blame him.

I ended up sitting with Quinn, and some of the other bridesmaids, raising a glass to the bride and groom.

"Drinks are on me, Poppy," she said, making her way toward the bar. "Because you did exquisite work today, and should I ever get married I'll need you to make my cake."

"Should you get married, I'll be the last one standing."

"You'll probably get married before me," Quinn said. "You and Josh have been together forever."

Seven years. But I didn't feel like we were any closer to marriage now than we had been the day we'd moved in together. Why change what wasn't broken? Why do something as drastic as say wedding vows and linked taxes? It seemed excessive.

"I'm not in a hurry. Besides, I go to more weddings a year than anyone I know. I've had my fill of weddings."

"I'm sure he goes to as many as you do. If not more."

He.

"Sure," I said.

Then, it was like her statement conjured him up. Out of thin air.

Because there he was, striding toward the bar – and maybe us – with intent and intensity. A hallmark of his entire . . . thing. It irritated me. We were at a wedding. Well, the afterparty. It wouldn't kill him to smile.

Except then he did, and I'd never be able to explain the reaction I had to it.

It shifted his whole face.

I'd known him since sixth grade. It wasn't like I'd never seen him smile.

But on his thirty-year-old face, it seemed new.

And I found myself smiling back.

Only to realize he hadn't been smiling at me. Or heading my way at all.

He stopped at the bar and clapped a man sitting there on the back, who stood and greeted him like they were long lost brothers.

"Who is that?"

Quinn was looking over at Ryan and his friend with very intense interest.

I wanted to say something cutting and clever about the fact that he was clearly someone important because he'd made Ryan, of all people, smile, like an actual human man and not a robot; or maybe something about how I couldn't possibly know if Quinn didn't know.

Instead, I managed a shrug.

And Quinn marched right over there as I shrugged, so I had to hurry and follow along.

"Hi, Ryan," she said.

This time, Ryan did look at me. And then back at Quinn. "Hi, Quinn." He looked at me again. Then at the man sitting at the bar. "Quinn," he paused for a beat, "this is Noah."

And Quinn looked lit up. "It's nice to meet you."

Josh joined us then, beer in hand. "This must be Noah!"

Why did he know who Noah was? Oh right, because he and Ryan were friends. And Ryan didn't like me.

"Yeah that's me," said Noah, who everyone now knew but me.

"Josh," said Josh.

"Ah, good to meet you, mate!"

Ryan looked at me. "Noah was my roommate in college. In New Zealand. Noah, this is . . . Poppy."

No explanation of me and Noah didn't have that same spark of recognition he'd had when Josh had introduced himself. Because Ryan didn't like me.

"Nice to meet you." I looked around the group and I could see that Quinn was completely felled by the beauty of that man, and he was gorgeous, so I couldn't blame her.

But I had Josh.

And I was attracted to Ryan.

Who didn't like me.

Oh God, I was going to have to scoop my brain out and put it in rice or something because it was short circuiting.

"I'm going to go get a round of drinks," I said. "Who wants a drink?" I looked around the group. "Drinks?"

A few hands went up and I nodded in the affirmative and migrated to the other end of the bar. The bartender came over and I smiled. "Can I get a round of whatever you have on draft for the group down there?" I gestured toward the knot of people at the other end of the bar.

"I can help you carry drinks back."

I turned around and Ryan was standing far too close. I hadn't expected it. Or him. "Go visit with your friend," I said.

"It's fine."

"No. No. I . . ." I bit the inside of my cheek.

"What?"

"Nothing," I said.

"Why hold back now?" he said. "You usually have no trouble speaking your mind with me."

Wasn't that a weird truth. I had a lot of trouble with it with most people, but not him. Because the damage was done already with him. Because there was no saving us.

"Fine. I don't get why you are helping me when you don't like me."

He paused. "What?"

"Yeah, I hear you don't like me."

His dark blue eyes shone with that same hardness I'd seen all those years ago. When we were kids and he'd hated me on sight, but for some reason it felt different now.

And then he took a step toward me, and I couldn't breathe. It was too much like New Orleans, and too much like the realization I'd had in the kitchen earlier today and I wanted to run away.

Because I had Josh. Because he was wonderful and safe and he liked me, and Ryan didn't, so why did he get to make me feel this way?

But I didn't step back.

"Here you go."

The bartender slid five glasses down the bar in front of us and Ryan reached into his back pocket and took out his wallet, putting his card on the bar top.

"I offered to get the drinks," I said.

"I got it," he said.

Then he picked up three of the glasses, balancing them like an alcoholic triangle in his hands, his forearm brushing mine and sending a sharp shock through my body.

He turned away and walked back to the group.

He didn't like me. But Josh did. Quinn did. Hell, maybe Noah would. There was no point in wasting my time worrying about Ryan.

Josh looked up, and his eyes caught mine.

It was a reminder that I had what I needed already.

CHAPTER 11

Present Day

A few days later the other bridesmaids flew into Queenstown, and we split our activities more firmly off from the groomsmen. I was ready for that. I needed a little bit of space from Ryan. Every time it seemed like we were on some kind of even footing, things went wrong. But with Quinn's words from the other day, and the energy from the other women, I was feeling stronger, a little less broken than I had been for a while.

We drove to Glenorchy, a very small town around forty-five minutes from Queenstown, where we walked a lovely, flat hiking trail that gave an incredible view of the mountains, marshes and wildlife. We ate ramen at a tiny shop at the end of a row of buildings, and then bought souvenirs at a yarn store that also had pottery and other items made by local artisans.

The next day we went to Arrowtown, which was much closer to where we were staying. A charming town that reminded me of Pineville. It also had its roots in the 1800s gold rush, though half a world away from the one I was familiar with. Yet, it was the ultimate reminder that people were people.

They were greedy, relentless, brave assholes who pursued wealth at the expense of happiness, for the promise of an easier life later.

The human condition really was something.

We stopped in a candy store and got caught up trying flavors of fudge, and possibly bought more sugar than any group of people could reasonably consume. Though I was intent on trying it.

We went into a souvenir shop where I bought a sweatshirt and some possum/merino wool gloves.

"The possums are a big problem for the environment," the man in the store told me as he rung up my purchases. "They wreck the trees. Not native."

"Oh," I said.

"And you know how we got the possums, eh?"

"I . . . don't."

"Well, we had a big problem with rabbits, and so we introduced stoats to kill the rabbits."

I blinked. "I see."

"Only then the stoats overpopulated and began to kill the native bird life. They're a massive threat to kiwis – the birds not the citizens. So the government figured, as stoats and possums are natural enemies, maybe possums would do the trick. So, they introduced possums, but instead of fighting and killing each other, they leave each other be. They don't have a common dietary need which means the stoats and possums get on famously. But the possums wreak havoc on the trees, which is also bad for the birds. But, handy thing, possum fur makes wonderful garments."

"Well . . . guess I'm doing my part," I said, indicating the gloves.

We went into a clothing store, where a woman explained just why clothing made from possum was so coveted for its warmth and softness.

As we walked down the street later, Quinn took some fudge out of the bag and took a bite. "Do you think that there is a possible lobby somewhere, trying to do a hard sell to get people to wear possum, just because they're actually overly plentiful, or do you suppose it actually is extra nice?"

"I'm going with possum lobby," I said. "Which both wants to drive up the price of possum fur and eradicate possums."

"The perfect crime."

Because that seemed as reasonable as anything.

We did go to the aviary, and I got to see the kiwis running around in their habitat, which simulated nighttime, so the guests could catch glimpses of the round nocturnal animals as they scurried around in their enclosure. They were much bigger than I had imagined kiwis would be. It was such an amazing thing to be outside my life for such an extended period of time, and feel grounded still. To not feel quite so desperate to go back home and cling to my grandmother's house. To not feel quite so much like I was losing touch with who I was and what I was meant for.

Or even sadder, my whole identity.

I was really beginning to feel that no matter where Quinn lived, we would always have a connection.

My mother had taught me that wasn't possible.

Because she had left me, and since then contact had been minimal. The person I cared for most, the person I had wanted most when I had been a little girl, had convinced me that out of sight really was out of mind, even with people you loved.

I realized how brilliant Quinn was, setting all this up. And I told her so one night when we were having hot pots at a restaurant in Queenstown.

"I'm so glad that we got a chance to see your new life," I said. "It's going to make me feel part of it, even though we're far away."

Hannah raised her glass in salute. "To Quinn! The bravest one."

Sierra laughed. "I don't know, I feel like your great skinny-dipping escapades in eighth grade were pretty brave."

Hannah laughed. "Only because the water was cold."

"Nah, it was brave," Caitlin said. "There's a reason I wouldn't do it."

I had done it. Because I didn't want Hannah to think I was a chicken, even though I was. I'd admired that Caitlin hadn't felt the need to do that.

I didn't really feel the need to just say or do things to go along with the crowd anymore, I realized. And even if I was tempted to, Hannah, Caitlin and Sierra would never make me feel like I needed to.

This dinner, this moment, was a reminder that while Quinn was my person, I did have other supports back home in Pineville.

I had friends.

And now I had a piece of my heart here, and it wouldn't be inaccessible to me. It wouldn't be impossible for me to reach it.

I wasn't going to be lost from it forever.

Intermittently, during the trip I had gotten texts from Josh, telling me about a road trip that he was on. And even that made me feel pretty good. Because I felt like there was something repaired in that relationship too. It had been important to me for a very long time, and I was glad that we were back on pretty decent footing.

Three days before the wedding, Quinn's parents, and Noah's parents, took the bride and groom out to dinner, and most of the wedding party went their separate ways for the evening. And I decided that it was the time to get started on the cake, since I was also going to be busy with the rehearsal dinner the following night. And that was when I allowed myself to really get in my feelings. To think about Quinn and our friendship. And how we had talked about our weddings when we were children.

I put every ounce of love that I had for her into that cake. I thought about all the years we had known each other, and shared our hopes and dreams. I thought of how knowing her had changed my life. How being her friend had genuinely opened up a part of me that had been closed off before.

She was my first friend. And my dearest. And her vanilla and lemon wedding cake would taste better than anything else I had ever made for the amount of feeling that was baked into it.

I heard footsteps coming up the stairs and turned toward the staircase. Ryan. Of course. He had his camera bag slung over his shoulder. It wasn't lost on me that the both of us were sort of set apart from everybody else in some ways. We had wedding duties, and that was part of it. But also, he was the lone American amongst the groomsmen. But there was also just something . . . separate about him.

In general.

He had friends. Josh was one of them. But there would always be that piece of Ryan Clark that felt inaccessible. I had to wonder how much of it was from his childhood. From feeling like there was something fundamentally wrong with him because his mother hadn't kept him.

That was how I felt sometimes. It was the wound I carried around underneath everything. That deep fear that there was something fundamentally different about you, and everybody else could see it. That there was something wrong with you, and it was going to come out at some point, and people wouldn't want to know you.

Because what must be broken in someone for their own mother to not want anything to do with them?

I wondered if that was the real reason he and I always seemed to be the ones that were left behind in a quiet moment.

"You didn't go out?"

"I have a cake to bake," I said.

"I see."

"I don't mind. It's nice to have a little bit of time separate from all the activity. As much fun as it's been."

He nodded. "I can only binge drink so many nights in a row."

"Is that really what you guys have been doing?"

"These Kiwis can drink me under a table. I don't have the energy for it."

I laughed. "Oh, well. That hasn't been happening at our girl outings. They've been very sophisticated."

"Maybe I should have gone with you guys."

"Maybe," I said.

I knew better than to let out a breath. I knew better than to totally believe that things were going to feel normal between us for the duration of this conversation.

I was far too familiar with the rhythm of our particular dance.

A smooth tango for a few beats, and then a catastrophic failure.

We were a beautifully risen cake taken out of the oven too soon. The end result of that was a crater.

And nobody wanted a cake crater.

I was determined to be vigilant in my watch for that.

Both metaphorically and literally.

"What were you doing?"

"Taking pictures."

"It's dark outside."

"I have a star tracker," he said. "That way I can take photos of the night sky on a really long exposure, and the stars stay sharp."

"I don't really understand how any of that works," I said.

"I can explain it."

"I dunno, I kind of like the magic of it."

"Fair enough. I guess I like the magic of cake without understanding how it all works."

"I never did get the feeling that you especially liked cake."

"As a matter of fact," he said, "I do. You know I've had a piece of wedding cake at every wedding we've been at together."

I looked at him, trying to see if he was teasing me or not. He looked serious.

"You never said."

"Because I'm a dick, sometimes even in spite of my best efforts."

An unexpected olive branch, and I wasn't above reaching out to take it.

"Well, I am open to praise."

"You're very good at what you do," he said.

I sniffed. "Feels a little faint."

"Best wedding cake I've ever had."

"That's better." In spite of myself, I was warmed.

"Glad you could be pleased."

"I'm actually not that hard to please."

We stood there and looked at each other for a moment. I couldn't decide what the feeling was that expanded between us. I wasn't sure I wanted to.

I saw a message flash up on my phone, sitting on the counter, and I turned away from Ryan, grateful for the slight break.

It was another one from Josh.

I drew back in surprise when I opened it and saw that it was a picture of him with a woman.

Met this girl Rose at the Grand Canyon. We decided to travel together.

I gaped at that.

I couldn't quite figure out what he meant by that. Except it was Josh, and I genuinely didn't think he meant anything awful by it. He was sending me a picture of himself with another woman. And I wasn't sure how I was supposed to react to that.

But this was what he had said he wanted to do. He wanted to travel around, he wanted to adventure and all of that.

He had wanted to be with other people.

And I didn't even know how I could fault him for that when he had been honest.

Enough time had passed that it wasn't like . . . it wasn't like it hurt sharply. It was just . . . I still couldn't quite fathom what he expected me to do with the information. If we were friends, I supposed it was fair.

But I wasn't sure that we were friends quite like that. I had been feeling like we were. I wasn't jealous. It was just odd.

I looked up and saw Ryan staring at me.

"What?"

"You look upset."

"I'm not upset."

"Liar."

"I'm not," I said.

I was lying.

"Who's that from?"

"It's really not your business."

"Really?"

"Really." I turned away from him.

"There's not a faster way to make me even more convinced that is something weird."

"It's just Josh, okay. He's traveling around the Grand Canyon, and he met somebody. Which is fine."

"What the fuck? Why do you accept that from him?"

"He's your friend, Ryan. You should know that he doesn't mean anything by it."

"All the hell he doesn't. He does mean something by it. He knows that you're here in Queenstown, saying goodbye to Quinn. He knows that you're here with me."

"What does that have to do with anything?"

"Are you serious?"

"I . . . yes. I'm serious. I don't know what that has to do with him. He doesn't . . . know anything."

"He's fucking jealous," Ryan said. "He's always been insecure when it comes to you, do you really not realize that?"

I tried to think back on my extremely unremarkable, extremely placid relationship with Josh.

Nowhere along the way had it ever seemed to me that he was jealous. Why would he be? I had never . . .

I had been attracted to Ryan.

Had I telegraphed that?

I didn't think so. I had only ever really been exposed to Ryan when we were away.

Was there something that we both put off? Sparks that I hadn't even noticed until a year and a half ago?

That had been there, but that I had been oblivious to.

"Yes. He's insecure. That's why he . . . that's why he's sending you those pictures. He wants you to be jealous. You've been broken up for nine fucking months, did you really not get that he wanted you back the whole time?"

"No," I said. "Because he broke up with me. Why would I think that he wanted me back?"

"I think he wanted you to respond to the breakup differently than you did."

"You think?"

"No. I *know*. I mean, I know him. He was miserable as fuck after the breakup and he was . . . waiting for you to call and you didn't. From my perspective, that was what he wanted. For you to chase him down. To beg for him to take you back."

"I don't . . . I never saw any of that."

"Why not? I don't understand that you were with him for that many years and you didn't see how . . . insecure he was?"

"You're his friend. If I said anything like that about Quinn you could be certain that I had been body snatched."

"Yeah. I've been friends with him since middle school. Which means I am pretty well versed in his bullshit – intentional or not. I think he means well, Poppy. But he didn't always do well, not with you. And he always thought he was punching above his weight."

"*That* I just can't believe."

"Because you don't see yourself the way that . . . everybody else does. I don't know what you see. I can't fucking imagine. How you look in the mirror and see somebody that . . . had to work to keep somebody like Josh."

"He was a good boyfriend," I said. "He was a good boyfriend who . . ."

"What? I'm all ears. What did he do for you? What did he do other than sit around in your house; he was practically a throw pillow on your couch. What did he give you?"

I felt something furious bubbling up inside of me; at Ryan, at Josh, at myself. Because how dare he, how dare he come in here and lecture me about my relationship. My seven-year relationship that had been so defining to me.

How dare Josh actually be less than I had realized until that moment? And how dare I be so oblivious to it because of my own feelings about myself?

How dare Ryan again, for being right.

For not being wrong about what I accepted. For not being wrong about what I had wanted.

"He needed me. And he made me feel safe," I said.

"Is that it?"

"What more is there, Ryan? What more is there when you know what it feels like when somebody abandons you. When you know what it feels like to have somebody that you love completely cut you out of their life?"

"That's not love, is it?"

"Security? It feels a lot like love to me. I'm not . . . the thing is, I don't want him back. I don't. Losing him just showed me that I needed to see my life differently. I'm not an idiot. And you're not any better than he is. Coming in and trying to tell me what I should and shouldn't accept. I am aware that Josh isn't the one for me. I'm not looking at that picture and wishing that I was Rose. At the same time, he is a person in my life and I'm glad that he's still in it—"

"Just because you're afraid of losing people."

"I'm sorry, is it better to act like you? Like none of the people in your life matter? Like you don't give a shit about anything?"

"I give a shit about plenty of things. Maybe you should stop acting like you know everything. About everybody, including me."

"Why should I stop when you're doing the same?"

"I do know you. That's something I think you really don't get. I don't connect with people the same way that you do, no. But I know you. I have watched you from the time we were twelve. I have watched you assume that your presence bothers people, that you have to work double time just to keep friends around. I have watched you treat yourself like you matter the least. From upside down wedding cakes to . . . to freaking out about the cake when a bear tears your car apart and your biggest worry is disappointing someone, not your own sanity or safety."

I ignored how deep that gouged me. "And I watched you use your camera to keep everybody at a distance. To build a barrier between yourself and anybody who ever wants to get close to you. To the point that you can come to me and trash your friend because . . . I can't even fathom why."

"You can't?"

His words ground against something inside me.

"I don't want him," I said.

"But you're not really over it." He shook his head. "I don't have the patience for it."

He turned and walked away, and I felt like someone had taken a giant spatula and scooped my insides out. The last two big blowups with him had more warning.

That the fifth wedding was history we might be doomed to repeat, if we weren't very, very careful.

And I did not want to repeat that history.

Not even a little.

I pulled my cake out. It was perfect.

The only crater was in my communication with Ryan.

I had no idea how to fix that.

Maybe I didn't need to.

It was a radical thought.

Somewhere along the line, I had lost track of one of the most exhilarating things about Ryan Clark.

Which was that I couldn't please him. So, for a long time I hadn't tried.

Ever since the fifth wedding, I had fallen into trying to fix whatever we were.

Maybe it just couldn't be fixed.

Maybe I had to be okay with that.

CHAPTER 12

*I*t snowed on the day of the wedding. It was perfectly beautiful, and perfectly terrifying to think I had to get the cake to Jack's Retreat in the weather.

Luckily the rental cars had four-wheel drive and there was a gorgeous tent with heaters inside for the reception.

Nobody would freeze. The cake made it just fine. Everything was fine.

I was more nervous than usual, pulling double duty, and still feeling a little bit off kilter from the confrontation with Ryan, that shouldn't have even been a confrontation. In a way he had been defending me. In another way . . . it hadn't felt like defense. It had felt like he was calling me out. Attacking me by way of Josh.

I really didn't need to be thinking about that right now. Today wasn't about me. It was about Quinn and Noah. And luckily, I was very good at putting on an uncomplicated smile even when everything inside of me felt like a tangle. The forest green bridesmaid dresses that Quinn had chosen for us were beautiful and complemented the greenery on the cake.

This wasn't a Christmas wedding, but it had wintry wonderland vibes. I hadn't fully appreciated, though, the complication of getting our pictures taken beforehand with Ryan.

Quinn invited him into the room where we were getting ready, once everyone was dressed. She wanted some photos of us getting our makeup done.

Quinn had a makeup artist, the rest were doing our own. I leaned into the mirror and began to dab a berry color onto my lips, and I heard the sound of a camera shutter.

I turned and looked at him. I had smiled for his camera multiple times. I couldn't find it in me to do it now.

He didn't seem to mind.

But he was watching me in a way that felt weighted. Heavy.

That made me feel all the years, all the weddings, all the everything.

He was still handsome. Even though I was mad at him.

I had trouble tearing my eyes off of his. But I managed it.

Afterward, we went into a field adjacent to the building we had all been getting ready at and the mountains serving as a glorious backdrop. And when he took photos of Quinn and I together, I was less distracted.

Quinn looked beautiful. Her red hair hanging down in simple ringlets past her shoulders. Her white dress simple, with long lace sleeves, swishing with each step she took.

It wasn't hard for me to smile when we stood together. And when the other bridesmaids joined us, it was even easier.

I forgot that I had made the cake. I forgot that I was feeling tortured about Ryan. I forgot everything but the fact that I was Quinn's best friend, and she was the most beautiful bride I had ever seen.

"Off to get the groomsmen," he said about a half-hour later.

That left us standing in a field, wearing beautiful dresses. I looked out at the mountains all around us.

"This is going to be amazing," I said. "You've been waiting for this your whole life."

Quinn squeezed my hand.

"You know, I've always wanted to ask my brides . . . did you ever have any doubts about this?"

"When?"

"At any point. You were engaged for such a short amount of

time. You knew each other for an even shorter amount of time. Were you ever nervous? Did you ever question it?"

She smiled. "I used to question so many things before I met Noah. I questioned what I wanted, if I wanted to stay in Pineville. If I wanted to take over my dad's accounting firm. If I wanted to get married, if I wanted to have children. Then I met him, and I knew that the answers to all of those questions were details. I wanted to be with him. I have questioned a lot of things, but never if he was the right choice. I still don't know the answer to some of those questions. If I want to do accounting here. If I want to do something else. If I want to stay here forever. If I want to go back home. But I'm certain of Noah. And that's enough."

I let out a slow breath. "Well. I couldn't . . . I couldn't understand that at first. But you guys are special. I get that now."

"You thought we went too fast?"

"I thought you went too fast because I couldn't quite understand it. You know, given me and Josh. We went so slow and . . ."

"You weren't certain about him."

"I was."

"No, you weren't, you were certain about how you wanted your life to look, and he was a really great set piece."

I let out a hard breath. "I didn't realize that everybody had such terrible opinions about my relationship."

"It wasn't a terrible opinion. I thought that you could be happy with him. But I don't think I was terribly secretive about the fact that I didn't think it was a great, sweeping romantic love. I also just figured we wanted different things."

"Romance would be nice," I said. "I've just never been carried away like *that*."

That was a lie. I had been. Once.

And I'd put a bowling ball through it.

"Why don't you think you can have it?"

I looked around to see where the other bridesmaids had gone.

I'd been abandoned. And my best friend was clearly determined to give me a talking to before we were separated.

"I don't want to anymore. That was what I learned from the whole thing with Josh."

"That's a shitty lesson from a shitty guy."

"He wasn't. He was good. He was . . . do you think that he was insecure?"

Quinn looked like she had whiplash. "What?"

"It's just . . . it's something that Ryan said to me."

"Is that why the two of you are acting weird?" Quinn squinted at me.

"No. He's acting weird because he caught Trev and I skinny-dipping in the lake."

Quinn snorted. "That's a lie, because you would've gotten frostbite and died." She paused for a moment. "I mean, it's a lie for several reasons, but that's one of them."

"Yes. Josh was texting me, and he was mad, because Josh sent me a picture of him with some other girl. But I wasn't mad about it. I was fine. But he told me that Josh was always jealous of me and other men. But he never acted like that to me."

Quinn winced. "I think you didn't notice. He was always right on top of you whenever you went out."

"Well, he was . . . I don't know, shy I guess."

"Insecure," Quinn said.

"Isn't that kind of the same?"

Quinn shook her head. "No. Because it was . . . like he was afraid if he let go of you, you'd run away. Or some guy would steal you."

I didn't know what to do with that. I'd always felt like I had to worry about losing him, and then he'd broken up with me so it had felt founded. I'd always thought he needed me but right then I thought of the word needy and I wondered if that was more accurate.

I frowned. "Am I the only one that didn't realize that? I just thought . . . I really thought that he and I were compatible. Like *really compatible*, because it seemed like he was happiest when we stayed at home and that was what I wanted."

"I don't think it makes him wholly an awful guy that he was worried about losing you. But I do think it sucks that he didn't transfer it into making you feel like you were a queen. I think whether he meant to or not he felt that insecurity in a way that made him hold you back, instead of having the confidence to build you up."

He had never been mean to me. But my own issues had left me feeling insecure, and combined with his . . .

We'd been a bad combination. And the worst thing was . . .

When I thought of missing him, I thought of missing my hope of security and certainty, not *him*.

He'd wanted me, and I'd wanted a relationship.

Of course, he felt like the right kind of relationship because in the beginning, especially, his brand of needing me had felt so good.

But it had never occurred to me to ask him to give us another try. I had been so upset it was over but I'd never wanted him back.

I hadn't loved him.

"I just wanted to . . ." A realization crashed over me. "I wanted to fast forward the part of my life that felt precarious, and I wanted to get to a place where I was settled. Where I knew what was going to happen. Where I knew how the rest of my life was going to go. That was what I really hoped for. And maybe you're right, I wanted that more than I wanted him."

Maybe I hadn't been devastated. Maybe my plans had just been thwarted.

Maybe I had been more broken about the loss of the future, than the loss of the man himself.

And I wanted some time, some time to excavate the truth about that relationship, but I didn't have it, not right now.

Maybe I didn't want it. Because I certainly hadn't taken any time over the last nine months to do any digging into it. I had just assumed that I knew the truth of it.

After all, I had lived with him. But how could I be completely attuned to what he had been doing and thinking when *I* wasn't even completely attuned to what I was feeling and thinking?

Right then, I was worried I had built up so many walls inside of myself, that I was never going to be able to get down to the truth.

"I'm glad that you found the sure thing," I said. "And if I ever feel tempted to think I'm falling in love, I'm going to remember that."

"I didn't think you wanted love anymore."

"If I found something I was that certain about, maybe I would."

I didn't think I would. I didn't think I could ever be that certain about anything.

Apparently all those funfetti trust issues that were baked into my very core weren't just limited to the people around me. But to myself.

It was like I'd had a giant wall demolished at the center of myself, and I was standing there staring at a landscape I didn't understand.

Yes, there were things about my relationship with Josh that hadn't been great. He hadn't always contributed to the housework in an equitable way. I could tell when he didn't like certain outfits that I wore out. And gradually, I had started to adjust what I wore to avoid any pushback.

He had also told me that Ryan didn't like me.

I sat with that.

I had felt like Ryan didn't like me, it wasn't as if it had been pulled out of thin air, but my boyfriend had been open about the fact that his best friend hadn't liked me, and when I really went back and thought that over, I wondered if it was true.

If there was jealousy there. He had wanted me to keep my distance from Ryan for a reason.

I suddenly wanted to ask Ryan more about it. More about what he knew, about my own life that I didn't seem to. That was galling. To realize that the people around me had made observations that I hadn't.

And I didn't have to ask Quinn why she hadn't said anything. It was because I wouldn't have listened. Because she was right; I was clinging so hard to what I had decided was safety, I wouldn't have been able to view it objectively.

I didn't have time to spiral about it, because it was almost ceremony time.

The chairs were set up facing the mountains, and the wedding party met behind a little rise on a hill. Ryan and I looked at each other. The best man and the maid of honor would be walking in together.

I linked arms with him. His suit jacket smooth beneath my hand. And he was hot beneath that. I could feel it.

I did my best to calm my fluttering heart, and when I couldn't comment any further, I decided to attribute it to the nerves of the wedding itself.

The music cued our turn to go, and I walked forward with him, feeling like my insides were pressing against the walls of my being.

Like there were too many big emotions. Too much of everything.

Happiness, grief, and all the things he made me feel.

I remembered what Quinn had told me only moments before, about all of her certainty.

I realized that I had never once in my life felt that certain about anything. I had been raised to believe that life itself was precarious. How could I ever have that certainty?

So many people were given that certainty from the moment they were first placed in their mother's arms, and I simply wasn't.

I had been an inconvenient accessory. One that had been picked up, carted around, and then eventually abandoned when I got too heavy.

My whole life had been viewed through that same lens.

I felt hollow then. Because how would I ever . . .

It's why you gave up on all this.

Maybe.

Maybe it was.

But maybe . . .

I shoved those thoughts aside. I hated that my friend getting married was creating such a landslide of peril inside of me. I wanted it to be about her. I wanted it to be uncomplicated. To just be happy. I get for me it was a loss, and also a strange confrontation with the immeasurable grief inside of me that I struggled to understand.

So I stared ahead at the mountains. Those mountains had been there for so long.

They had seen so many things.

So many different people. So many different stages of earth and time. I was small.

I tried to find comfort in that.

As I had done before.

We separated at the head of the aisle, with me on the bride's side, and him on the groom's.

I stood there, holding my bouquet of red flowers. I turned my thoughts off.

I watched Noah's face as Quinn came down the aisle. Looking ethereal and beautiful. I could see tears in his eyes, and that was when I knew for sure that he was good enough for my friend. I hadn't realized that part of me had still been held back. But, of course, it had.

He saw her. Everything that she was. All the value in her. That was what I wanted for her.

It would be a perilous thing to want for myself.

Because I struggled to figure out my own value.

I blinked seriously.

When Noah and Quinn joined hands, and said their vows to each other, I didn't bother to stop the tears.

I wept. Because I was happy.

I wept. Because I was sad.

And then, just like that, this wedding that had been ahead of us for so long was behind us.

I took Ryan's arm again, and we walked back up that aisle. I clung to him like I might fall this time, because I was afraid that I would. So, I let him hold me up, even though I probably didn't deserve that. Not from him.

That thought was like a knife, twisting inside me, and slicing clean through parts of myself I tried not to examine honestly.

But there was something about this changing nature of a key relationship in my life, this last crumbling of a foundation that had built me when I had first come to Pineville, that had me scrambling, looking for something to hold onto. And as I looked at all the rocky spaces inside of me, as I tried to find something to cling to, it forced me to examine dark corners I normally left alone.

It was time to take photos of the bridal party altogether.

But, of course, Ryan wasn't in the photos.

I smiled. I didn't look right at him.

I watched as he took pictures of Noah and Quinn.

And then, when I made sure that everything with the bridal party was done, I went to begin making sure that everything with the cake was as it should be.

The tent was lit up gloriously inside, with heaters and string lights. With greenery and roses.

When Quinn and Noah came into the tent, the crowd of their friends and family cheered.

And I felt my whole soul lift.

At the same time, I felt like I understood something I hadn't before.

I tried to picture myself on this day, with Josh.

I tried to honestly, truly, imagine it.

He would have left most of the planning to me. Not in a malicious way. But it would've been something that he'd have said he was having a hard time handling.

I went back over so many things with a fine-toothed comb, trying to see what Quinn and Ryan had told me they saw.

It wasn't obvious.

It wasn't like I had been living unhappily, without knowing it.

But when I looked at Quinn and Noah, I could see what we were missing.

We had been friends. But it hadn't been a partnership.

He had needed me, but it had been about him and not me.

And I was no different. I'd needed stability and security and he'd been an emblem of that for me. He deserved to be a whole person to someone, though.

So did I.

I had learned to shrink certain parts of myself because his reactions to them weren't favorable, and I was so in tune with other people's emotions because of my childhood.

But I wasn't the point of today. It was Quinn, and we were getting to the part of the reception where speeches would be given.

The pressure that I felt to make sure that I gave a fitting tribute to Quinn had been gnawing at me, and I felt like I had to make a whole new country understand why they should welcome her with open arms. Why they should be so lucky to have her.

Why Noah was so lucky to have her when I wouldn't have her all the time anymore.

New Zealand, and Noah, better be adequately grateful.

I'd found it so hard to distill our friendship and what it meant to me into a single speech, but I'd done my best. I'd sourced memories from Caitlin, Sierra and Hannah, talking about our high school days, and laughing so hard that I forgot I was a little bit sad.

I looked at Quinn, sitting at the banquet table with Noah by her side, and I knew a moment of such pure, intense pride and happiness, I thought I'd burst.

Quinn had found the one she could be her whole self with. And she was radiant. My best friend was absolutely, gloriously radiant. A beautiful mermaid of a woman who'd found love and happiness and I genuinely couldn't be more thrilled.

The reception dinner was a lovely, elegant affair, and the speeches were wonderful. Quinn's parents spoke about her early years, and Noah's family talked about his life, in a way that made me feel like I knew him, and made me feel even better about my best friend moving across the world to have a life with him. He did seem like a singular sort of guy. Which was exactly what my singular sort of friend needed.

But then it was the best man and maid of honor's turn. We both moved from where we were, and our eyes met. I felt it like when he'd taken my arm.

He and I had already touched one another. We'd walked down the aisle together. But I was struck right then with how gorgeous he was. He'd taken his jacket off, the sleeves of his white shirt were pushed up to his elbows, revealing muscular forearms that made me weak.

I asked myself, was I actually attracted to Ryan, or was my attraction to him part of my obsessive need to make him like me?

You know it isn't.

I winced.

But really, a blow job probably *would* make him like me more.

My mouth went dry. I shouldn't be thinking about blow jobs and Ryan. Not now or ever, really.

I couldn't untangle the tension between us just then. If it was the regular sort of tension we always had, or if it was sexual.

Or maybe the tension had always been sexual, and I had never called it what it was.

I was the antagonist of Taylor Swift's 'All Too Well'. The ten minute version.

That was unflattering.

I looked at him, and he stared back at me. Waiting for me to make the next move. So I did.

I moved forward and took the microphone from its stand so that I could face the wedding guests. "I'm Poppy Love. I'm Quinn's . . . maid of honor." I cleared my throat. "I met Quinn when I was seven years old. And I think she might've saved me. At that point in my life so many things had changed, so many people had disappeared from my life. I moved in with my grandmother, I moved away from the school that I had been going to, from the state that I had always called home. And I met Quinn." I looked at Quinn, who was smiling with tears in her eyes. "That was when I knew everything was going to be okay. Because all I have to say about Quinn is . . . take care of her and let her take care of you. Because when I let Quinn take care of me, my life became exponentially better. Because she makes everything better. She'll make you better too." I raised a glass. "To Quinn and Noah."

Quinn stood up and walked to me, wrapping her arms around my neck and I didn't bother with not crying because . . . I was going to cry.

But I wanted Quinn to be a whole person. And I had to figure out how to be a whole person too. Suddenly it felt okay to let go.

So I did. And when I did, I smiled. And I really, really meant it.

Then I looked at Ryan, and handed the microphone to him.

He didn't look overwrought or sad or nervous. He was just . . . himself. Always. "I'm not a big believer in fate." For some reason right then, his eyes connected with mine and I felt it all the way down to my toes. "But if anything could make me believe in it, it would be this. Meeting Noah was great. It made me feel at home in a country I had never been to before. It made me feel I got a great gift when I met Noah. I got a great gift when I met Quinn too. I was twelve and I had just moved to town. Quinn is one of those people that just makes you feel welcomed. She and Noah are both that way. They give me too much credit for introducing them, when the truth is, they did this. They made friends with a guy who didn't have many, at different times, in different countries, and that's what brought them together. Maybe that's fate, I don't know. I do know that theirs is the kind of love that challenges even cynics like me to see the world a little bit differently."

I was lost in the beauty of that statement, of the speech. Of the way it painted their relationship as something they'd built with their own kindness.

But the way he talked about Quinn . . . about her being nice to him. She had been, but so had I. I'd tried so hard and he'd been mean to me. But, somehow, he'd managed to see that Quinn was trying to be his friend.

He vexed me.

He always had.

Why did I specifically offend him? I thought about that as the reception moved on to dancing, as it was time to cut the cake. I thought about it and I felt . . .

Wounded. Maybe I had no right to be wounded where Ryan was concerned but I really felt it.

I was serving up the last piece of cake when he took a photo near me. Our eyes met.

"What?" I asked.

"Nothing," he said.

You could say nothing, Poppy.

I could. But where had it ever gotten me with him? He didn't like me no matter what I did, so there was no point in not calling this out.

"Oh. I thought maybe you were going to comment on the fact

that apparently you and Quinn have been besties since you were twelve. When . . . I don't know. Why did you immediately think that I was an awful person, Ryan? When you were able to see that Quinn was being nice to you."

His jaw went tight. "You're not Quinn."

That made me feel like I'd been stabbed. I wasn't Quinn. I was Poppy. Did that mean I was inherently wrong?

"No. I'm not. But all I ever was, was nice to you, and you were mean to me immediately, and you tried to hold the science fair thing against me, but the very first thing you said to me when I met you was . . . unfriendly. And dismissive. *Admit it*."

I needed him to at least say it. To acknowledge that for some reason he didn't like me. That it was me personally. Me who offended him, long before . . .

"Well, I was warned about the Love family. Because of the feud," he said.

Lies.

"The feud is bullshit. It's something that happened years ago, and you just said that you don't even believe in fate. I think you would basically have to believe in fate to believe that because some people . . . fucked each other back in the 1800s and our families have had beef ever since, you were destined to have beef with me."

"But it seems to be true, doesn't it?"

"*Why?*"

"I don't know," he said, his voice rough. "I can't explain it to you. But you have to admit we can't seem to get rid of each other. And it never ends well."

I tried not to think about the fifth wedding. I tried hardest of all now.

But with his eyes; glittering, intense and blue right there, it made me think of that night. Of how he'd looked at me then.

And I knew he was thinking of it too.

CHAPTER 13

The Fifth Wedding
Leavenworth
Nine Months Ago

*T*he radio was on, but I wasn't singing. My hands had been frozen in a single spot on the steering wheel since I had finally pulled out of my driveway an hour later than I was supposed to.

It was a nine-hour drive to Leavenworth, and the weather was iffy. I wasn't going to get there until well after dark.

I was angry. Upset.

Devastated.

There weren't enough words. Or maybe, I was just tired of repeating them over and over again. Because I was . . .

Angry. Upset.

Devastated.

It had been the single most fantastic implosion of our entire seven-year relationship, and it had been the end.

He had broken up with me while I was standing in the kitchen putting cream in my coffee.

Like he was asking me what I was doing today. Like he was asking me about the weather.

Just casually.

I don't feel like we're on the right track.

I had . . . asked him a thousand questions. Gone over all those years in my head. Nothing that made sense.

Nothing that felt real.

What do you mean by that? How can we not be? Look at this . . . place, this place we share with each other, how is this not that right track?

Then why does it never seem like the right time for us to get engaged?

It had felt right to me. Or I thought it had. But then he'd said that and it made me question everything. How I'd never brought it up, and how I'd never pushed for it even though it felt like something I wanted.

I think we've been together since we were so young and we've never had a chance to really . . . play the field.

Play the field?

I really hadn't seen that one coming.

We haven't married each other, and maybe there's a reason for that. Maybe we need to go out and spread our wings and see what else is out there? Maybe . . . maybe that's what we have to do and if we're meant to find our way back to each other we will, but we have to—

You want to have sex with other women?

It was all I'd heard.

My stomach felt hollow. And I just stared at the road ahead.

I was borderline catatonic.

I still had a wedding to go to. I had a cake to bake.

This was about love. Somebody else's love. And I couldn't afford to let my thwarted love affect it.

But I felt awful. Sick.

I felt like I was dying.

This was my nightmare. My stable, perfect life was falling apart around me.

Everything that I had ever hoped for. Everything that I had wanted.

I had invested so many years in the relationship because I had been so sure of where it was going.

You don't want me?

He'd deflated.

You're the only woman I've ever . . . He'd cleared his throat. *And you'd been with someone else before we were together.*

I really hated that. That he was using me having been with someone before him against me, especially when . . .

It had never been that important to me. Sex had never been a huge deal to me. *He* had always been more important. The relationship had always been more important. No, we didn't exactly make for a hot, erotic romance novel. And I can certainly appreciate the fantasy aspect of some guy calling you *baby girl* while he put his hand around your throat, but that wasn't love. And it wasn't real.

I had already been rejected because somebody had bigger fantasies than being with me. And it got me. Right between the ribs.

He'd apologized. He had told me he would be gone by the time I got back. I had cried.

I was going to spend Christmas by myself, and it made me feel like being a child all over again and not knowing when I would see my mom again. It made me feel like myself, when my grandma died and I knew I was going to have to face the holidays without her. Even though all she would do was complain about them. And make cookies even through the complaints.

Lonely at Christmas was far too familiar a feeling. I could barely breathe past it.

The drive was a blur. And the hotel that I was staying and working in was beautiful.

The whole town was. A snow globe brought to life.

Beautiful historic buildings, built to look like a Bavarian town and thoroughly bedecked for Christmas.

Normally, I would have enjoyed it. Immensely.

Instead, I was just sadly unloading my car.

And getting angrier and angrier. Some of the numbness from the drive up had faded.

And I was just starting to feel . . .

Did he think I might want something more? But I had decided that I wasn't going to take it. I had decided that what we had was more important.

I understood that love and security were the stuff of life, not . . . roaming around indulging yourself in fake passion. And anyway, wasn't that the privilege of men? That he could think maybe he would go out and get laid and satisfy some need he had for variety. He knew that he would come. A woman could never know that.

You picked a random partner at your own peril. Even with Josh it had been a grab bag. The prize, or whether or not I'd even get one, had been uncertain.

But I just wanted to be close. Maybe.

My rage was starting to feel like it had teeth.

Oddly, it made me feel closer to my grandmother, who had always had choice things to say about men. She'd cursed my grandpa's name as a daily prayer.

She hadn't liked Josh, but the thing was, she didn't like anybody.

I tried to breathe past the pain in my chest.

I checked in, and I went and introduced myself to the restaurant manager, who was allowing me to use the kitchen to make the wedding cake.

I managed to do it without being a puddle, and without imploding. I felt personally quite pleased about that. Maybe the bar was low, but at least there was a bar.

My hotel room was pristine. The bedspread was velvet and berry, and the details in the room were all gilded and ornate. It was hands down the nicest place that I had stayed during all the weddings that I had done.

I sat on the bed and I cried. Because I was by myself, because he couldn't see it, because nobody had to know that I felt like an abandoned child.

I wanted my anger back, but it had been far too fleeting for my liking.

I ordered room service and stayed under the covers to eat it.

The next morning, I got up early and collected everything that I needed to bake. The wedding was early in the day, because it got dark so early this time of year. I needed to get moving.

I got a cake baked and assembled quickly. I knew the process so well now. I was good at baking in strange kitchens.

I was good at things.

I told myself that repeatedly as I decorated the cake with fondant evergreen trees and tiny reindeer. With sugared cranberries and little sprigs of pine.

I had a life. It wasn't completely upended.

I had put too much weight on another person, and I could never do that again.

What if I was untethered? What if I didn't make marriage and love my goal?

What if I sold the bakery and I started my own business. What if I planned weddings, from top to bottom, and used all my creativity and my business degree?

What if I was just me and I wasn't trying to earn anything or pay anything back?

I stood there at the counter, feeling like I was having a revelation.

What if I was in charge of how happy my life was? I really had been this whole time, it was just that I had convinced myself that I needed to make a family that looked a certain way in order to truly have security. But was that even true?

I just felt miserable.

But . . .

He was going to go out and travel. He was going to sleep with other people.

I had suppressed parts of myself in order to maintain that

relationship, because I had decided that it would be the safest. And here I was, completely not safe.

Completely undone.

That wasn't fair.

I had hotel staff to help me move the cake into the reception hall, and I was walking through the ornate lobby when Ryan came in.

He was wearing a black coat, wool, with a sprinkling of snow-flakes on his shoulders and in his dark hair.

The strangest sensation gripped me then.

I wanted to yell at him. I wanted to ask him if he'd had any idea that Josh had intended to break up with me.

But that wasn't all.

There was something else. Something dangerous. Something that gripped me down deep and held onto me. Held me fast, kept me motionless there in the lobby.

"Ryan."

I would never know for sure if I'd meant to say his name out loud.

He turned his head, and the momentary ferocity there pinned me to the spot. I wondered if he knew. Did men call each other about things like that? Did they ring up and have a chat about the recent and random breakup? Did the breakup even seem random to Ryan?

Maybe Josh had talked to him about his changing feelings, his insecurities.

The idea that somebody could know more about my relation-ship than I had filled me with a deep sense of rage.

"What's wrong?" he asked.

I hated that I looked wrong. I hated that I looked like I felt.

Nobody wanted to look like the dried-up husk they felt like.

"You don't know?"

He moved closer to me. "No. What happened?"

I didn't know what to do with that expression of genuine

concern on his face, because I had never seen anything like it. Not just from him, but from anybody.

The intensity there was something entirely foreign.

"Josh broke up with me."

I couldn't read what happened to his expression after that. But the end result was something like the face of a mountain. Remote, and craggy. Completely solid.

Impossible.

"He what?"

"This morning. Before I drove up here to the wedding. Honestly, I would've thought that he told you."

"No. He doesn't talk to me about you."

I felt like I had been stabbed. He didn't even talk to Ryan about me? That was a huge part of what Quinn and I talked about. Not everything, obviously. My life passed the Bechdel test.

I had other things going on with Josh, and I always had, but I absolutely did talk to my friends about him. He didn't talk to Ryan about me at all?

"Well, that's a little defensive. I guess kind of telling."

"I'm not the person to talk to about things like that."

Of course not. Because he was the kind of guy who hooked up with women at weddings. He was the kind of guy that Josh wanted to be like.

"Well, even though you don't talk to him about things like that, apparently he idolizes you."

"Does he?"

I was so acutely aware that we were having this conversation in a lobby. That he had a backpack slung over his shoulder, black and utility looking, with his camera equipment inside of it, I'm sure.

Camera equipment that I had damaged last time we had been in serious proximity to each other. Not that I hadn't seen him since that incident, but we had barely exchanged a handful of words. Even with Quinn dating one of his friends.

We had taken avoidance to a level of high art.

And now here we were, talking about my devastated personal life in public.

"Yeah," I said. "He wants to travel. He wants to have sex with other women."

Josh drew back as though I had punched him. "He what?"

"Yes. Part of the very fun conversation that we had this morning. It's not me, it's him. Except, when your boyfriend wants to have sex with other people, it feels a little bit like it's you."

"I'm . . . I'm sorry, Poppy. I genuinely had no idea that he was thinking about doing that."

"And if you had?"

He shook his head. "Nothing. It's . . . It's not my business. But it just feels . . . hell, I feel shocked, so I can't imagine how you feel."

Of course, it wasn't like he was my friend. He wouldn't come talk to me if he had known about it. Why would he?

No.

I wasn't his friend.

"I have stuff to do," I said.

I turned away from him, and he grabbed my arm, stopping me in my tracks.

His touch was warm, and firm. His gaze like fire. And I found that I couldn't breathe.

I found myself immobilized like I had been looking through the window between my cabin and his in Lake Tahoe. I found myself once again breathless with the realization that I was attracted to Ryan.

Right now, there was nothing preventing me from doing something about it.

Except that he was Ryan. Except that he didn't like me. Except that I had never in my life made a physical move on a man that I didn't have a relationship with.

Except that I would have to walk down the street and see him, and face what had happened.

But everything already felt upended. I was going to have to go home and see Josh again too.

This feeling was so strong. It was almost bigger than the anger that I felt. And the shame and the sadness. I was tempted. Tempted to move closer. Tempted – in this hotel lobby – to close the distance between the two of us so that I didn't feel quite so alone.

I snapped back to reality suddenly and sharply.

"I have work to do," I said, going back to my room and sitting on the bed, curling my fingers into fists over the top of the velvet bedspread.

My heart was pounding hard.

I was running scared. Because that had been the single most disorienting moment of my life.

I had almost done something completely out of character.

That stuck with me for the rest of the day, for the rest of the wedding.

It was a beautiful wedding, filled with snow and Christmas cheer, and even in my heartbroken state, I couldn't be cynical about it.

I still believed in this for other people.

Families existed too. Families that were like mine. Mothers who loved their children, and who wanted to raise them.

Love could exist in its many splendored forms and still not be something that everyone had.

I had friendship. *Great friends*.

I'd had my grandmother.

I didn't need *everything*.

No one got everything.

After the cake was served, I melted back from the glittering reception and felt myself begin to crumble.

A tear slid down my cheek, and I wiped it away.

I wanted to be done with that. Every breath was like a different emotion, every moment passing bringing with it a different wave.

I had been angry. I had been sad. I had been fine. Resolved. But then angry again. And now sad.

It was a lot.

I sniffed, and walked out of the reception hall, taking the elevator back up to my room.

I slipped the key card in the slot, and watched the light turn green. Then I slipped into my room.

I meant to change into something comfortable. I meant to take a shower. Instead, I just sat on the edge of the bed. Staring blankly at part of the scrollwork on the brass lamp sitting on the nightstand.

I don't know how long I sat there. But there was a knock on the door, and I stood up.

I walked across the room and peeked through the peephole.

Ryan.

Without thinking, I jerked the door open. And without that standing between us, I felt it. That same thing that I had felt down in the lobby. But it was stronger. Because it was coming from him too. This wasn't just inside me.

He felt it too.

I knew that. As I drew in my next breath, I could taste it on my tongue. As I let my eyes meet his, I could see it.

The ferocity there. The intensity.

He felt it too.

I didn't think. And I'm not sure who moved. But I was suddenly pressed against him, my hands moving up his broad chest, around the back of his shoulders. And then he lowered his head, his mouth claiming mine hungrily.

The force of it was enough to make my knees buckle.

He wrapped his arms around me, lifting me onto my toes, then entirely off the ground.

He was hard. And big.

I had never been held by a man like him.

I had never felt anything like this.

My heart was pounding so hard I thought I was going to die, and he was kissing me so deep that it was like he was trying to consume me.

His tongue slid against mine, the most delicious friction, and I shivered.

My hands kept moving, up the back of his neck, into his hair. Ryan Clark's hair.

I was so painfully, acutely aware that he was the one holding me. That he was the one making me feel like a lit match.

I had never understood this. I had never understood passion with the absence of love.

But this was passion. And it was no less acute for being disconnected from those things. No. If anything, it was more.

There was an edge to this. An explosiveness that I had never believed was real. I thought it was the stuff of fiction. Something that made an exciting paragraph, but would be elusive in real life. But here it was.

Combusting between the two of us.

Josh had wanted to find this. He had wanted to find this sexual excitement out there, and I had found it with his best friend.

I couldn't let go of that thought. Of that momentary bubble of triumph that fizzed in my chest. It mingled with the desire that I felt, a cocktail that was stronger than anything I'd ever had before.

He loosened his hold on me, and I slid down the front of him, breaking the kiss. I could feel the hard ridge of his cock against my stomach.

I had given Ryan Clark a hard-on, and I didn't know what to do with that. Except go right back in for another kiss.

"Are you just doing this to get back at him?"

His words were rough, spoken close to my lips.

"Yes."

He went rigid. And moved away from me.

"I mean . . ." I felt stunned.

"I'm not here for you to fuck out your feelings for somebody else."

"I didn't say—"

He moved away from me, and the look in his eyes made me wish I could evaporate into nothing. I had always felt with him that he disliked me for no good reason. But right now, I felt like I deserved every moment, of every hour, of every day, he'd spent hating me.

Right now, I felt like I was as unlikeable as he'd always treated me.

Then he turned away, and he walked out the door.

He said nothing.

He just left.

I could have opened it again. Except I was just standing there, shocked. Unable to believe what had just happened. That I had just kissed Ryan, and that I had managed to ruin it a minute later.

But I couldn't lie to him. I had felt petty triumph at the thought of kissing Josh's friend, when he had hurt me so badly.

But I wanted him too.

Surely both of those things could exist together.

But I had run over the camera lens. I had dropped a bowling ball on the solar system.

I had broken everything with him, just like I always did.

CHAPTER 14

Present Day

"*R*yan . . ."

"They're leaving." He jerked his head back, in the direction of Noah and Quinn, who were waving at their guests.

"Oh I . . ."

"There's no point going over this," he said.

I could see that he wanted to, though. That he didn't want to pull away. And I felt the same thing.

He turned and walked away from me, toward Noah and Quinn, where he started taking pictures of their walk to the car. I tried to gather myself and join them, because I needed to help see them off.

They were going to the airport and flying to Auckland, and from there to Fiji.

Everyone else was getting flights out that night too.

Out of Queenstown, out of the country.

My flight was for the next day.

And I regretted that, suddenly. I wanted the familiar. I wanted to be at home. My memories of Ryan, and the acknowledgement of what was between us, coupled with the wedding, had left me scrubbed raw and I was longing for something familiar.

I wasn't going to get it.

I packed everything up, and Trev offered to take me back to the vacation rental.

"Thanks," I said. But I wanted to make sure he knew that it didn't mean I was going to sleep with him.

I didn't know how to do that without coming out and saying it. So, I decided to wait and see if he tried anything. He didn't. He just very pleasantly waved me off in the driveway. I opened up the garage to go in through the side door, and paused when I saw Ryan's rental car there.

I hadn't asked when he was leaving.

And suddenly, I had the very terrible, exhilarating feeling that he was staying here tonight.

And that the house would be just him and me.

What if.

Except I'd broken it. I could see it when I looked at him now.

But he wanted me. Even if he hated that.

Even if he hated me.

I took a breath, and unlocked the door, taking my shoes off before heading up the stairs.

He was in the living room, looking out the windows at the lake.

"I didn't realize you were staying here tonight," I said, knowing I sounded on guard.

"Yeah. I fly out tomorrow."

"For Europe?" I asked.

He nodded, clearly uninterested in fighting with me. I didn't know why that hurt a little bit. "By way of Sydney, I'll be flying there from here."

"Oh. That's . . . great."

Suddenly, without the wedding, without the distractions, and with that honest memory about the fifth wedding, it seemed like it bloomed between us bigger than it had.

I wanted to apologize. I also didn't want to say anything about it.

I wanted to move closer to him. And I wanted to move further away.

Without the conflicting feelings for Quinn's wedding and her new life in New Zealand there, I was left with nothing but the complication of Ryan.

I stayed on the other side of the room. I thought it was probably the better part of valor.

"I'm flying out tomorrow too. I have a midmorning flight."

"To Auckland?" he asked.

"Yes. And then to LA."

"You going to be okay on a long-haul flight by yourself?"

That he cared at all did more to my heart than I wanted to admit.

"Great. Great. I have my noise cancelling headphones and my eye mask. I may download some Shark Week."

"Seems a little intense for a plane watch, Poppy. I heard sharks are scary."

"In the *fun* way."

"I see."

There were so many things I wanted to say, but didn't feel like I could. I couldn't get any closer to Ryan, because I was never being really honest with him.

I never had been.

Or maybe it was myself that I wasn't honest with.

I guess in the end it didn't matter very much.

Because the end result was the same.

"I'm exhausted," I said. "I'm going to go take a shower and go to bed."

"I'll give you a ride to the airport in the morning."

"Okay."

I went upstairs and undressed. I got into the shower, and let the warm water cascade over me. I didn't do much else. Didn't wash my hair. Just let the spray beat down on me.

It felt like I was missing something. Missing a chance of something. But I felt that way once with him.

When I had been hurt and furious. I wasn't hurt or furious now.

And he was a much bigger part of my thoughts than Josh had been for a long time.

I stopped.

I had probably spent more time thinking about Ryan Clark in the last five years than I had about my own boyfriend.

Wondering what he thought about me and why. Watching his every move at all these weddings.

Making him mad. Accepting his help. Talking to him about the way our fractured pasts seemed to line up in weirdly synchronous ways.

I stepped out of the shower and dried myself. Put on baggie, warm sweatpants. And the oversized sweatshirt I'd bought in Arrowtown with the giant kiwi bird on the front, and *Aotearoa* emblazoned across the top and *Keepin' it Kiwi* on the bottom.

I went out into the hallway between mine and Ryan's bedrooms. And I decided to go out onto the small deck up there to look at the stars. I stepped outside, and startled, when I nearly ran into Ryan.

He had his camera out. Taking pictures of the stars, I realized.

"I'm sorry," I said. "I'll just leave you to—"

"Don't go," he said.

I turned to him.

He had his camera up. That wall. The one he kept between himself and the world.

I suddenly wanted to break it down. I wanted to get between that camera and him. But that would mean being pressed up against him. I had been once.

I felt exhilarated then.

Maybe this was inevitable.

This moment. Ryan Clark and Poppy Love, standing on the

deck on the other side of the world, with no one who knew them anywhere for miles.

With nothing but acres of misunderstanding, bad feelings, and the kind of desire that had never made sense.

Maybe it was what Ezekiel and Madeline had felt too. Standing on a prairie somewhere, with promises and obligations to other people that didn't matter as much as what they felt right then.

Maybe it was a true story. Maybe it wasn't.

I suspected Gran had told me that story to keep me from losing my head over a man. To keep me from ever giving into the kind of madness that consumed you, all the way down, and left you without thought, without breath.

It was dangerous. I knew it.

I didn't care.

For once, I didn't care.

My heart was beating hard.

I was terrified.

Terrified that he was thinking the same thing I was.

Terrified that he wasn't.

That would be horrible. To feel this alone. To feel this sense of inevitability, and to be the only one.

He lifted his camera up and took a photo.

And I reached out, and put my hand on the top of his camera, forcing him to lower it. "Put it down," I said.

"Poppy," he said, his voice rough.

And he did. He set the camera down on a bistro table out there.

And he moved closer to me.

So close that if I breathed, it would be the same air he was breathing in.

"Remember what I said last time?"

"Yes," I said.

"I don't care anymore. I don't give a shit why you want to do it. I just can't wait. Not anymore. I need you. And if that's not what you want—"

"I do," I said. My words hung there in the air, suspended on a cloud of my breath.

I thought that I was going to pass out, my heart was beating so hard.

I thought I might topple over completely.

I was terrified.

But it was fun scary.

It was Shark Week.

But then, he wrapped his arms around me, and I didn't have to be afraid of that. Not anymore. Because Ryan was holding me. His arms solid and strong, his chest hot and firm.

And then, he lowered his head and kissed me.

We were leaving tomorrow. That was unspoken. We were leaving tomorrow, and then after that he was going away. We wouldn't see each other.

At the fifth wedding, it had been a terrible idea because we were going to see each other again the next day, and the next day, and the next.

But we wouldn't now.

Because I was going back to Pineville and he was going to Europe. Because this was goodbye as much as it was anything.

I wanted to cry.

Because somehow, goodbye was a relentless, repeating theme in my life, and yet at least now the promise of goodbye was helping me get to somewhere honest within myself.

Get to somewhere honest between the two of us.

And so as he kissed me, I clung to him. His mouth was hot, the slick glide of his tongue against mine sending a shock of sensation to my breasts, down between my legs.

I was wet, instantly, needing him in a way I had never needed anyone else.

We were right back to where we had been that night a year and a half ago.

Zero to near orgasmic just from his mouth on mine.

"Don't stop," I whispered against his mouth.

And I would beg if I had to. Because I didn't have any pride left. I only had my desire for him.

My tangle of confusing need.

I had never wanted sex without love.

Ryan was the exception.

I didn't know myself. That was becoming clearer and clearer.

Because I had thought that Josh was the love of my life. And I had been forced to reckon with the reality of that.

So maybe I didn't know what I wanted. Maybe I didn't know what I felt.

And anyway, what I felt before didn't matter, because this was like nothing I had ever experienced. Not ever. Not with anyone.

He was still wearing his suit from the wedding. I pushed his jacket off his shoulders, right out there on the deck.

I would've let him take me out there if it wasn't so cold.

"Ryan," I said, his name a plea. A reminder to both of us that I knew full well who he was.

He growled, and walked me back a few paces, opening the glass door, and bringing us both inside. He closed it ruthlessly behind him. And I was momentarily immobilized by the intensity in his expression.

I had never seen anything like it. Not directed at me, that was for certain.

I wanted to ask him questions. I wanted to know what this was. Because it was only when I had destroyed this moment last time, that I had realized there might be more to it than just him being opportunistic.

That the possibility of me being more than that bridesmaid in New Orleans had made itself apparent.

Maybe.

Maybe.

But I couldn't speak, because I didn't want to ruin this. More than anything, I didn't want to ruin it again.

So, I just let him take me back in his arms. I let him pick me up, like I didn't weigh anything. And I reveled in his strength.

In all the things I would've told you I didn't care about.

That he was bigger than me, that he was stronger than me. That he was so unapologetically masculine.

He carried me into his room, and I felt a moment of pure terror. After all, it had been a very long time since I'd been with a man who wasn't Josh. And before that, there had just been my college boyfriend. Just the two.

And Ryan had probably been with more women than he could readily count. I wasn't going to have a special set of skills.

I wasn't going to blow him over with my fantastic hand-job technique, or my practiced deep throat.

The idea of doing both to him suddenly made me dizzy.

He took hold of my chin, and looked at me, his eyes fierce. "Get out of your head, Poppy."

"I can't," I said, my heart beating a scattered rhythm. "I've known you since we were kids. And you're Ryan."

"And I'm going to make this good for you," he said.

I couldn't keep my insecurity pushed down as deep as I wanted. "I'm worried I won't make it good for you."

The words escaped, as small and sad as they had sounded in my head, and I wanted to punch myself in the face.

He chuckled. Hard, strained. "I'm not worried."

"I am. Remember that time I saw you with . . ."

"She doesn't matter."

She doesn't matter. It was that easy for him.

After this, I probably wouldn't matter either.

But I was used to that. That was maybe the one good thing.

I knew how to say goodbye. Or, at least, I knew how to stand there and take it when somebody said goodbye to me.

And I wanted him. So it seemed worth it.

At least this time the goodbye was forced by flight schedules.

And it would mean . . .

No expectations that I built up in my head that were going to be dashed.

It was what it was. And this had a time limit on it. One that wasn't personal. That was all for the best.

He loosened the black tie he was still wearing, and I felt like I had been shot clean through with an arrow of desire, watching a large masculine hand undo the knot, loosening it and casting it aside. Then he began to unbutton his white shirt. First at the wrists, and then at his throat. I found myself shivering. He released one button at a time, each one exposing more of his skin. Of his dark chest hair. Those muscles. So perfect and glorious. I had seen them before. From afar.

But this time I could touch him. Suddenly, I was very self-conscious about the fact that I was wearing a baggy, yellow sweatshirt and voluminous sweatpants.

So, I did what any sane woman would do in that situation. I took the sweatpants off. Because the sweatshirt just went down to the tops of my thighs, and that kind of made it a miniskirt, which was infinitely sexier than what had been happening before. I thought maybe.

He stopped unbuttoning his shirt, his eyes zeroing in on me, a muscle in his jaw ticking.

He wanted me.

He really wanted me.

I couldn't breathe through that realization.

This wasn't about sex. Because Ryan could've had sex with any woman that had been at that wedding. Probably married or single. His power was that great.

He wanted *me*.

No man who didn't specifically want a woman would be immobilized by the world's saddest striptease.

But then, if anyone was forbidden, it was me.

It was him.

Because hadn't we built this up for all these years?

This *impossible* thing.

Maybe that was why it felt so essential, so inevitable, to me.

He was the one man I could never fathom touching, and so he was the one I wanted to touch most.

I walked forward, and put my palm on his bare chest, sliding it beneath that white shirt, shivering as I made contact with those hard muscles. He wrapped his arm around my waist, bringing his other hand down to the back of my thigh, moving it up slowly underneath my sweatshirt, until he found my bare ass. "Holy fuck," he said.

"I don't wear underwear to bed," I said.

"No . . . you don't," he said, sounding like he'd been stabbed.

And I thrilled at that. How much he wanted me. That was my kink.

Being wanted.

And I had never experienced it quite on this level. Not even close.

I stretched up on my toes and kissed him, and he tightened his hand on my rear, squeezing hard as he kissed me deep.

Until I was breathless.

Until there was nothing but this. Nothing but him.

He moved his hand slightly, and his finger grazed my slick, wet channel. I gasped as he teased me, tormented me, with the promise of penetration that he never made good on.

All the while he kissed me, deep and hot, holding me so tightly that he had full control over the kiss.

I was being conquered.

I didn't even mind.

I had been the driving force in my other relationships. I had never experienced anything like this. Surrendering like this.

And I knew that I could trust him. I knew that I could trust him to make it good. He'd said it, but he was proving it.

And suddenly, I felt utterly unburdened by all my insecurity.

He wanted me. So it would be good.

I would be good enough for him.

Because he had looked at me like I was a revelation, even in a baggy sweatshirt. I couldn't lose.

He grabbed hold of that sweatshirt, and tugged it up over my head, leaving me completely naked, pressed against him, still partially clothed.

I could feel the hard outline of his cock pushing in front of his pants. And I arched against him, hoping to feel more of that.

He growled, and walked me back to the bed, pushing me down on it.

I was tempted to look away from that sharp, hard gaze.

Because it was almost too intense. Because it was almost too much for me to withstand.

But if I looked away, I would miss this. If I looked away, I would lose this moment.

When a man looked at me like I might be everything.

Weird way to heal childhood trauma, but I would take it.

"I've fantasized about this for a long fucking time," he said, his voice hard.

He was Ryan. Still. Familiar. A man I had known for so many years. And yet he was a stranger now too.

I was naked in front of him, and he was looking at me. He was hard.

This wasn't part of how we knew each other. And changing it, rearranging the way that things had always been, was a magical sort of terror.

And all I could do was surrender to it.

CHAPTER 15

*T*he look on his face made me weak. In the very best way.

"First," he said. "I'm going to taste you. I'm going to lick you until you beg me to stop. And then I'm going to fuck you. You have no idea how much I want to do that. How much I want to feel you. Wet and hot around me."

So much for my belief that sex like this was confined to books.

I felt like a wall between us had just been torn away. And I could see the truth of him.

The truth that I hadn't wanted to see. That he was intense, sexual, unapologetic about it.

That he absolutely could give me the best fuck I'd ever had in my life, and possibly ruin me for all other men.

Part of me had maybe known that. At least since New Orleans. And if not from before.

Josh was jealous of Ryan.

Had it always been there? Was I just that committed to putting blinders on so that I didn't have to deal with the complicated things?

The things that felt like a threat to my safety?

Because this did not feel safe. It didn't feel easily controlled. It felt volatile and wild, it felt like jumping off the edge of a cliff. It felt like a million different things that I would never do, but there I was. Laying on the bed, my legs slightly parted, my eyes glued to his, desperate to hear what he would say next, to see what he might do next.

He pushed his shirt off of his shoulders, let it drop down to the floor. He was wearing nothing but black, low-slung pants.

He undid his belt smoothly with one hand, a sexual magic trick the likes of which I had never seen before. The ease and smoothness making my internal muscles squeeze tight.

A promise that my body responded to.

He would be that smooth and unerring when he touched me. I just knew it.

He stripped the rest of his clothes off, and my mouth went dry.

He was the most beautiful man I had ever seen. He was hard and thick, bigger than I've ever seen in person. His thighs were firm and muscular, and I couldn't say that I had ever given a lot of thought to a man's thighs. Until right then.

I wanted to lick him.

All the things he'd said he was going to do to me, I wanted to do to him. And yet I found myself immobilized. Pinned down to the bed by the intensity of his gaze.

"I'm going to make good on my promise," he said.

He prowled slowly to the edge of the bed, and got down onto the mattress. He moved slowly between my legs, his face inching closer to where I was wet and needy for him.

Then he moved his hands beneath my ass, and lifted me up off the mattress, bringing me down toward his mouth, his lips firm and sure as he began to lick and suck me where I needed him most.

"Holy shit," I groaned, as he went to work, eating me like I was the greatest delicacy he'd ever tasted in his life.

He pushed two fingers inside of me and fucked me with them while he continued lapping at my clit.

My hips shifted restlessly, my whole body on fire with need for him.

He was right. He was relentless. He pushed me to the edge, over and over again, and he didn't let me go over.

Normally, when I couldn't reach the edge of my orgasm, it was frustrating. Normally, there was no control there. It was just me not quite being able to get to climax. This was different. He would take me there, then pull me back, and I felt each and every time like I could go over easily, and every time he teased me, it didn't end with a sweep of disappointment, a raging feeling of irritation at my aborted pleasure; no, it only ramped up my need. My excitement.

It only brought me even more pleasure. I wanted it to end, and I also wanted to stay suspended there as long as possible.

I was strung out on a rack between pleasure and pain, and I had never loved anything more.

He lifted his head, made eye contact with me, and then slowly slid a third finger deep inside of me, and I exploded.

Everything in me shattered, cascading around me like a million stars, my orgasm blinding me, ripping through me like a violent storm. I was breathless. Lost.

He growled. "Come again."

"I can't," I said, breathless.

"Sure you can."

He began to move his thumb over my clit, back and forth. "Come again for me.

"Come on, Poppy. Be a good girl for me."

I had no idea that was such a trigger for me, but it was. Because I burst, bright and euphoric, another time, just as strong as before.

I was gasping, trying to catch my breath.

And he was moving to the nightstand, grabbing hold of a condom, and I wasn't going to ask how long it had been there, or who it had been intended for.

I hadn't gotten to touch him. I hadn't gotten to taste him.

I knew a moment of regret for that. But I also didn't have the patience to stop him now. I wanted him. I wanted him inside of me. So, I didn't tell him to stop when he took out the condom and rolled it over his thick length. I begged him to take me when he pressed the head of his cock against my slick entrance. And when he took me in one smooth thrust, I gasped. And I shook.

I looked up into his eyes, and I was overwhelmed. It was Ryan. Ryan Clark.

Quinn thought of him as the author of her fate.

I had always found that annoying.

And yet, in that moment, with him deep inside of me, I couldn't escape the fact that he was tightly wound around my fate.

I had just never been able to see it.

He began to move, each thrust taking me closer to the edge yet again.

I clung to him. If I didn't, I was going to fly off of the bed. Maybe off of the earth. Out of my body.

But I had also never felt more connected to myself. He was deep inside of me, and I could feel every inch, every stroke, so much more than I had ever experienced.

This was like something entirely new. And I felt broken apart by it. Shattered.

I couldn't breathe.

I didn't want to. I wanted to hold onto him and let him show me what was real. I wanted him to make me real.

And all the while, the realization of who this was kept roaring inside of me. I opened my eyes, I looked at his face.

Contorted with pleasure, as lost as I was.

I kissed him. Because his mouth on mine made sense. My hands on his skin. Sweat slicked beneath my fingertips.

Our breathing was fractured together.

We had never been so in sync. We had never both worked so hard toward the same goal before.

Except for maybe when he had helped me rebuild that cake.

Maybe I was wrong about him.

That made me falter. But then, he rolled his hips forward, and the new rhythm took hold of me. I wrapped my legs around his waist, he went deeper.

I didn't realize I was saying his name until he growled. Until he said mine.

"Poppy."

It sent me over the edge. I came hard, gripping his cock, pulling him deeper, and then he lost it. Any semblance of control. His thrusts became erratic, and I surrendered to it. To him.

I came again, shuddering, shivering. Begging for more, begging for a reprieve. It was too much. It was not enough.

It was everything, just like him.

Just like us.

When it was over, he rolled out of bed, and went into the bathroom. I lay there, the sheets warm and a little bit damp underneath me.

My breathing couldn't find its rhythm. My heart couldn't seem to settle down.

He came back into the room, and I swallowed a big gulp of air, then managed to make myself choke. On air. That was just how destroyed I was.

He came to the bed. "Are you okay?"

"Fine," I wheezed.

His face was unreadable. I had hoped that maybe this would make that wall go away forever. That maybe I would look at him and understand him. But I was maybe even more mystified now than I had been before.

I wasn't sure what this meant. Any of it.

I wasn't sure how to fit all these pieces together. Everything I knew about him from back then, everything this told me about now.

Except, what was there to know?

Attraction had been there, underneath the surface, all this time.

We both gave in when we knew we were going to have to see each other.

That said everything.

I sat up.

"Stay," he said.

I found myself laying back down, as he sat back down on the mattress.

He lifted his hand, put it on my cheek, held me like that as he leaned in and kissed my mouth.

I shivered beneath his lips.

When we parted, he was looking at me with that same intensity.

It was all the same with him.

He had looked at me like that so many times, and I had thought that he was angry.

I felt like I had a chest of drawers in my head that contained various things I had observed about Ryan over the years. And suddenly all the drawers had been pulled out and dumped upside down. I had that same collection of things I'd always had, but they were in disarray. I couldn't figure out how they were supposed to be organized or pieced together. What I felt like I knew, I clearly didn't know anymore. And maybe never had.

He lay down beside me, and pulled the covers up over both of us. I tried to relax, but my heart was still playing havoc inside of me.

"Relax, Poppy."

I tried. The absurdity of it. I had rarely had a conversation with this man that hadn't ended in an argument and here we were laying in bed together skin to skin. But I had to tell myself that. Because I didn't really feel that.

This didn't feel unnatural. This didn't feel wrong. It felt nice. It felt good.

I didn't feel panicked.

My heart was still beating fast, but it wasn't fear.

It was something else I didn't have a name for.

I turned over onto my side, and he wrapped his arm around me, his large hand on my stomach. I could feel him against my back, his chest hair crisp against my shoulder blades, the press of his cock against my ass arousing, even though I should be totally good.

He was getting hard again. Which seemed a little bit excessive. I couldn't complain.

After all, being wanted . . .

That did things to me.

He kissed the back of my neck. I moaned. And I thought of all the things that I still wanted to do to him.

He was leaving tomorrow.

Leaving. We both were. Getting on planes that would take us to different corners of the world.

This was our night.

I shifted, turned over so that I was facing him. He looked at me, and there were questions in his eyes. I wasn't sure what the questions were, so I really couldn't find answers. Except I pressed my hand against his chest, let my fingertips trail down the muscles there, down his abs, moved it down to his ever-hardening erection, squeezed him.

He groaned, closing his eyes, letting his head fall back. His Adam's apple bobbed up and down, and I followed the rogue desire that I had, and licked it.

He growled, suddenly gripping my wrists and pinning them up over my head. "You're playing a dangerous game."

"Am I?" I asked, panting.

I wanted to be. This kind of sex, this kind of intense, consuming sex, had never been part of my experience. I licked my lips, and I watched as his eyes flared with desire. I couldn't help but respond to that.

I was wet and throbbing again, even though I had come more times in the last fifteen minutes than I ever had in a single night.

I had a feeling I was going to again. And maybe even again.

I pushed him onto his back, and he let me. Then I ran my hands down his chest and back up again, kissing his neck, kissing down, until I reached his cock. I had never been especially bold sexually, but then, the kind of sex I'd had hadn't really necessitated boldness.

I felt it all now. Need, mixed with an incredible desire to make him feel what I was feeling.

I felt wild. Like something elemental had been stored up inside of me.

I didn't care right then how I looked. What he thought.

I was beyond that need to please. It was something earthier than that. Something deeper.

He was so beautiful. I couldn't say that I had ever thought of a man's penis as beautiful. But his was.

Thick and glorious, and it had given me so much pleasure. I owed it a debt of gratitude.

I didn't care if that was silly.

I licked him from base to tip with the flat of my tongue, swirled around the crown.

The sound he made was feral. It turned me on.

His hand went to my hair, pulling hard.

This was definitely a different side to sex than I'd ever experienced before. Maybe that was what I was feeling. This need that bordered on violence.

That space that contained both pleasure and pain.

I sucked him in deep, and he made a sound that was inhuman. I loved it.

I loved his reactions, but I wasn't working just for those. His pleasure was mine. It was that simple. That mystifying.

It was like I knew what to do next, exactly. Perfectly.

I swallowed him down, pushed him to the brink, and when he couldn't take it anymore, he gripped my hair hard and pulled me away from him. "Not like that. I'm going to fuck you again."

"Okay," I said.

He wasn't going to get an argument out of me. I probably should have said something sexier. I needed to work on my porn dialogue. His was great. Mine was probably lacking.

"Ask nicely."

Oh. Well. He was coaching me.

"Please," I said. I looked up at him, gave him my best innocent expression; hilarious, given everything that had happened in this bed in the last half-hour.

"Please what?"

"Fuck me," I said.

He pinned me down, taking hold of my wrists again and deftly applying a condom with one hand as he held me fast.

Then he slid into me, and my body welcomed him, in spite of a little bit of soreness from the last time.

It was wild. Fractured.

Somehow more intense and electrifying than the first time.

He was breathing hard, so was I.

He held onto me when his pleasure built, and mine reached the same peak. We went over together.

This time, he didn't immediately get out of bed. This time, he just held me.

Like we had both been shipwrecked together, tossed by the waves.

I clung to him. I fell asleep. And when I woke up, he was breathing steadily beside me.

I panicked.

I was in bed with Ryan.

We'd had . . . we'd had sex twice.

And in the morning, he was going to leave. We were going to go to the airport together, and say goodbye. It made me want to throw up. I couldn't stand it.

I was too embarrassed. By the intensity of all of it. By everything.

I couldn't bear it.

I knew that I couldn't.

I scrambled out of bed, and thankfully he didn't stir.

Heart hammering, I collected my clothes, and slipped out of his room, and into mine.

I went into the bathroom and looked at myself.

My hair was wrecked. A reflection of my innermost self.

I turned away from the mirror, and finished packing the few remaining things I hadn't gotten to the day before. Then, as quietly as I could, I took my suitcases down the stairs, slipped my shoes on and walked out of the house. I walked my bags down three houses, and pulled up a rideshare app on my phone.

There was a driver pretty close by, and I put in the location of the Queenstown airport, and waited.

It only took five minutes. He helped me get my bags in the trunk, and I got into the backseat. I called myself a coward in a hundred different ways.

He would be in the international terminal. Since he was flying directly out of the country. I would be in domestic.

I was wrecked after last night. And I still couldn't say what I felt for him.

I just knew that I didn't want to say goodbye.

CHAPTER 16

*H*e didn't text me, and I figured I should be grateful for that. No awkwardness. But then, part of me felt like that meant I wasn't all that important. Which was ridiculous. I was the one that had snuck out under cover of darkness.

The car pulled up to the front of the airport. I hastily got my bags out, and was thrust into pandemonium. The small airport was overly filled with people. And there was a long line by customer service.

I moved quickly to check my bags, and then I wove around all the people to get into the domestic security line.

I looked up on the board and saw that about four flights had been canceled.

Not mine, though. Still, seeing that much red on the outgoing flights filled me with dread. I stood there, a lump forming in my stomach. I made it through security. I went and sat by my gate. And I saw three more flights change to canceled on the board.

Slowly, the gate area began to empty. More and more people going out to the other side of security. My flight was still scheduled. I still didn't have a text from Ryan. Those two things were unrelated. Or at least, I tried to make them unrelated.

Somehow, it was all swirling together in a big knot of dread.

And then, every last flight on the board changed.

Canceled.

There were audible groans from the gate area, and from those still in the security line.

Slowly, we all began to filter out into the main area of the airport. It was utter chaos. The line to customer service stretched all the way down past both domestic and foreign security.

The line around baggage claim and the rental cars was even longer.

I got my phone out and tried to call Air New Zealand. Their lines were of course jammed. Busy.

I decided to wait on hold as I got in the end of the impossibly long line.

People were grumbling, complaining. I overheard somebody say that there were no hotel rooms available.

There was a woman in line in front of me, and I tapped her on the shoulder. "Excuse me. Do you know what happened?"

"It's the wind," she said, looking annoyed. "Flights can't land."

"Oh," I said. "Is that normal?"

"So far, so Queenstown," she said, grimacing.

Then she turned back toward the front of the line.

I saw that on the international side, there were still a few flights scheduled to depart, and gathered from conversation around me that it was because the planes had already been there. They could take off, they just couldn't land.

There had been a round of flights that had left this morning, but they had corresponded with flights of people coming in, and now Queenstown was overfull, with those who had just arrived, and those who couldn't leave.

I heard his voice.

I couldn't hear what he was saying. I couldn't even explain how I knew it was him. It was more a deep rumble cutting through the voices around me. And I knew.

I turned, and there he was, on the phone. He was looking at me.

His gaze was . . . dark. Stormy. He was mad at me.

That was probably fair enough. I likely deserved it.

I had run out that morning without a backward glance. But then, he hadn't texted me.

"Great." I could make his words out now that I was looking at him. "Thanks, mate. Great."

He hung the phone up, and then he walked over to where I was in line. "Good luck getting through this," he said.

"Ryan . . ."

"Save it. Your flight's canceled?"

"Yes," I said. "Is yours?"

He nodded. "I got a place to stay."

"How?"

"I called the rental management company from the house we just checked out of. There's a place they have, it's not listed yet, so no one was scheduled to check in today. They said there won't be any cleaning service, but we're welcome to go."

"*We?*"

"Did you want to sleep in the airport?"

"No. Of course I don't want to sleep in the airport, but . . ."

"And I'm not leaving you in the airport, Poppy. No matter that you're a coward who tried to run away."

I had been thwarted. Well and truly. Caught in my cowardice, and in my inability to face what had happened between us.

"I don't know what to say," I said.

"Say let's get out of here now, and we will worry about getting booked on two different flights later. Because this line is going to take hours, and we're never going to get through on the phone now. But if we wait, we are never going to get a fucking Uber."

He had a point. "I have to get my bags."

"Fine."

All the bags were spit out at the baggage claim, and mine were already sitting there, tagged for a flight they were not going to get on. I noticed that he only had a backpack.

"Is that all you're bringing to Europe?"

He shrugged. "It's all I need."

I suddenly felt extremely extra with my two suitcases.

We walked back out of the airport, which was just as chaotic as it was inside. The snow was coming down hard and fast, and the gusts of wind were freezing cold. We managed to get a car with about a fifteen-minute wait, and we both stood there. If I felt anything like fanciful or romantic, I would be tempted to believe this was fate. Instead, it felt more like the inevitable bowling ball that always arrived when Ryan was involved.

The wind whipped around us, I shivered.

And I found a heavy coat being placed on my shoulders.

I looked up at him. "You don't have to give me your coat."

"I'm fine," he said.

"You know, you're a human being with the same core body temperature as me, regardless of gender. I'm not quite sure why men feel the need to pretend that they don't experience cold."

"I'm cold. Fucking freezing, I think you should have the coat anyway. How do you like that?"

I didn't know what to do with that at all.

"Ryan . . ."

"Poppy. You told me that we were going to ride over together."

"I didn't want to say goodbye to you," I said, the words scraping the inside of my throat like a knife.

He looked dumbfounded. And right then the car pulled up.

"Fuck," he muttered.

He gave the driver the address, and we piled inside.

"Flight canceled?" the guy asked.

"Yes," Ryan answered, clipped.

"You got somewhere to stay?"

"This address," Ryan said.

"Lucky. Because I've already heard that a lot of people can't find a place. No rental cars either."

"What a shitshow," Ryan said.

The driver left.

The new rental house was a block above the other house, down the street just a bit, further out of town.

It was newer, and quite a bit smaller. Part of the duplex that overlooked the lake.

The living room was huge, with sweeping views, and the kitchen was modern and open.

There was one bedroom.

And one bathroom.

So that was that.

I tried to take a breath. It was cut off by Ryan. He put his backpack down on the ground, the sound harsh in the quiet space. "Now what was it you said to me?"

I closed my eyes. "I don't like saying goodbye. And I didn't know what to say to you after last night. It wasn't like . . . it wasn't like anything was going to come of it, Ryan. You were headed to Europe. I was headed back home. I just didn't . . . I didn't want . . ." I started to hyperventilate, which was stupid.

"What's wrong?" he asked.

"Sometimes . . . it just . . . it sucks to say goodbye. I was grateful that Quinn left last night to all that fanfare. It wasn't personal. I hate looking at somebody in their face and saying it right to them. Because I said goodbye to my mom. When she left me with my grandmother, I thought that I was only staying for a vacation. She never came back. Not really. She visited a couple of times, we went to see her once. But everything changed after that. I just didn't see the point of it. Especially when it's inevitable."

"Well, a man doesn't really like to wake up ghosted either."

"Don't they? I was under the impression that most men would be pretty happy if their one-night stand took off and left without any awkwardness."

"Who fucking said it was a one-night stand?"

I nearly choked. "What else was it ever going to be?"

He snorted, and walked away from me. He went into the kitchen, rested his palms flat on the countertop. "Let's get one thing straight. There's one bedroom here. One bed. When do we skip the part where we pretend we're not going to fuck?"

CHAPTER 17

I was completely immobilized by his directness.

"Does that word make you blush now, Poppy?"

"Always did," I said, trying to force the words out through my strangled throat. "It's just . . . I was so horny the last time you said that to me I didn't have time to turn into a stuttering wreck."

"My mistake. But I don't see the point in beating around the bush."

"Fair. I . . . yeah. Okay. We won't pretend."

"My next request is that we stop pretending altogether."

"I don't understand what you mean."

"You don't?"

"No," I said.

"You want me. You have. For a long time."

I closed my eyes. "I'm still sorting through all that."

"Great. We have time. Here we are, stuck in Queenstown. It's snowing outside, we're probably going to have a hell of a time getting a car anywhere. Going to be a lot of walking in the snow."

"I can't believe this."

"Well, maybe it would be better if we just started over. With a little bit of honesty."

"What honesty?"

"I want you," he said. "I have. For as long as I can remember. I wanted to strangle fucking Josh when you came back from college and started dating him. But, I didn't have any right to my feelings because you and I weren't even friends."

I was completely stunned by that. I didn't know what to say. I had assumed this whole time that he didn't like me at all. That he didn't think of me when I wasn't there. But he was attracted to me? I knew he was attracted to me, in the sense that we had sex, and he had clearly enjoyed it. I'd had the sense that he wanted me, in a much more specific way than I had realized before, but finding out that he'd wanted me all the way back then . . .

"I don't know what to say to that."

"Of course not. It's too weird, right? Why do you think he was jealous? He knew. I think on some level he knew."

"If he knew then why . . ."

I looked at Ryan. Who was so tall and so handsome. Who had that quality about him. That golden boy quality.

I knew that his life had been hard. I understood it, I respected it, because it so closely mirrored the hardship that I had gone through.

But I had to wonder what Josh saw when he looked at Ryan. If he saw him as somebody who got things in life easily.

Because he was the one who had become the hometown hero even though he had only lived there since he was twelve.

The town was proud of him, he was a credit to the people that lived there.

They considered him their favorite son.

He had been adopted into one of the richest families in Pineville.

I knew that I had feelings about how easily he had risen to the top of things in town. But that was because I often felt like a square peg that had been shoved into that particular round hole just like he was, but hadn't been quite as universally loved.

"He's jealous of you," I said.

He nodded. "We're friends, I don't want to make it sound like we aren't. But we have . . . there's competition there."

"How can there be competition?"

He lifted a brow.

"I only mean, if it's sports, you're going to win. If it's . . . I really hate this, because when I get into comparing Josh with you, I just feel like I'm being mean. I feel like you beat him at everything. That makes it sound like I wasn't happy with him when I was with him."

"He's not here. Maybe stop trying to be so damned fair."

I swallowed hard. "Okay. Maybe I will."

It occurred to me then that maybe one of the real reasons I had enjoyed my time with Josh so much was that I had felt like maybe I was punching below my weight. Maybe that had made me feel secure.

Maybe that was why I had been so blindsided when he had broken up with me.

"You just seem like you're good at everything," I said.

He chuckled, and made his way over to the coffee pot. He dug around until he found some coffee, and then he started to make some in the percolator on the stovetop.

"You should understand why," he said.

"Oh," I said. My heart sank just slightly.

Because, of course I did. Because of course I knew it wasn't because he was just so happy; effortlessly happy to do everything and succeed at it.

I understood overachieving that came from a place of desperation. That came from a place of fear.

I understood exactly what he was talking about.

"Because you are afraid if you didn't do it, they would think that it was a mistake to have adopted you."

He nodded. "Yeah. And you know, they are relentlessly proud of me. Even when I decided to be a photographer, and not a . . . not a doctor, or whatever I might've been. They never made me feel like I had to earn my spot, but I felt like I did anyway. Because when you know what it's like . . . when you know what it's like to not be important enough to be kept, you figure you might have to earn your place."

"I get that," I said. "You know I do."

"Josh doesn't. He doesn't get why I wanted the top spot in everything. Just like he didn't understand that you weren't just the world's greatest girlfriend who lived to do everything for him. Just like he didn't understand that he was benefiting from you feeling insecure, and that he did little things to keep you that way."

"I just don't like thinking he did that on purpose . . ."

"It sounds like I'm saying he's a shitty person, and I'm actually not. He just doesn't get it. And why would he? He has two parents who love him. And he never had to earn it. He doesn't get it. He never has. And so, there were things that I did that he took as a threat to him. That made him feel like he was competing with me, when I sure as hell wasn't. I was just trying to . . . survive. So yeah, there was a little bit of a thing. And I think he thought because he got you, he won something."

"I didn't know," I said.

He shook his head. "Of course you didn't."

"Why would I? It never occurred to me that you . . . I didn't think you liked me at all, Ryan. You weren't nice to me."

"Yeah, I wasn't, back when I was in my phase of trying to push people away."

"But after that, I still didn't know what to do with you. I still did not talk to you. I had no clue what might . . . what might make you like me. But you know, there was always something kind of nice about it. Because there was a point where I accepted that you just never would. And you were the one person I didn't have to perform for."

"I know," he said.

He took the coffee maker off the stove and poured two cups. "I never hated you," he said. "You were the first time I was ever faced with . . . liking a girl when I wasn't going to leave six months later. I handled it badly."

"I haven't handled everything perfectly myself. I . . . I know I've been attracted to you for a while. I just . . ."

His eyes sharpened. "Since when?"

I felt myself sinking deeper and deeper into the floor. "I don't know."

He made a short, masculine sound and looked away. "Well. Figure it out. Get back to me."

"Oh . . . I . . . okay." I started to turn away from him.

"I wasn't dismissing you," he said.

I stopped and turned back to him.

"Are you asking me to stay?"

He moved toward me, and my breath abandoned me. "I told you," he said. "I'm done pretending."

"It's early," I replied quietly.

"So?"

"I'm not a big fan of morning sex," I said, pressing my thighs together, trying to do something to deny the rush of need that pounded through me right then.

He didn't say anything. He just . . . laughed. Deep and sexy, and powerful enough to make an absolute mockery of my previous statement.

Because my body didn't care what time it was. It just wanted Ryan.

It wasn't that the tension was gone. It wasn't that everything was fixed.

But something had changed.

Maybe I had.

I wasn't sure.

He wrapped his arm around my waist and pulled me up against his hard body.

Then he dragged his thumb along my lower lip, and I liked it. He tasted like salt and Ryan. I already knew. His unique taste. And what it did to me.

Then his mouth was on mine. I wasn't worried anymore. About

the flight delays or being here with him or what my life would look like back home.

I wasn't even worried about saying goodbye.

Because right then, we were together. And I didn't need to know anything else.

It was bright inside the rental house, everything bright white and modern. There was a fireplace with a sheepskin rug in front of it, and beyond that the windows that faced the water.

He kissed me all the way to the rug, laid me down on top of it. He stripped me beneath that glorious natural light. And I did the same to him.

I marveled as I moved my hand over his chest, watched myself touch Ryan.

It was amazing, and so was he. It didn't feel quite as frantic as last night, though there was still an edge to it. Still an edge to us.

Because this was the culmination of so many years of frenetic energy between us.

Maybe the energy was everything.

Maybe it was dislike. And like we had never known what to do with it. Attraction and reaction and compulsion.

Maybe he had always scared me more than anyone else because of the way he could see me. Because of the way he understood me.

Maybe we both scared each other.

He kissed me, and rolled onto his back, bringing me with him, so that I was on top of him, straddling him, the hard press of his cock against me. I rubbed against him, slick and needy for him. I had never been one to have sex like this. In the full light of day, with no shadows, no secrets. I felt dimly like maybe I should be embarrassed to show how much I wanted him.

It hit me then that maybe I had never enjoyed sex all that much because there was something so exposing if you wanted someone so badly.

So I never really had.

I had enjoyed the closeness, the niceness, and when everything went well, the ripple of release.

But just touching Ryan was better than an orgasm. Anticipating that moment was even better than the moment itself. Or maybe not, because I couldn't think clearly. Couldn't remember much of anything.

I only had the moment.

In the moment he was all I wanted.

I leaned down and kissed him, my hair making a curtain surrounding us.

I kept my eyes open. My nose pressed against his, and I looked at his face. I ran my thumb around the outline of his upper lip, and he bit my palm.

My heart jumped hard against my breastbone.

I didn't feel afraid to want him. Because I could see how much he wanted me back.

Because when he kissed me, he agreed to be as vulnerable as I was.

I arched my hips forward and back, teasing us both, and he grabbed a condom from somewhere to his left. I assumed he had taken it out of his pocket before he had stripped his clothes off, but I hadn't noticed.

I was just glad that he was thinking clearer than I was.

He applied the protection swiftly, cradled my face and kissed me again as he guided himself inside me.

My breath hissed through my teeth as he filled me, inch by satisfying inch.

And then I began to move, never looking away from him, keeping my eyes fixed on the pleasure on his face.

I had never seen anything so beautiful in my life. Maybe it was a hideously narcissistic thing to think. But watching that man, that glorious man, wanting me, was indescribably healing. It filled places inside me I hadn't realized were empty.

He moved his hands up, spanning my waist, cupping my

breasts. He looked at me like I was art, and I knew for a fact that *he* was.

He brought my head down, and kissed me, firm, didn't release his hold, raised his hips upward and took control, even with me on top. He held me fast, tight, one hand on my hip, bracing me so that each and every thrust went deeper, harder.

A ripple of need expanded inside of me, and my release hit unexpectedly, entirely without me striving for it, or expecting it.

He growled, and came, pulsing inside of me as he did.

And then he held me. Against his chest, as his breathing normalized. I didn't know if mine ever would.

"I'm not falling asleep," he said. "Because you might run away."

I laughed. "I don't have anywhere to go."

"Don't sweet-talk me too much. It might go to my head."

I rolled off of him and sat up. I was dizzy. I couldn't believe we had just had sex on a rug in front of an open window. Not that anybody could see up and inside the house, but still.

"You make me act like . . . not myself. You kind of always have," I said.

"In what way?"

"Normally, I am a lot more cautious than this. And also, normally I'm a lot nicer to people than I am to you. Because I always felt like I had to be nice and accommodating and please everybody else."

"Maybe you're more yourself with me," he said.

I let out a hard breath and pushed my hand through my hair. "I . . . more my evil self."

"Why is it evil? Do not give everybody what they want all the time. Including me. Also, I am impossible to deal with sometimes."

I looked at him and I laughed. "Yes. You are. I didn't know you knew that."

"I've lived with myself for nearly thirty-one years, Poppy. I'm pretty familiar with the ways in which I'm a difficult asshole."

"Then why are you?"

"Probably for the same reason you're accommodating?"

"Except I'm not with you."

I was a little bit annoyed that I acted different with him, and he didn't act different with me. But for some reason, as he sat there, staring straight ahead, and the light from outside caught his profile, I couldn't breathe. And I couldn't find the words to say anything about that. Because I just knew that it was a lie. I knew that even if I couldn't quantify it or articulate it, he did treat me differently.

For some reason, I couldn't bring myself to ask him about it.

"Well, what do you want to do today?"

"We should probably try to call the airline."

"I doubt there's any point."

I groaned. Then I stood up, and crossed the room naked, grabbed my purse and took my phone out of it. I checked my email. There were a few from Air New Zealand. One of which promised that when we were rebooked, we would be notified.

"I guess they're going to get in touch with us. Though, we may not be flying out on the same day," I said.

"First the weather has to clear."

It was still windy outside. The lake was choppy, the waves crashing against the shore with all the intensity of an ocean.

"That could be a while."

I looked at him, and he stared back at me. Tension gathered in my stomach. There was the very real possibility that we would be stuck here for days. And part of me wondered if it would be wrong for us to do nothing but have sex.

"Bad news," he said.

"What?"

"We're out of condoms."

I nearly choked. He had read my mind.

"That is terrible news. Please tell me you didn't go through a bunch of the ones that you brought with you with random women you met about town in the last couple of weeks."

"No," he said. "I just had a handful with me. All used with you."

"That really shouldn't make me feel good about myself. I feel like the bar is low."

He laughed. "You're here with me. The bar is very low."

I couldn't let that pass, though. Not knowing what I did about him.

"The bar is not low. Trust me. This is the best sex I've ever had."

He lifted a brow. "I'll take that."

"You like that," I said.

"Yeah. I do. What man wouldn't?"

I wanted to say more. I wanted him to tell me that I was the best he'd ever had. But that was probably reaching, given the number of lovers he'd undoubtedly had, compared to my paltry two other dudes.

He stood up and went back into the kitchen, and leaned against the counter, scrolling through his phone. "There are no cars. No taxis, no rideshare. The wait for them is insane."

"Seriously?"

"Seriously. Grocery delivery, food delivery. All busy."

"The town is overrun," I said.

I realized just then how extremely lucky we were to have secured this house.

I walked over to him, and wrapped my arms around his shoulders, stretched up on my toes and kissed his cheek.

For some reason, that felt even more bold than what had just happened down on the rug. "Thank you," I said.

He looked at me like I was unhinged. "For what?"

"Taking care of me."

CHAPTER 18

I felt my chest cave in just slightly.

I hadn't realized until the words came out of my mouth. Very few people took care of me. Not since my grandmother had died.

Josh never had. I took care of us. Some of that was being afraid to need anybody too much. Some of it was my own fault. I didn't tell people how to take care of me. But Ryan had never seemed to need to be told.

He had taken care of me when the bear had eaten my cake. He had taken care of me that day of the breakup. And I was the one who had been terrible to him. Even after I had run out on him after sleeping together, he had made sure I was taken care of.

He did it like it was breathing.

"Why don't we get dressed and you can come with me. I was wanting to hike the Queenstown trail and take some pictures. Then we can go to the grocery store for . . . food."

Condoms also, I hoped.

"Sure."

I took the suitcases into the bedroom. The bedroom we were going to share. I felt a little shiver of excitement go down my spine.

It was so weird, though. To be with this man that I did know, but not in this way. To suddenly be launched into the intimacy of not only sleeping together, but living together.

I put on my very warm snow pants, and a sweatshirt. Then I

drifted into the bathroom and fussed with my hair for a while, ultimately doing braids and putting a beanie on. When I came back out, he had gotten dressed as well, and then he took his bag and deposited it in the bedroom. I swallowed hard.

"Okay," I said, trying not to marinate on why I felt gravity because our bags were cohabitating. "Let's go."

We went outside, and I had to brace myself against the intensity of the wind. I shoved my hands deep into my pockets, and I followed him, trusting in his sense of direction to get us where we needed to go.

His camera bag was slung over his shoulder, his hair pushed back off of his forehead. He always looked so rugged. Like photographer Indiana Jones or something.

"You're staring," he said.

"Well. Because I think you're hot. And I'm not worried about you knowing that now," I said.

He looked at me. "I think you're hot too. If that hadn't been made clear."

That made me blush. My whole face was hot. And suddenly the beanie felt too warm.

"Thanks," I said.

"I should've told you that back in high school."

"I would have run away from you," I said. "I wasn't . . ." I squeezed my eyes shut for a second. "I was not in the space to hear that from anybody then."

"Especially not me, probably though," he said.

I grimaced. "I didn't know what to do with you. I think . . . I could never have put this into words until just now. I kind of realized it earlier today. I was always afraid that you would look at me and see what I was lacking. Because you were like me."

"Ah. Right. The outsiders club. Where you don't even reach out to each other because you're feral and you don't know how."

I laughed. "Yeah. That's exactly it. But I had done such a good job of not being part of that club. I had Quinn. And I had my grandma, and I was hiding it."

"I didn't hide it. Not at first."

"No. But then you began your descent into golden boy territory. It was intimidating."

"There was a point," he said, the only sound other than our voices our feet on the sidewalk. "There was a point where something flipped inside of me. Where I realized they weren't just going to send me away. But even more so, I realized I didn't want them to. And once I didn't want to be sent away. That was when I started trying. To do better. Be better. Be worth it."

"How did you even meet them? How did they find out about you?"

"They were looking for an older child. One that had been stuck in foster care. They took me in because they felt sorry for me. It's tough, because when you're a foster kid like I was, you kind of need the pity of the well-intentioned. But I never wanted it."

I could feel it then, another sharp difference in our experiences. My grandmother had taken me in because I was her granddaughter.

Mary and Michael had been doing a good deed. And it didn't mean they didn't love Ryan. They absolutely, obviously did. They were his parents. But I knew how much those shitty experiences from childhood could affect you. And when you were in Ryan's position, a teenage boy who had been in foster care all of his life, and the people who adopted you did so as an act of charity, a good deed, because of your need, not necessarily their burning need to have a child, it must linger inside of you.

You must wonder at what point the good deed was no longer worth it.

When the balance of the scales would be thrown off altogether.

"I feel ungrateful sometimes," he said. "Feeling the way that I do about those years. About my childhood. Because they really did give me something spectacular. Something that I had never had before. I think I have every right to be a little bit messed up from foster care. I don't really have the right to be messed up over them taking me in."

"Well, funny thing, you don't get to choose what emotionally scars you. Believe me. I tried to sort through all that. Because what I would really love is to just be grateful that I had a grandmother who took me in and took care of me. What I would really love is if I could just be okay, because I was okay. Eventually, I was okay. That isn't how it works, though."

Neither of us said anything for a while. We continued on up the trail, the view around us stunning. The town itself on one side, the vast wilderness on the other. The lake, the mountains. We were surrounded by beauty, just like everybody else who ever came up here. We still carried all that same pain around with us.

"Good things don't make the bad things go away," I said. That realization suddenly crystallizing within me. "We had both. Standing here, looking at the view doesn't make us not abandoned children."

He huffed a laugh. "All right. That's a good point."

When we reached the top of the mountain, the end of the trail, he got out his equipment, his camera, his tripod, and began to take pictures. I sat down, grateful for my waterproof pants, picking a spot in a snow drift as I watched him work.

I was fascinated by this part of him. By the way he used photography.

His exhibition about the town; the way that he had captured and held the people that were around us all the time. Froze them, so that we could pause and make sense of them. For better or for worse.

When you were a kid that was thrust into unfamiliar, strange situations all the time, that must be a gift.

The opportunity to pause and breathe and make sense of your surroundings. To capture it and hold on.

To make the memories you didn't have from before.

There was so much to it.

There was so much to him.

He turned around and faced me. He lifted the camera up and covered his face. I smiled. He took my picture.

"Come over here," I said.

"Why?"

"Ryan," I said, "come here."

He did, and I wrapped my arms around his neck and took my phone out of my pocket.

"I don't do selfies," he said.

"Now you do," I said, taking the phone out and turning it to face us. And right as I was about to take the photo, he kissed me. Deep and hard, and I was dizzy.

I clung to him, and kissed him back, there at the top of the mountain, where anybody could walk up and see us. Of course, we weren't home, and everyone we knew had left, so it wasn't like happening upon the two of us making out would mean anything to a stranger.

It still felt like something to me.

He pulled away from me, and I looked at the picture. Us kissing. His eyes closed. It felt bizarrely intimate to look at it, even though we were the people in the photo.

I let out a long, slow breath. "I like it."

Even though like didn't quite cover it. Even though like was too simple.

"Everybody thinks they're a damn photographer with their iPhones," he said.

"Well, at least you're in the picture."

We walked back down the mountain together and went to the grocery store.

I chose a couple boxes of frozen meat pies. Bread for toast, which we had decided was superior in New Zealand for some reason. He bought a jar of Marmite and insisted that I try it on my toast.

Then we went down the aisle that also contained shampoo and paracetamol and grabbed a box of condoms. I grabbed a second.

"We don't know when we're getting a flight out," I said seriously.

We went to the checkout line, and I felt like a teenager, caught doing something a little bit naughty, but I didn't hate it.

I did my best not to look at the checker as she moved the two boxes of condoms across the scanner.

When we were back out in the parking lot with our scant bags, I burst into a fit of giggles.

Ryan took the bag I was holding and proceeded to carry everything back to the rental house.

"You don't have to do that."

"I want to," he said.

And that brought me back to my earlier thought process. About the way that he took care of me.

I felt a little bit wind-chapped by the time we got back into the rental. Ryan took the groceries into the kitchen, and I flexed my fingers, which were frozen, in spite of being encased by my new gloves. Maybe possum wasn't all it was cracked up to be.

I was back to believing in the possum lobby.

Ryan moved to me, and brushed his thumb across my cheek. "You're freezing," he said.

"Only a little bit."

He reached down and tugged at my gloves, pulling them loose one finger at a time. Then he curved his fingers around mine, rubbed my hands between his palms, before moving his lips to my freezing fingers and kissing them.

I wanted to lean against him. My full weight. Into all of his strength.

I had never wanted something that scared me so much so desperately.

Because I had never once leaned against someone with everything I had. I knew better than that. He made me want to.

I felt so desperate to know him. To really know him. But I wasn't sure I even knew myself on the level I wanted to puzzle him out. I wanted to burrow inside him. To get down beneath all the layers of rock and stone and see him.

We were here together after so many years of . . . whatever we'd been.

After how I'd . . . hurt him.

Had I hurt him?

It seemed important to know. And important for me to tell him the truth of that night.

Suddenly, he lifted me up off the ground, and carried me like I weighed nothing, right into that single bathroom we had to share. There was a large, deep white tub in it. He turned the water on and set me down.

"You're freezing. And I think you could probably use a bath."

"I think you probably have lascivious intent," I said.

"I absolutely have lascivious intent," he said.

He stripped his shirt off, and I discovered that my intent was pretty lascivious too.

"Wow," I said, when his bare chest was revealed. "You are really . . . you are really hot."

He growled and moved toward me, and took my shirt off, began to make quick work of my clothes. Something was nagging at me. Chewing at the back of my mind.

I wanted to say something, but I was in a lust fog, who could blame me, and I was having trouble making sense of what was quite so pressing, since really, the only thing I wanted to be pressing was his cock against me.

The fifth wedding.

"I just need to—"

But he kissed me.

And I ended up arching against him, rubbing my breasts against his chest like an absolute hello, and I wasn't even ashamed.

I took his jeans off of him, making quick work of the belt, button, zipper.

And then, I wrapped my hand around that hard length, velvet-covered steel. Which I had read in romance novels before, and laughed at, but found it so apt now.

I had never given that much thought to the textures of sex. To all the different aspects of it. And now I found myself obsessed.

Yes. Maybe I was different.

But then, he lifted me up and deposited me in the warm water, coming to sit behind me, planting me firmly between his thighs, my ass pressed up against his insistent arousal.

"You're so sexy," he said, kissing my neck.

No one had ever said that to me before.

He said it with intensity. A guttural sound. Like it was an imperative truth.

I had never been so enamored of anyone as I was of him in that moment.

Maybe because no one had ever seemed so enamored of me.

And that was when the fog cleared. "Ryan, I need to say something about Leavenworth."

His hold on me went tight, his body went still. "When I said that I wanted to get back at him, I did mean it, but that wasn't . . . that wasn't the only reason. And I was too stunned by the whole thing to articulate myself. I was angry. And yes, part of me wanted to hurt him for that. But it wasn't . . . it wasn't what it sounded like."

"That you only wanted me because I was the person that would hurt him the most?"

He did believe that. It was my fault. I'd been so in my own head, in my own feelings, that I'd let him believe I only wanted him to hurt Josh.

It seemed like such a stupid, stupid thing. Especially now, when I could see how pale what I felt for Josh really was.

"No," I said. "It wasn't. Because you made me feel exciting and beautiful and desired. In a way that he never did. And he made it really clear that he wanted to go out and have sex with other people in part because he was bored with me. So having you . . . you, who didn't even like me . . . want me like that, that made me feel good. And it did feel poetic. I can't separate your relationship with him, and my relationship with him, and my feelings for you. Not entirely. Because we're human beings who don't exist in vacuums, however much we might want to. But it wasn't the only reason that I wanted you. It never was."

He didn't say anything. He moved his hands up to cup my breasts, and I figured that was . . . well, him not hating me.

I leaned my head back against his chest, desire making my words slow. Making it hard for me to think. Hard for me to speak.

"I wanted you. And I knew that. In New Orleans when I saw you with the bridesmaid, I was sick to my stomach. But I couldn't figure out why. But I know you felt it. Under the awning."

"Is that when you were first attracted to me?" he asked.

"I'm sure it wasn't. I don't know when that happened. It was the first time it felt like something I couldn't just dismiss. I've told myself for years that you make me feel uncomfortable because you don't like me. And every little bit of discomfort I've felt around you has been easy because I could blame it on you. But not that moment in New Orleans. Not that evening in the rain. I didn't want to label it. I didn't want to say what it was, not even inside my own head. I protect myself from it. Because I was determined to . . . I just wanted for everything to stay the same. So badly. And in that moment, I felt precariously close to letting go of something. To losing it completely, and that terrified me. But I couldn't handle seeing you with her. And I also had a very hard time rationalizing that response away."

"But you tried," he said.

"Yes. I did. And then I had a hard time looking at you. I had a hard time being nice to you. In Tahoe I saw you through the window. Without a shirt on. And it was like I got slapped in the face. I couldn't deny it anymore. No matter how much I wanted to. So, when we kissed in Leavenworth, I was free to do something with wanting you. And it felt good. It was never only about him. It never could be. Because we've never been *only* about him. We had our own thing *first*. Even if it was dysfunctional and filled with dead science fair projects."

"Don't be dramatic," he said. "It was just one." He paused for a moment. "Do you know why I hooked up with the bridesmaid?"

"No," I said.

"Because I wanted you. Because I wanted you, and that moment outside, in the rain, it tested me. And I knew I would be the biggest asshole on the planet if I showed up to your hotel room and told you how much I wanted you."

That hurt my feelings, actually. That he'd been with somebody else while wanting me. It made me feel small and hurt. I was kind of glad. Because I had hurt him. It was kind of nice to know that he had also responded to this thing between us badly.

That I wasn't alone in my ineptitude.

"That's sort of terrible," I said.

"Yeah," he said. "It is. But I told you, I've . . . I felt things for you that I shouldn't and I had to come up with ways to handle that."

"I genuinely thought you just didn't like me."

"In a way it's true. I didn't. Because I didn't want the complication. Josh was my first friend and it was the same as it was for you and Quinn, in the beginning. Not in the same way always, but at first. And I felt a hell of a lot of loyalty to him for a long time. I didn't want to want the woman that he was dating." He moved his hands over my skin, I shivered. "Anyway, I didn't think *you* liked *me*."

"I didn't," I said. "Because you were so unimpressed with me. And I really need people to be impressed with me."

He tightened his hold on me. "God, that was a lie though. I was."

"You were just like a feral cat."

"Still am," he said.

"Me too, I think," I said. "I don't really want to be. But . . . old habits die hard, I guess. And protective measures can die really hard."

"I'm familiar."

"I really didn't mean to drop the bowling ball on your science project."

"I really was mad about that," he said.

"I know."

"That was the first thing at school I ever really tried on, you know?" He was quiet for a second. "And my . . . my mom helped me with it."

"Oh," I said.

He kissed my neck, moved his hands over my skin, began to tease my nipples. He was obviously done talking. Sharing feelings was over. And I was a swirl of revelation and contradiction.

He had wanted me. He had disliked me.

He had resented me. But of course he had.

Right now, he was holding me, and the feeling of his rough hands moving over my sensitized flesh was good enough that I didn't really want to think about complications, or the future. Not about the inevitable goodbye that I had tried to outrun this morning.

Who knew when we would leave here?

We were together now.

That was what mattered.

I didn't know what to think about it. I didn't know how it was going to end neatly. What lesson we were supposed to learn from each other, or what this meant as the end result of our issues with each other. I just didn't know.

Maybe I didn't need to. I was always trying to make everything chronically okay, and I had never really been able to do that with Ryan.

That was the beauty of him. And the pain.

I maneuvered so that I was facing him, straddling him in the water, rubbing against him right where I was desperate for his touch as he kissed me deep, his hand fisted in my hair. I didn't need to rationalize. I didn't need to reason. I just needed him.

He fisted his hand in my hair and pulled my head back. I arched forward and he leaned in, taking my nipple into his mouth and sucking hard.

There was something feral about him now, and I loved it. Craved it.

Suddenly, I was being lifted out of the water, his arms strong around me, as he carried us both safely out of the tub. I clung to his neck as he took us into the bedroom and flung me down onto the bed.

"I would have killed us both trying to get us out of the tub like that," I said breathlessly.

"I had you," he said.

He had. He'd had me. And I trusted it. I trusted him, which was the most amazing thing of all. Because the list of what and who I trusted was short. Very, very short.

"Wait here," he said.

"I'm not going anywhere!" I called, as he disappeared from the bedroom and returned a moment later with a condom box.

Then he laid down on the bed, his naked body pressed against mine, our skin still slick from the water. This was frantic. Frenzied. Perfect.

He pinned me down, kissed me hard. Kissed his way down my body and forced my thighs apart so he could lick me right where I needed him most.

He lapped at my clit, his fingers buried deep inside me, as he called an effortless climax from my body. As he made me cry out his name.

Ryan.

It blew my mind less that it was Ryan now. Because somehow now it just made sense. Of course, he was the man who made me feel like this. Of course, he was the best kisser, the one who touched me exactly how I wanted him to. How I needed him to.

How long had it been him?

When he was inside me again, I clung to him. Locked my legs around his hips, and took him. I felt like I understood things I hadn't before. About songs, and poetry. About books and about myself. If it hadn't felt so good, I might've been terrified. But I was lost in the moment. Lost in him.

He said my name against my mouth when he came, and I followed him over the edge, clinging to him until the storm passed.

I lay against him afterward, my hand resting on his chest.

"When was the first time you saw your mom on TV?"

I turned to face him. "That's a weird question."

"I've always wondered. But we've never really done the getting to know you stuff."

"This isn't really a small-talk kind of question."

"Yeah, and what we just did isn't really an introduction either. So, I figure I'm allowed to skip the weather and go straight to parental issues."

"Fourth grade. She was in a movie about a talking pig. You probably remember it. He played basketball."

"Oh. Yes. I do remember that."

"Everybody was seeing it. But, of course, my grandma didn't want to go. And I wasn't sure if I did either. But the trailer would come on all the time on TV. I ended up seeing it at a friend's house. At a sleepover. But I couldn't say anything to anybody. I didn't want them to know. That my mom was famous. She wasn't, not really. I mean you don't get famous after one movie part, but ten-year-olds don't really know that." I huffed, and looked at the texture of the ceiling. One shape looked a little bit like a sheep. I let that distract me for a second. "Of course, after that, she was in that erotic thriller, and that actually made her famous. And I never saw that. I would actually rather die."

"I know she's on a sitcom."

"She wanted to do something different. And that presented itself. At least that's what she said. I suspect that maybe she was just having trouble getting roles because Hollywood is ageist. And it isn't like she was Meryl Streep. She had a couple of movies that did well."

"What was it like, seeing your mom on TV like that? At a party?"

"I went in the bathroom and cried. And threw up some of the birthday cake."

He wrapped his arms around me and pulled me close. "I'm sorry, Poppy."

"You get used to it. But you might see your mom in a newspaper or a magazine. On a billboard. On a poster by the movies. Eventually, that image of her kind of became . . . not my mom. It's weird, though, because I know her more as a Hollywood version of herself than I do her."

"And you never wanted to go join her? I mean, surely when you were older . . ."

I shook my head.

"No. She didn't want a mom image." I laughed. "And, of course, she ended up on the sitcom playing a mom. That's actually been the hardest one for me. Because she's so many things on that show that she's never actually been for me. And I have watched it. Because . . . I was so curious. What it would look like. If she had kids that she loved. She's good at pretending."

"What a mindfuck."

I snorted out a laugh. "Tell me about it. It's ridiculous. And it's not like anyone around me relates. It's just such a weird thing. I've always felt alone that way. I thought you probably would understand the most. Or at least, it's dawning on me that out of everybody I know, you probably understand it the most."

"It's different. I don't even know what my birth mom looks like.

Maybe she is famous. Maybe she grew up and got clean and got away from everything. But I have a feeling that's a fantasy. It's what I kind of like to believe though. I'd like to believe it was worth it. Not having the kids. I mean. Like maybe not having us let her get sober? I don't know."

"Well, that's kind of my thing too. Sometimes I need to believe that it was worth it. That what she puts out to the world is helpful for other people, and I am an acceptable casualty. She has her dreams. In my life is . . ." To my horror, my chest hitched, and my throat closed. And suddenly I was crying. Which I really hadn't expected. To go crying about my mother, who was an old, old wound. It wasn't the grief over losing my grandma, it wasn't even the disorientation and the sadness over losing my relationship with Josh, which I knew now wasn't heartbreak, per se, but had still been something difficult to contend with. I hadn't thought that it could still hurt me like this.

But I hadn't had anyone ask me these questions before. I hadn't talked about it.

"You know, sometimes I feel like . . . fuck her," I said. "Because *I am* her daughter. And I really wanted to matter. The way that daughters do. The way that they're supposed to. But I don't even have kids, and I don't know if I'll ever have them. I probably won't. I probably won't, and I feel like I don't have a right—"

"You were hurt by her. It still hurts you. You have a right."

"I just . . . it's pathetic to want somebody who didn't want you. I hate it. I hate it so much. I don't want to feel it anymore. Most of the time I think I don't. And then something like this comes up and . . . I don't think I've ever actually talked about this with somebody. No. Not even Josh."

"Why not?"

"Because it's well-trodden lore. Everybody knows my mom is famous now. They didn't when I was ten, but everybody does now. They all know that I don't live with her. What is there to ask?"

"How it makes you *feel*."

People had gawked at it before, but I'd never gotten the sense anyone had wanted to dig into how I felt. Not out of a lack of care just . . . no one else I knew connected quite as deeply to being separated from the mom who'd given birth to you like Ryan did.

We both remembered what it was like to live in a time before we'd landed with the people who'd raised us.

We both knew what it was like to feel the abandonment. He might not remember his mom, but he remembered the consequences of her losing custody of him. The years being bounced from home to home.

"It makes me feel like shit. How else should it make me feel?" I scrubbed my forearm over my eyes. "I got raised by the grumpiest old lady in the entire world. And I loved that woman to death. I still do. She hated you, Ryan."

He laughed. "Yeah. I know."

"That was probably my fault. Because I complained about you a lot. She didn't like Josh either. She didn't like men. Her husband left her, and it hurt her. I think she blamed him for what ultimately happened with my mom. Like his abandonment twisted her up and made her into the kind of mother that would abandon her own kids."

I hadn't fully realized the way we were all sitting in abandonment issues. My grandmother. My mother. Me.

All hurt people lashing out in weird ways. Except I had tried really hard not to lash out. And now I kind of wanted to. I kind of wanted to call my mom and tell her that she sucked. I wasn't sure I even still had her number.

"Who was the last family you were with?" I looked at him. "Before you came to Pineville."

I wanted to know his story too. And I wondered if anyone had ever asked him these questions. If the bridesmaid that he had sex with in New Orleans had cared. If she had known. If anyone ever had.

"They were one of those foster families with like fifteen kids. A bunch of them were theirs, but a bunch of them were wards of the state, like me. Huge house. Lots of bulk food and label bins. They were nice. But you really had the sense that everybody was just passing through. All the kids were kind of interchangeable. Because we would be switched out in a few weeks. It was a short-term placement. I had a lot of anger issues. That got me kicked out of those houses."

"You did?"

Ryan was grumpy. And he could definitely be an ass. But I couldn't imagine him having anger issues. Even the boy that I had met at twelve had been a very particular sort of difficult.

"I was just mad all the time. One of my foster parents told me it was because people like my mom were broken, and they had broken kids. I couldn't believe it when someone actually wanted to adopt me. Because I already knew that I was . . . I knew I was broken."

I didn't even know what to say. I was wounded. Bleeding for that little boy. There had always been somebody that loved me. I had never been on my own completely. I had never had to look out for myself entirely. He had.

I rolled over and pressed my face against his chest, tried to hold my tears back. "I wish I would have been nicer to you."

"You were," he said.

"I smashed your science project with a bowling ball."

"You didn't mean to."

"I held it against you that you weren't nice to me," I said. "I made it about me. I wasn't understanding. I never asked you why."

"I was mean to you for smiling at me. Because I didn't know how to be cared about anymore. But even . . . with everything, it wasn't all bad. I swear to God. And my parents did a pretty good job rebuilding me. And most people wouldn't have tried. Do you have any idea how much more common a story it is to become a kid that just ages out of the system and finds themselves on their own?

Hell. People who had families just turned out when they're eight-een with no support. I have more than most."

"Good. Because you need it. Because you had all that other stuff besides."

"Do you know something," he said, his voice rough. "Hope is the most painful thing on the planet." It was. He was right. The hope that something would work out when you didn't have a guar-antee, and God knew we never had guarantees. Nobody did, it was true. But, of course, we wanted guarantees more than most.

"Have you ever had a real girlfriend?"

He laughed, and I realized he did that when I surprised him. And when he didn't really want to answer. "No. Because what the fuck's the point?"

I had arrived at that place. The whole *what was the point* place. Because I had tried to have a relationship that I could control. One that wouldn't hurt.

"Right," I said.

"It's not that I don't . . ." He looked at me, his expression sud-denly serious. "It isn't that I don't want those things. Who doesn't? But to me, it's like being a foster kid and wishing that you could have a family. You can. I do. But I'm still not the same as a kid that was born into a family with parents who wanted them. And loved them. I lived twelve years of being passed around, unwanted, and that leaves scars on you. I'm lucky to have the parents that I have. I'm lucky to have my family. But sometimes I wonder if they wish they had a son who wasn't so messed up."

"I think your parents love you," I said, my heart squeezing. "Because you're . . ."

I wasn't sure that I had words for it. To me, he had always been magnetic. Yes, historically, when things had happened between us, they had gone wrong. But the truth was, no matter what, we were always drawn to each other.

I had been drawn to him from day one. How could I not be?

He had always been a fascination, an obstacle. I had been as drawn to him as I was afraid of him.

"You were always meant to be something. And nothing was ever going to hold you back. That much is clear. Because if it could have, it would have. But you . . . you're amazing, Ryan Clark. The photo exhibition that you made for the town, the way that you brought Quinn and Noah together . . ."

"Entirely unintentional. Noah and Quinn."

"Quinn thinks that you're the very hand of God."

He squinted. "Does she?"

"Now, I can personally attest to the fact that your hands have made me see God."

"Don't get me hit by lightning, Poppy."

"I'm not trying to." I sobered. "You're not broken forever."

"I wish I could believe that. But it's like you said earlier. We can have the views, but it doesn't take away the hard things. Especially after I got adopted, I thought maybe I could just be normal. But a lot of other experiences showed me differently. And I've found a life that makes me happy. It really does. Traveling around. Taking pictures. I get to meet all kinds of different people, move around to a lot of different places." He let out a long breath. "There are things that happen to you, Poppy. Moments that change who you are. There are some things you just can't fight. I'm just realistic about who I am."

I wanted to fight with him about that, because I really wanted to believe that there was hope. That all the damage could be healed. Maybe because I wanted mine healed so bad.

But hadn't I written off love and relationships too? Was I any different?

I had tried, with Josh. At least, I had told myself that.

"I'm hungry," he said.

"Meat pies?"

"Sounds good."

CHAPTER 19

I'd fallen asleep in his arms. I'd woken up at least three times during the night and peered through the darkness at his profile.

I couldn't stop marveling at the fact that I was sharing a bed with Ryan. The sex was one thing – holy cow was it ever – but actually sleeping with him was . . . so warm and wonderful and I wanted to hang onto him all night like a desperate sugar glider, but I also didn't want to freak him out.

I didn't want to freak myself out.

One day ago, I'd run away from him so that I didn't have to say goodbye.

And the goodbye was still looming. I couldn't afford to forget that.

When I woke up the next morning, Ryan was gone. He had texted me saying that he was going out to take pictures of the sunrise. I also got a text from Quinn.

Husband is off doing physical pursuits that I'm uninterested in. Do you have time to talk?

I hadn't even told her that I was stuck in New Zealand. She probably thought she was texting me midday in Oregon.

Yes.

My phone rang. I picked it up. And I realized that I was about to have *the* conversation.

The one where I told her about me and Ryan, and everything.

"Hi," I said immediately to my glowing friend on FaceTime,

looking like a bedraggled rat who had just woken up, after a long night of being ravaged. Because that's what I was.

"Hi," said Quinn. "Where are . . .?"

"I'm in New Zealand," I said. "I got stuck trying to leave."

"Oh no. You can't get a flight?"

"No. Ryan and I are stuck, actually."

"Oh?" Quinn asked. Her expression became wary. "Are you . . . together?"

"Yes," I said. "We got one of the last few vacation rentals remaining. Well, he did. He rescued me. If it wasn't for Ryan, I would be sleeping in the airport."

"No way."

"It's the weather. All the flights were canceled."

"Oh no! I'm so sorry."

I laughed. "I'm stuck in Queenstown, Quinn. It's not a struggle."

"With Ryan," she said.

I let out a slow breath. "Quinn. I . . . I'm sleeping with Ryan."

Suddenly, the image on the phone blurred as Quinn screamed. The phone stilled and I realized I was looking at the ceiling in Quinn's hotel room.

I watched the screen, as Quinn appeared over the phone. "I'm sorry," she said. "I had to throw the phone across the room. Thankfully it landed on my bed. *You are not.*"

"I am."

"No. Are you . . . are you going to marry him and have babies? Please say that you are, because I would love that more than anything."

"No," I said, sadness twisting my stomach. "It's not . . . it's not like that. But there have been a lot of things. The last few years. And then at the fifth wedding . . ."

"The *what*?"

It took me a moment to realize she didn't have a running

number in her mind of all the weddings Ryan and I had been at together.

That was a me thing.

"The wedding in Leavenworth. Right after Josh and I broke up. The Christmas wedding that I did. We . . . something happened. He and I kissed. But it ended really badly. Because of me. It was my fault."

"You always said that you hated him."

"Well, I thought that I did. I thought that was why things were weird between us, because we hated each other. But it turned out that actually we were attracted to each other. Surprise."

"I really hate to tell you this," said Quinn. "But I knew that you were."

"*What?*"

"I'm sorry. I don't mean to say it like that. Like there are all these things about you that you don't know that I do. That isn't what I'm trying to get across here. But you're very certain, Poppy. About how you feel. About everything. Everything you think, everything you do. And nobody can tell you anything."

I had always thought of myself as a people pleaser. Not somebody who was stubborn.

"I don't think that I'm like that."

"Just about really specific things. Because you have a way that you want your life to go. You don't want to be afraid. You latched onto Josh after college and I didn't think that you were a great couple, but I saw that he made you feel safe. And I knew that for you that was the most important thing. But I could see that when it came to you and Ryan, you both protested a little bit too much. And I always thought that you guys would be a way better couple."

"We aren't a couple," I said. "He's never had a girlfriend before."

"Did it occur to you that it's because he has feelings for you?"

"What?"

"I think he has feelings for you."

"He's *attracted* to me," I said. "He has been. That's not the same as having feelings."

"I think he does."

For some reason that made me feel panicked. Like standing at the bottom of a mountain I knew I couldn't climb without dying.

"How is your honeymoon going?" I really wanted to change the subject. "How is life as a married woman?"

"Amazing. Fantastic. Fiji is great. And I love my husband."

"You want to tell me about the sex?"

"We didn't wait till our wedding night, Poppy. You've already heard about the sex. In fact, I seem to recall I gave you the world's most graphic monologue when I screwed him in Tahoe two hours after meeting him."

She had. It was true. I knew things about Noah I couldn't unknow. Things that made it hard to make eye contact with him sometimes.

"The sex we haven't discussed is the sex that you and Ryan are having," Quinn said.

I pressed my hand into my right eyeball. "I don't know what to do. I don't know what I'm feeling. I've never done anything like this before. This sleeping with a guy when I don't have a commitment thing. I don't know why I'm doing it now. It's just that it didn't work anymore. To resist him. To not want him. But I decided that I didn't want to do the love thing, and he really doesn't want to do it. And we hated each other until a few days ago, so there's no way that it's something more than sex. Right?"

Quinn looked at me regretfully. "I really can't answer that. Because I have never thought that you didn't want love. I have never believed that you didn't want to get married. I sure as hell never believed that a guy as lame as Josh had the power to take that desire away from you, and at the very least I didn't think he had the right."

I felt panicky. "I want to be safe, Quinn. And this thing with him doesn't feel especially safe."

"I have bad news for you, but caring about somebody doesn't feel safe. Ever."

"That's really unfair. And easy for you to say. Because you have these great parents, and you have a good example for ways that life can work out and neither Ryan nor I can feel that level of certainty."

"It's not easy for me to say. I understand that your mom made it really hard for you to trust people."

I was angry, because Quinn knew me. I was angry because she actually was one of the few people who could comment on my issues. But I didn't want to think about what I could potentially have with Ryan. Because I didn't want to care about him. Because if I did I knew that he would actually be able to hurt me. He had been there. Always there. This angry, completely unknowable presence in my life. He had been a constant.

What if I did something or said something, or asked for too much, and then there was nothing. The tenuous thread that had held us together all these years suddenly cut.

I felt like I was freefalling. Like I was on the edge of a revelation that I didn't want to have.

"I'm never going to be able to hold onto him," I said. "All this is ever going to be is the two of us dealing with this attraction that we have. This thing that we feel for each other. It's not love. It's not anything that domesticated."

"You're the one that managed to convince herself that love had to be domestic."

"You and Noah haven't done anything to convince me otherwise."

"You haven't seen us fight."

"You told me that you were always certain of him."

"I am. I'm still certain of him even when we fight. Even when things are hard. I was certain of him even while I told myself I was falling in love too fast. I tried to rationalize my feelings away, and that was foolish. It was bigger than we were. And something like that isn't ever going to be comfortable the whole time."

I didn't like that. I didn't like her challenging me. Because I had gone and put her and Noah into an unknowable, unquestionable box, and I preferred that.

Preferred the idea that they were experiencing something that mere mortals never could. Something I certainly didn't have to worry about.

"I'm not certain of anything. Except for my house back in Pineville. And my career, I guess. When I go home, things are already going to be different. And Ryan is going to Europe. And I don't have time for this."

"You can't plan everything."

"Yes, I can. It worked for a really long time. I planned all the things. I planned my feelings. I planned my future. And it all fell apart, and nothing has been as easy since."

"But have you ever wanted him back?"

No.

Never.

I'd been fine. Making cakes and living in the house by myself. And seeing Ryan across the street, and our eyes clashing and making sparks go off inside of me.

Hovering around the edges of memory, of kissing him.

I had been happier.

These past few days, finally being with him, talking to him. Getting to know him. To understand this man that had always been there, this unfathomable mystery, yes, I had been happier. But it wouldn't last. And there was no way that I could force it to.

And I hated that.

But I couldn't see a way around the fundamental problem here. I enjoyed being with him. He was . . . he was always going to be traveling. My life was back in Pineville. My grandmother's house. My grandmother's bakery.

And, even if we could ever integrate our lives, he was right. You couldn't take the good only and leave the bad.

We were both carrying an awful lot of bad.

"Why do you look desolate?" Quinn asked.

"Change," I said. Because it was true.

Suddenly I wanted to weep. Beneath the weight of everything that was different.

Quinn leaving, and Ryan and I sleeping together, and me knowing that I didn't want to say goodbye, all the while knowing that I would. That I had to.

"Life always changes," Quinn said.

"I don't like it," I said.

"I know," she said. "But someday . . . someday you'll be the one that wants to make a change, Poppy. And when you do, I think it's only going to be for the best."

"I hope so."

I didn't know why I said that. Because she was wrong. I didn't want things to change. I wanted everything to go back to the way it was. I wanted my grandma. I wanted to sit at her kitchen counter and watch her make cookies. I wanted to be a little girl again. In Tahoe. Sitting between my mother, and my grandmother. Not understanding or knowing that everything was about to change. I wanted to go back to that one moment in my life when I felt like I had the two people I loved most in my life right there. When it felt like everything was going to be okay.

When I hadn't been hurt yet.

But my grandmother was dead, and my mother might as well have been.

I needed to get back home. But I wasn't in control of that.

There were just so many things happening that I didn't like. I didn't have control.

And the feelings in my chest were so much bigger than any I wanted to carry.

"Are you okay?"

"Yes," I said.

Because if I said no she would leave her honeymoon and come back to New Zealand to check on me. She was right. There were things in your life that you were supposed to want more than safety and staying the same. She had that. I wanted her to have it. But I didn't want it. I desperately didn't want to.

I also didn't want to put a wrinkle in her happiness.

"Well, keep me posted on your travel situation. And the Ryan situation."

I heard the front door open and close. "I better go," I said. "The situation is here."

Quinn pulled an over exaggerated excited face. "Go. Make the most of it."

"Bye," I said.

I stood up, and my phone vibrated, flashing an email notification. I paused and opened it, as I walked out into the front room of the house.

Ryan was standing there looking at his phone.

"I have a flight out," he said.

I read my message. "So do I."

CHAPTER 20

"*T*omorrow morning," I said, staring down at the screen.

"Me too," he said.

"Oh."

I was flying back to Auckland, and then would be taking an evening flight to Los Angeles.

"I'll be flying to Sydney, and then on."

"Oh," I said.

"Have you had a good morning?"

He wasn't acting like it was a big deal. Wasn't acting like it was sad. I had just been thinking that I needed so badly to get back home, and now I didn't want to go.

Because at least here it was like we were outside of time. At least here, I didn't have to know anything. What I felt about him or my life, or anything.

I didn't know how I could want so many different things so badly. How I could want things to go back to how they were, but also want to stay on a vacation from everything forever.

It was that game I played. Imagine what my life could be like when I was somewhere else.

If I were a different person. If I weren't quite so broken. If I were brave.

If I was the kind of person who took off to parts unknown to live there just for a while. Who could get on a plane without taking lorazepam, and without wearing noise canceling headphones and an eye mask.

"We should go downtown tonight," he said. "Have dinner."

"Yes," I said.

Because surely a dinner date would fix it. It would make this feel good. Likely to draw a line under it. Like everything would be fine.

Like it could all go back to normal. Just something we got out of the box in New Zealand, but back in Pineville, it would be safely packed away. Stowed with our suitcases. Yeah. That would work.

I wouldn't even have to worry about it for several months, because he wasn't coming back. Not for a long time. I didn't even know when.

He hadn't told me. Because it wasn't my business. Because we were . . . whatever this was. Taylor Swift had an invisible string, and we had a long, torturous rope with so many knots in it we could never begin to untangle it.

"I have a couple of places I'm going to try to get pictures of. Do you want to come?"

"I should pack," I said. "Make sure I have everything in order. I have to figure out my connecting flight home. Because it's on a different airline and they didn't rebook it. Separate reservation. It's just . . . it's going to be kind of a headache."

It was true, but it was also kind of an excuse. When he left, I went to work in my Alaska Airlines app trying to rebook my flight. I couldn't manage one until the day after my flight got to LA.

Los Angeles.

That always made me feel weird, because of course my mother was just a skip away over in Hollywood.

I didn't loiter down in that area of the world for a reason.

I can remember the first time I drove to Hollywood. I had been down in the area for a wedding convention, and I had thought that it would be a good idea to see the glittering place that she had left me for.

It hadn't glittered at all. I had been shocked by how old and dilapidated it was. How the streets were cracked and the buildings were faded. The brightest colors on the pink oleander blossoms and the spindly palm trees. The Hollywood sign on the hill had seemed somehow less in person than it did on the screen.

I had been more confused after seeing it. Nothing felt resolved.

I ignored the feeling that the world was throwing deliberately difficult things my way.

The world was giant.

The world outside the window with its big blue skies and ancient mountains didn't care about my emotional issues.

Only I did.

That gave me perspective.

I packed. I made a hotel reservation by LAX. I ignored the weight pressing down on my chest.

I took a bath, by myself, which was infinitely less interesting than taking one with Ryan.

For the first time since I got to New Zealand, I got out my paper planner and looked ahead at my calendar. I had a few weddings to try and manage when I got home. Only one coming up quickly.

Weddings Ryan wouldn't be at.

Weddings I wouldn't number, because I didn't assign numbers to the ones he wasn't there for.

For another moment, I wondered what it would be like to leave. To do something different.

To run away with him.

But what would happen to the bakery? To the brides?

What would happen to that safe space I'd made?

That echoed inside of me.

I didn't want to let anyone down. I never had.

And yet, I always felt like it wasn't enough. Like *I* wasn't enough.

For God's sake. I was so melancholy.

I got dressed for dinner, and just as I finished, Ryan rolled in.

"I'm going to get in the shower," he said.

He disappeared into the bathroom. I wasn't sure if it was an invitation. But I was already dressed and I had done my makeup, so I didn't take him up on it. Even though I wanted to.

There was something so domestic about this. We had been cohabitating.

Even listening to the shower running, knowing he was in it, it felt like something it wasn't.

It was so easy to feel like we were something we weren't.

When he walked into the living room wearing only jeans, his chest still wet from the shower, my body went into overheat mode. He just did that for me. Every time. And now that I had given myself permission to react to him, it was just over the top all the time.

I had never been like this before. I had never been so hungry for sex.

But it wasn't just that. It was the living together, the sleeping together. Waking up in the morning together.

It was everything. And going back home would mean leaving this.

"Did you have something in mind that you wanted?"

"I don't mind," I said.

"You sure?"

"No. I'm into whatever."

"We're going to have to walk down. There still aren't any cars."

"We should probably feel lucky to be got flights out so early."

His expression was unreadable. "Yeah."

"I didn't mean . . . I didn't mean because I was in a hurry," I said.

"I know," he said.

Except, I didn't think he did. I was frustrated at myself. For sorting through my own thoughts and feelings just . . . way too slowly.

I wanted to say something reassuring, but I couldn't even reassure myself.

"How about hot pots?" I asked. "I went there with the other girls. And it was really great. I think you would enjoy it."

He looked pleased at that. "I would enjoy that. Thanks."

He finished dressing, and we left the house together. He reached out and grabbed my hand, just casually. He laced his fingers through mine, and I just enjoyed the moment. Our hands linked together as we walked down the street. Like we had nowhere pressing to be. Like it was normal. Like this was who we were.

"How many more weddings do you have this year?"

"Six," I said.

"Wow."

"Yeah. It's a lot."

"I think I'm pretty much done with it," he said.

"Really?" It felt like something inside me had torn.

"Yeah. It was good for a while. Like I said, and helped pay the bills. But it's not what I really want to do."

There was something about the way he said that. It turned something inside me on its head. It also made me feel like he was being honest about something I wasn't able to.

"I really love baking. It makes me feel closer to my grandmother."

"I can tell."

"I went to school for business. I wanted to figure out how to help run the bakery a little bit better. I don't know that I would've opened a bakery. It was what my grandmother did. I mean, I really enjoy baking. I like the artistic design of cakes. I guess you can't know the answer to that question, can you? What you would be if you didn't feel tangled up in . . . obligation."

I felt guilty calling the bakery that.

"Is that how you feel it is?"

"I don't know."

"What business would you run if you weren't doing wedding cakes?"

I had always liked doing other people's weddings. I got a lot out of it. I got to see people making commitments to each other. It was artistic. It was fun. And nobody was ever happier with you than a couple who was pleased at their wedding.

It was the ultimate high for me.

That made me feel so small and sad.

At the same time, I felt like as long as I did cakes, I had grounding for it. A basis to start from. The baking my grandmother had taught me to do, her legacy and reputation with her bakery.

I didn't feel good enough to try for more. And that was even sadder.

"I . . . I had the thought it would be fun to help plan the whole wedding."

"You want to be a wedding planner?"

I nodded. "I mean, I'm close enough. But think about all of the things we've seen. Bears in my car and missing wedding rings."

"Why don't you do it?"

I shook my head. "I'm not sure. Maybe I wouldn't really like it. It seems silly, to still be waffling on all that at thirty."

"It's okay to not know what you want."

"You don't strike me as the kind of person that's ever been uncertain."

He looked up at me. "I mean, I have been, about plenty of things."

"I don't mean about life, or what was going to happen to you. I mean about what you wanted."

He nodded slowly. "That is true. The reason that I went to school in New Zealand was because I can remember very clearly seeing a picture of Waimangu Volcanic Valley hanging on the wall at one of my parents' friends' houses. They were those kinds of people. They had traveled the world, you know? Suddenly I knew rich people, and before I never had. But I remember seeing that. And thinking it looked magical. The water was so blue. It didn't seem real. And they said that it was. Even bluer in person. I wanted to see it for myself, I wanted to capture it for myself. And suddenly,

I realized it was possible. That was one of the first times I set my mind to something. Because suddenly I could dream. It wasn't too expensive."

I was in awe of him. He had looked at a photograph of a place around the world and had seen it as a place he could go.

I felt like my own dreams were so small in comparison. I couldn't see past the four walls of my grandmother's house because they represented safety. I had been able to dream as far as getting a degree to help run her bakery better.

And then I had taken that and turned it into my wedding cake business. It was a small thing. I was proud of myself. I wasn't downplaying it. It was only that I could see my own limitations. Limitations I put on myself. The way that I was sort of cautiously circling the same basic thing. In ever widening circles, but they weren't all that wide.

"You made your dreams come true," I said.

"Some of them," he said. He tightened his hold on my hand, and we dropped down into town. We walked past the now familiar fern statue, down to the walk in front of the lake. Past the statue of the man and his sheep. All the way through to the hot pot restaurant.

The light was low inside, and faintly red.

We sat down at a table and ordered an array of vegetables and meat for our broth.

I looked at him across the table, and had the sudden, terrifying feeling that I could look at him across the dining table for the rest of my life and be happy.

I pulled way back. Way, way back. I didn't want to have thoughts like that.

But they were so insistent. And futile all at the same time.

He was leaving.

I had escaped in the dead of night when I had thought we were going to be separated the first time because I didn't want to say goodbye. Because I didn't want to have thoughts like this. I didn't need to romanticize what had occurred.

But I also couldn't reduce it.

I couldn't just tell myself that we were two people blowing off steam that had been building up for years. It was something that I could've done a few days ago. But not now.

Because yes, there was something to the steam. It was amazing. Better than anything I had ever experienced before.

But I didn't just like being with him when he was naked. I liked being with him in every way.

I liked walking with him. Holding his hand. I liked learning about him. I liked watching him work. I liked sitting across from him at a dinner table.

That was more than sex.

I looked down, and concentrated on picking up a piece of meat and swishing it around in the broth.

"Where are you going first?" I asked, trying to loosen some of the tightness in my chest.

"Croatia," he said.

"Oh. That sounds great. Where are you staying?"

"Dubrovnik."

"Have you been there before?"

"No. I'm only going to places I haven't been before."

I wish I had something to say to that. I felt like a tear had started to form at the center of my chest. Or maybe it had been there for a long time and it was just now beginning to expand. One side was being pulled right, the other was being pulled left, and it was going to leave me split.

Ryan didn't seem split. He seemed to have found a way to be everything to everyone, and himself, and I had no idea how he did it. I had no idea how he was all the things he was without fear.

I wanted to figure out how to stop the horrible tearing in my chest. The one that wanted to go back to my safe, quiet life, and the one that wanted something more.

Everything.

No. I already knew no one got to have everything.

"And you're going to go back home?" he asked.

I nodded. "I have a wedding cake to make."

"Of course," he said.

I looked up at him and it was like everything, all the feelings from the past few days and forever, bubbled over inside of me.

"I don't want to stop this," I said.

The words tumbled out of my mouth, I hadn't been aware that I was about to say them, and I really didn't know quite where I was going with it. Just that I couldn't stand the pressure anymore. I just couldn't.

"What?"

"This. When you get back to Pineville, I want the two of us to still be . . . I like this. I like that we're friends now. And I want to keep sleeping with you."

It would change so many things. We would be walking around the town where everybody knew us, holding hands. People would have opinions. Josh would probably be upset.

I didn't know his parents very well, and my grandmother had hated them, because I was a Love and he was a Clark. And as much as I was pretty sure only my grandmother had ever put much stock in that, I didn't really know what his parents would think.

It made my mouth dry. It made my heart pound so hard I thought I was going to be sick.

"Let's talk about this when we get back to the house."

"I want to talk about it now," I said.

"Poppy, eat your food."

I did. But it was difficult. Because he was maybe on the verge of protecting me. Or something. I didn't . . . I didn't know what.

He was very certain. He was certain in ways that I never had been. Maybe he found me too timid. Maybe I was only good for sex, and now the sex had been demystified he wasn't interested anymore.

We finished our meal, which I could no longer enjoy, and when we were out on the street I turned to him. "I really do want to know what you think."

"I thought you were supposed to be a people pleaser."

"Not with you. I want . . . to keep doing this."

"Is that it?" He stopped walking, he looked at me. People were milling around us, walking across the gray cobbled path, but we were frozen. Totally in the way. I didn't care.

"I think we can try for . . . something," I said. "Because no matter how many years we've known each other, no matter how many different things we tried to be to each other, nothing has felt quite right, has it? But these last few days have felt really good. And I want to hold onto that."

"You're proposing that we do a friends with benefits thing?"

That he found such an easy, neat label relieved me. Because I could see that working. I could see how that was what we were. We had told each other secrets. And we had touched each other in ways I had certainly never been touched before.

We were friends. But there was more to it. I could handle that. It felt finally like a good category that I could put Ryan into. Not the messy, fascinating thing he had always been, but something that sounded so nice and permanent and would let me have my life and him have his.

"That's exactly what I want. Exactly that. Because the idea of going back home and pretending that none of this happened just isn't something that I want. I don't want to pretend that this didn't happen."

"Neither do I," he said.

I was relieved to hear that. "Good."

"I'm not your fucking friend."

He started to walk ahead of me.

"Ryan," I said, trailing after him. "What you mean? Of course you're my friend."

"No. I'm not going to let you downplay this. I'm not going to let you hide. Yes, you are a people pleaser, Poppy love. You are also the most ridiculous little control freak that I have ever met. You're always shocked when something doesn't go according to plan. When a bowling ball falls on something, or when a bear eats your cake. But that's life. You can't stop it. Things are going to happen, just because you didn't mean to hurt somebody doesn't mean that you're exempt from the consequences of it."

"It's not . . . it's not a bowling ball, Ryan. I really want this. I'm not trying to ruin things."

He looked so angry. Furious. He had been mad at me before, but not like this. The closest thing was the fifth wedding.

"Maybe it could be something else, but maybe it won't be. And we have to live in the same town. I know that you travel a lot, but you're going to be home, and I can't face it if we . . . I don't want to implode."

"And I'm not taking your half-assed offer."

"It isn't a half-assed offer, I mean it. It's a big deal for me."

"It's a big deal for you? To get to keep safe? To keep your little house, to keep your life exactly the same way it is except you get me in your bed when I'm home from an assignment. What changes for you? Nothing. And that's what you want. That's why you liked Josh, and it's why you ignored the little undermining things he did and said to you. Because what you really wanted was somebody who wouldn't challenge you. What you really wanted was some-body you wouldn't have to give anything up for."

"He never asked me to give anything up for him."

"I know."

"I don't understand why you're mad at me about this."

"I told you. One of the first things in my life I was ever sure about was that I wanted to be a photographer. But you know what the first thing was?"

"No," I said, my heart suddenly dipping, fighting against my breastbone.

"When I saw you, sixth grade. And you smiled at me. I knew what love was. For the first time in my goddamned life. I was sure. I have been sure every day of my life, ever since. It didn't matter that you tried to avoid me, it didn't matter that you had that same easy smile for everybody else for all those years after, and you didn't have it for me anymore. I do."

. I couldn't believe what I was hearing. I felt like I was in a free-fall, there on the sidewalk in New Zealand.

What he was saying didn't make any sense. There was no way that Ryan had loved me since we were twelve. It didn't seem possible or reasonable or rational. He had hated me.

Except I started to circle around all the things he had said to me. And all the things he hadn't.

"Love felt a lot like resentment to me," he said. "I didn't want to feel those things for you. I wanted to push you away. You were scarier than Mary and Michael. Scarier than anything. And you never looked at me like that. You were kind, but I was never special to you. Not like you were to me. I was kind of grateful for that, because . . . I wouldn't have known what to do with you even if I could've touched you. I would've broken you. It would've been worse than a bowling ball on a science project, believe me. But when we came back from college, I wondered . . . I thought that maybe we could try something. But then you started dating him."

He closed his eyes and shook his head. "And you were everywhere. You were *everywhere*, I never got away from you. It didn't matter how many women I slept with, it didn't matter how many photography assignments I took. It didn't matter how good I made myself feel about all of my achievements, I still didn't have you. And then there was the . . . the wedding photography. Being constantly in your path. It was like a joke. Finally, finally he broke up with you, and I was just mad that he hurt you. But then you were kissing me, so it didn't matter. Except you were only kissing me because you wanted to get back at him."

"I told you," I said, feeling like I was being scraped raw. "I told you it wasn't that simple."

"Yeah. That's what you said."

"I meant it. Ryan . . ." I felt like I was dying.

He loved me?

He loved me.

All those years, I have felt weird and awkward and alone. Afraid. Just marinating in the precariousness of everything. Of being a middle schooler, of missing my mother. Of being afraid of losing friends, because I was afraid of losing everything. And he had loved me? All that time. I couldn't make sense of it.

"Stop trying to rationalize it. Stop trying to make it a math problem. If it was that easy, if it was that simple, I just wouldn't feel it," he said.

"What am I supposed to do with that? You love me, but you don't want to?"

"No," he said. "I don't want to."

"Well that's not . . . very nice."

"Why should I want to? Because all it has been is me caring more for you than you do for me. And I've had enough of that. I spent my life dealing with that. And I didn't need to meet you and fall right back into the same pattern."

"It isn't the same," I said. "I have feelings for you. I do. But it's not reasonable to think that we can just jump into the deep end. We have to figure out how our lives are going to work together. You have a job that takes you overseas all the time, and I can't even get on a plane without taking pharmaceuticals."

"Is that the real reason?"

"I don't know. It's enough of one. Why can't we take things in steps?"

"Because I don't want half measures. I know what I want. I have known what I wanted since I was twelve. Since I saw you for the first time in my grandpa's restaurant delivering the mail. I want to marry you. I want you to belong to me. I want to belong to you. I love you, Poppy. It's not ambiguous, it's not a question. I don't need to get my toes into the shallow end. And more than that, I can't. I am not a man who does halfway. And I don't deal in uncertainty."

"That's not fair. You can't let me have one moment to try and process this?"

"You didn't ask me what I felt. You started making proclamations. You started trying to control it. Because that's what you have to do. You have to shrink everything down to fit inside that little box that you want to stay in. But I can't fit in that box. And my feelings for you sure as hell can't."

"So it's all, everything, right now or nothing?"

"It fucking is," he said.

"I can't . . . I can't make a decision that quickly."

"Quickly? We have known each other since sixth grade. I'm not asking you to make a decision quickly. I'm asking you to finally make a decision. You can't even tell me when for sure you were first attracted to me. And I think if you are genuinely honest with yourself, you would know. You would know that we both felt something, all those years ago. But you have been running from it. And I've been waiting. Waiting for you to look at me and see me the way that I see you."

"I do. I think that you are the most incredible, amazing man that I have ever known. You're so strong and you're so talented and you—"

"And it doesn't matter. Because you don't care about me any more than you care about whatever fantasy you have about the perfect life."

He started to walk away from me again and I hurried after him.

"That's not fair," I said. "Everybody wants to have a perfect life. Everybody wants to be safe and happy. Everybody does. Don't turn it into some kind of psychosis that I alone am suffering from."

"You don't just want to be happy and safe. You want to have everything be comfortable and on your terms. That is not what everyone wants. Because if you have another person in your life, it has to be about them too."

We were back at the rental house. I hadn't even been aware that we had been walking that quickly.

"I'm going to the airport," he said, picking up his backpack.

"Ryan," I said. "Don't run away from me."

"I'm not. I'm not running away from you. I have been here the whole damned time. But if this doesn't do it, if it doesn't show you what we could have, if it doesn't show you what you feel, then nothing is going to. And I need to have permission to move on. To go live my life."

"So you're just going to swan off into the darkness and have some kind of sad man fantasy? Are you going to bang some Croatian girl against an ancient wall when you get to Dubrovnik?"

"If I did, it wouldn't be any of your business. It would only be your business if you were in love with me."

I wanted to say something, but the words got stuck in my throat. Everything was jumbled up inside of me.

I couldn't figure out how we had gotten here.

And before I could say anything, he had picked up his backpack, and was headed out the door.

"You can't walk to the airport," I called after him.

He didn't answer me. He didn't turn around.

He didn't say goodbye.

And it hurt so much worse than saying goodbye ever could have.

CHAPTER 21

For the first time in memory, I didn't need to take pills to get on a plane. I was like a zombie. Shellshocked and eager to get home. To get into my own bed. To get back to familiarity so that I could try and make some sense of myself. I needed that. I couldn't do it while I was away. I needed comfort and safety. I needed a grandmother that was dead, and a mother who had never particularly cared. I needed my friend who was in another country, and going to stay around the world from me. I needed a lot of things I couldn't have, so the indignity of flight wasn't quite what it normally was. I was like a husk of a person the whole way to Auckland, where I sat by my gate, occasionally wandered listlessly, and sat more for the hours long layover I had before the plane departed for LA.

I didn't sleep.

Not on the whole eleven-and-a-half-hour flight. We landed at one p.m., the same day that we left. Like we had gone back in time. But, of course, we hadn't. Because if we had, maybe I could redo everything with Ryan. Except I didn't know how. Because I wanted him. That was the problem. It was just impossible. If it was as easy as just deciding to have him, then maybe I would've done it.

But one of us would have to give something up. When we would have to . . . risk so much. We could barely get along for extended stretches. We had only just tested out this whole relationship thing.

How could we dump ourselves into forever?

But I kept thinking back to how he had looked at me. The way he had told me that he was sure. That I was the one thing he had ever been sure of.

He loved me.

But it couldn't be that simple. He couldn't just love me. He couldn't have just looked at me and seen what no one else ever had.

My own mother hadn't wanted to keep me.

When I dragged my bags out of customs, out of the airport and into the California sun, I squinted against the harshness of it.

It felt far too bright, and far too optimistic.

I hated it.

I took a car to my hotel and was too early for check-in. I stashed my bags at the concierge, and I went back outside and stood there on the sidewalk for a long moment.

And then I decided.

I got a car, and I gave the driver an address I usually pretended I didn't know.

Maybe she wouldn't be home. The odds were low, after all. She might be on location.

But, I unfortunately also knew which lot her show was filmed on, which meant not even that was an excuse. Though the layers of security would make it a little bit harder to get there.

Not that there was an absence of security at her home.

I sat with my hands folded tightly in my lap the whole drive to my mother's gorgeous house in Beverly Hills. There were high walls and a gate around the outside. It felt like a metaphor. It felt about right.

We pulled up, and I got out.

"You're stopping here?" my driver asked.

"Yeah. Why don't you . . . just one second. I might need a ride straight back."

I walked up to the gate and pushed the button. "I'm Poppy Love. I'm here to see Caroline Love."

"You're who?" A man's voice came back over the speaker.

"If Caroline is home, if you could just tell her that Poppy is here. And ask if she has a minute to see me."

I waited. It was torturous. And insulting, really. Having to wait to see if your mother had a minute to check in with you.

When you were there in person for the first time in five years.

"You can come in, Miss Love," said the man's voice.

I turned and waved my driver off as the gate opened.

And then I stepped inside my mother's world.

I hadn't been to her house before. The last time we'd seen each other, we'd had dinner at a restaurant. I walked up the glorious, paved path, surrounded by beautiful flowers and plants.

My mother had always loved beautiful things. I had just never been beautiful enough. Interesting enough. Fulfilling enough. I couldn't be sure. I wanted to be.

I wanted to know. What was it that made me less? That made me so unimportant. What was it about me that made me so easy to forget?

So pale next to the oleanders and Hollywood sign.

I walked up to the front door, and stood there, unsure about whether or not I was supposed to ring the bell. But then I didn't have to worry anymore, because the door opened.

"Hello," the woman said. "Caroline will see you in the sitting room."

I followed her, my heart pounding hard.

The woman was about the same age I was. Working for my mother.

Maybe if I was willing to take a job for my mother, I would be able to see her more. I would probably finally have a use as far as she was concerned.

The house was done all in white, bright and airy.

The sitting room was even more aggressively clean. My mother was sitting on a long white sofa, dressed in bright pink. She was the only color in the room. Suddenly I understood the color scheme.

Nothing was ever supposed to outshine her.

Her face was unlined, her hair dark and shiny. Her makeup was pristine. She didn't look surprised to see me. But that could be a function of the Botox I was sure she got regularly. Because while good genetics could certainly account for use to a point, her aesthetic was more *frozen in time* than *well rested*. And that, I figured, could only come from procedures. I probably had more lines when I smiled than my mother did.

"I wasn't expecting you," she said.

"I wasn't really expecting me either. I had a flight delay. I thought that I would stop and say hi."

There was no point getting into the details.

"I'm glad that you did," she said. Ever gracious and smiling. You didn't read bad stories about my mom in the media. She was never rude. She always tipped. She was very conscious of her image. I didn't think she particularly wanted me there, but she would never say that. Because what if I went to the press? The truth was, I always could have. It wasn't like the existence of her daughter was a total secret, but it was definitely little-known. I had never gone to a single event with her. I could make sure that the world knew that Caroline Love had abandoned her only daughter in order to pursue her dreams. But to what end?

Still, I always had the feeling that my mother was careful with me just in case I ever did decide to do that.

But doing so would only expose my own insecurities. My own issues around being wanted.

Not high on my list of things to experience. The problem was, though, I wasn't just there to say hi. I hadn't known why I had come here. Not until that moment. But it wasn't to say hi.

I needed to understand. Because . . . a man had just stood in front of me and told me that he loved me. That he always had. That I was important to him, and I hadn't been able to tell him I wanted that. That I loved him too. Thinking those words was like a knife wound straight to the soul. Because I realized then that they were true. It was just I didn't know how to claim them. I didn't know how to say yes to him. I didn't know how to stop being so afraid. And instinctively I had gone back to the source of that fear. Of that abandonment.

I wanted my mother. But not in the way a lot of people did. I had wanted my mother because I needed to ask why. To ask if it was worth it.

"It's amazing that you caught me. The show is on hiatus right now, but I just landed a role in an upcoming rom-com."

She would be great in a rom com. She was beautiful and vivacious. She had the kind of sunny energy that made everyone want to get closer to her.

I was eighteen years younger than her and that gap had never felt smaller. She really could have been my sister.

"Great."

"We're going to be filming in the Pacific Northwest."

"I live in the Pacific Northwest," I said.

"Oh, not there, honey."

"Okay."

Meaning she wasn't going to visit me, and wasn't inviting me to visit her. But adult daughters hanging around on sets would probably ruin her mystique.

"I need to talk to you about something," I said.

"What about?"

"I . . . was there something that I did? Was there something that I did to make you leave me? Like specifically. What's wrong with me?"

She frowned, at least, I was pretty sure she was trying to frown. "Honey, I didn't abandon you. You went to be with your grandmother because it was just a much better life than being bounced around film sets. You always got taken care of."

I stared at her. "Mom, I was seven years old and you just left me with Gran without explaining it. I didn't know that you weren't coming back."

"It's too hard to explain those things to children. When you're a mother you'll understand."

As if she was a mother. As if she had really been a mother. "I don't think I will ever understand. And if I have my own kids, I think that I'll understand even less."

"Are you pregnant? Is that why you're here? Because I think it's pretty unbelievable that I'm the mother of a twenty-five-year-old, much less that I could be a grandmother."

"I'm thirty," I said.

"If anybody asks in context with me tell them that you're twenty-five. I can't have people thinking I have a thirty-year-old."

"Mom," I said. "You abandoned me. I can't have a normal fucking relationship because of what you did to me. I . . . a man just told me that he was in love with me. He stood in front of me and said that he loved me, and that he wanted everything, and I couldn't give it to him, because I feel like there's something wrong with me. And I can't for the life of me sort out exactly what it is. And I came to you to find out if you could tell me. If you could help me make sense of it, and you don't even . . . you don't even know what you did to me. You don't understand how much you . . . screwed me up."

My mother's face went stony.

"Honey, you say that, and you have no idea how much being around this industry could've screwed you up. I did you a favor. Do you know how many pervert directors would've wanted you on the casting couch the minute you got a training bra? I was giving you a different life. A better one. You didn't choose to have a mother who was famous, and I wanted to protect you from it."

Her eyes were round, her voice affected with sympathy and a small amount of sadness. It was tempting to believe her.

She really believed it. She really had absolutely no insight into what she'd done, and she wasn't going to. She had written a new story. One where what she had done was benevolent. One where her actions somehow made her the *best* mother, even though she hadn't raised me.

When she knew full well she never talked about me in an interview, when she knew full well she didn't even send me cards on my birthday. I couldn't be certain if she actually didn't know how old I was, or if she just couldn't admit that her daughter was thirty, but either way, my mother really did live in La La Land. In all the ways that it could apply.

And the fortress that she had constructed for herself was so strong I wasn't going to be able to demolish it. Not just because I showed up wanting a reckoning.

"You didn't protect me. You fucked me up. I just want you to know that."

She sniffed. "I get that it's popular to blame your parents for everything, but this is taking it a little far."

I didn't even have the power to hurt her. Because she didn't love me enough. What she cared about was nothing disrupting her narcissistic story. The one where she was good at everything. The one where she had done the only thing.

She loved herself and this house and her career. She didn't love me.

That meant that standing there screaming at her wasn't even going to work. Wasn't going to accomplish a damned thing.

I could hate her all I wanted, but it wouldn't change it.

"I'm not going to come back," I said. "I'm not going to worry about you anymore. The only time you were ever a good mother was on a TV show. And I get that you actually don't care about that, but I did. And someday, when this place spits you out, when you need somebody, and you don't have them, I hope you remember what I said. *That you hurt me.* You didn't do it for me, you did it for you. And I . . . I thought all this time that maybe you loved me. So there had to be something big that was wrong with me to make you treat me the way that you did. But you don't. You love yourself. The problem is not me. The problem is *you*."

I turned around, my heart thundering hard.

And I walked right out of the front door, right out of the house. I ended up wandering up and down the sidewalks in Beverly Hills. I ended up walking until my legs hurt.

Only then did I get a car back to the hotel. I wanted to call Ryan. But I couldn't. Because he didn't want me now either, because I had messed that up.

But there was nothing wrong with me. *There was nothing wrong with me.* My mom didn't want to be a mom. She wanted to be an actress. She didn't want her actions to affect other people, even though they had.

It hadn't hurt her to leave me behind. And that wasn't a problem with me.

I sat there, dry eyed. I wanted to cry about it, but I couldn't even bring myself to do that. Because I was just so . . . shellshocked. Because this had taken my wound and aggressively flushed it out. It hurt. But it also felt cleaner. It felt better.

It felt closer to healing.

I just needed to get back home. Because back home things would feel better.

I ordered dinner in my room. And the next morning, was at the airport ridiculously early. I took the morning flight back to Pineville, and by the time I got to my house, I was ready to weep.

But once I got inside I didn't feel what I had hoped to. I didn't feel home.

Panic clawed at my chest. Because how could that be? This place was the most important thing to me. This house.

I was supposed to come back home and everything was supposed to feel like it made sense.

I had exorcised the demon that was my mother, and I . . .

I didn't feel anything.

I just missed Ryan.

I wanted him here with me.

I had felt more at home in another country than I did here, because I was with him.

I sat in my living room. In that place where Josh had broken up with me. But hadn't broken my heart.

I looked around, and I couldn't make it feel right. I couldn't make it feel real. I couldn't make it feel like it was mine.

But Ryan wasn't here. And for all the years before the possibility of him had existed, he had always been there.

And whatever I felt for him had been an underlying presence for so many years.

It had always been him.

That sudden thought hit me. Out of the blue.

It had always been him.

And I had been so uncomfortable with it, that I had pushed him away at every opportunity.

I had dated the wrong man. The one that didn't make me feel even half as much as Ryan did when he was looking at me. I had done everything in my power to push him away.

Because I had known that losing him, really losing him, all the way, was the one thing that I couldn't bear.

But I . . . I couldn't be safe. Not with the way I felt with him. It was too much. It was too intense. I couldn't control it.

And if I lost him . . .

You did. You lost him, and it wasn't because something was deficient in you, it's because you're too scared.

I had. I had lost him. And that was why this place didn't feel right anymore. I had changed. What I wanted had changed. But I was trying to force it to stay the same. Because stepping out, taking hold of something new, that was . . . it was terrifying. Because being with him would mean stepping out of my comfort zone. In a huge way. It would mean leaving this life behind. It would mean leaving behind all of my comfort, all of my defenses.

It would mean stripping myself bare, and finding the heart of who I was.

It would mean trusting somebody else to love me. To be there.

I had chosen Josh because I could fit him into my life. I couldn't fit Ryan into the life that I had. I was going to have to change and rearrange. I was going to have to be different.

I was going to have to disappoint people. And take risks.

I kept thinking that I had done it all. That I had fixed myself. That I had solved my issues. I had known that I was a people pleaser, so I had been convinced that knowing it meant fixing it. I had thought that being in a relationship, being in love, meant that I was healed.

But I was just putting Band-Aids on wounds that were bleeding out. I was covering up all my own issues with incomplete self-awareness and everything that I did was about fear.

I had been so sure that wasn't true anymore. I had been so certain I had broken generational trauma when the truth was, I had just become an expert at bending around it. Finding ways to contort myself into new shapes but didn't push against that pain.

And maybe I had always known about Ryan too.

I'd had the realization earlier that I was worried he would see me. But I hadn't really figured out why being seen would be a terrible thing.

I had thought maybe it was that he might see my inadequacies. But there was so much more to it than that. I had been afraid of wanting someone so much that the loss could actually destroy me. And if I was really seen, if I was really understood, if I was really cared for, then that relationship could become everything.

But that was how you became the kind of person who was afraid to stay. The kind of person who was afraid to love. The kind of person who shut everything off.

My grandmother. My mother. I wasn't as different from them as I wished I was.

Fear was a fist, balled up at the center of my chest. It kept me from being open. It kept me from love.

And I knew that.

Because I hadn't loved Josh. Because I had closed myself off to the reality of that relationship, to the issues in it, because I was so dedicated to constructing a life that made me feel safe. And in that way, I wasn't as different from my mother as I wanted to be.

Of course, I hadn't realized that Josh was trying to play games with me. He hadn't mattered enough to me for the game to resonate. I hadn't meant to do that to him. But I had just been so obsessed with things going the way I wanted. I had thought because I was open to love, I was different than my grandmother. I had thought because I was happy to be in Pineville, I was different than my mother. I was repeating that same cycle of trauma. That same closed fist.

I took my phone out of my pocket and scrolled back through my photos until I got to the selfie.

The one with Ryan.

The one where we were kissing.

I saw myself, away from home, on a mountain, happier than I'd ever been. I saw him. I really saw him. And I saw how he loved me.

I was so focused on how I loved other people, and how I could get them to want me, that I'd never given any thought to how I wanted to receive love. What I had wanted was for people to stay. I hadn't cared how.

Poor Josh hadn't been horrible. But his insecurity had changed me in small ways. I had become his mother, cleaning up after him and paying the majority of the bills, because I wanted his life with me to be easy.

I wanted to be a soft place for him so that he wouldn't go somewhere else.

But Ryan wasn't looking for a soft place to land. Ryan wanted me. The me who had dropped a bowling ball on his science project. The me who had said the worst thing possible to him the first time we'd kissed.

But he needed me to stop being scared. Because his love wasn't a soft place. And I could recognize now that a love like that wasn't real. It wouldn't stand up to hard times. It wouldn't endure.

I touched the screen. I touched us.

We had already been through so much. We already knew how to survive. We knew how to climb the mountain and take in the view, even though that view didn't erase the bad things behind us.

We didn't need them erased. We just had to choose to make a better future.

I had rejected a man who loved me. A man that I loved.

Out of fear.

But safety didn't mean what it had meant before I left Pineville for New Zealand. And home wasn't the same either.

Because home was Ryan.

It was an idea as thrilling as it was terrifying.

As revelatory as it was obvious.

It had always been him.

Always.

When I had first seen him, when I had smiled at him, I had known something too.

I knew that in order for the two of us to make it work, we were going to have to give something up.

But I suddenly felt more than willing to drop everything I was holding to grab onto him instead.

I had good employees to help run the bakery. I could hire a manager. I could delegate my next wedding.

And maybe the bride would be upset. Because I had said that I would do it, and it was going to be somebody else.

But there was time, and if she wanted to get someone else, she could.

What I needed was more important than making someone else happy.

I stood up. I was going to have to get on another plane.

I picked up my phone, and I called Josh. "Where exactly is Ryan?"

"What?"

"I need to know."

"He's in Dubrovnik."

I sighed. "I know that. But do you have any idea where he's staying?"

"What, like the hotel?"

"Yes."

"I'm sure his mom does. She always gets that information."

"Do you have his mother's number?"

"Yes."

"Great. I need that."

"Why?"

It wasn't his business. I didn't have to tell him. But I decided that I was going to.

Because I decided that I was going to throw myself into this with everything. "Because I have to go to Dubrovnik to be with him. Because I love him."

There was a strange pause on the other end. "I knew you did," he said.

He didn't even sound angry. "You knew?"

"Yeah. I mean . . . I don't know. I always thought there was something between you guys. And then you were traveling with him . . ."

"Nothing happened until after we broke up."

"I know that," Josh said. "Because neither you nor Ryan are shitty people."

Josh wasn't really either. That was the thing. He probably had done some things during our relationship that weren't very good, but I had allowed it. I hadn't done anything about it. I hadn't asked for different.

Because I wasn't really in the relationship that we had both thought we were in. It wasn't only because of him. It was also because of me. Because my emotions had been tied up, not just in Ryan, but in my own fear. My own issues.

"He said that you were jealous of him," I said.

Josh coughed. "Well, who wouldn't be?"

That was honest.

"I actually do hope you find what you're looking for," I said. "And I really mean it now. I wasn't actually in the relationship the way that I thought I was. So, if something felt wrong, it wasn't just you. It was definitely me."

It was complicated. It was like he was the world's best boyfriend, but it was also understandable that he'd had insecurities. I hadn't been in love with him. I had been hung up on somebody else.

"It's okay," he said. "I really did think we might get back together. But . . ."

"Then things changed," I said.

"Yeah," he said. "Things have changed."

It was the most real thing either of us could have said.

Things were just different now. We didn't want the same things. I didn't need to be in Pineville.

And it was a change I wouldn't have been able to make for anybody else. Anybody but Ryan.

He gave me Ryan's mom's number. And I hung up. And called her again. "Hi . . . Mrs. Clark?"

"Yes."

"This is Poppy. Poppy Love."

"Oh," she said, clearly confused about why I might be calling her. "Nice to hear from you."

"I know our families are feuding," I said.

She paused for a moment. "I don't think we're actively feuding."

"Well. Ryan seemed to think we were. When we were twelve."

She laughed. "I told him all about our family history because I wanted him to realize that he was part of it now. And . . . so are you."

So was I.

We were like Quinn and Noah in that way. Except we didn't get brought together because two people were nice to someone. Maybe we *were* doomed because two people fucked in the 1850s.

Or we weren't doomed at all.

We were connected because my mother couldn't handle me. Because my gran held onto me. Because his parents had seen a little boy who needed them, and they'd known he wasn't broken.

Because my gran and his grandpa weren't speaking to each other, so I'd had to deliver the mail.

Maybe we were meant to be all along.

Maybe it was fate.

Because of all the people who had held onto us, when the wrong ones let us go.

It had just taken me an absurdly long time to see that.

To realize I had to hang onto him.

"I . . . I was wondering if you could tell me what hotel Ryan is staying at in Croatia?"

There was an even longer pause. "Why?"

"Because I'm in love with him. And I need to go tell him that."

"Then I'll get you the address right away."

CHAPTER 22

I didn't take any medication for the flight to Dubrovnik either. I was fueled entirely by my desperation to get to him. As quickly as possible. By my need to see him. Grovel. To get on my knees and tell him what an idiot I was.

What if he rejected me now? What if what I was offering was too little too late?

Those old fears manifested inside of me. It was just so easy to fall back into that space.

It was just so easy to let old fears rise up to the surface.

I wasn't going to let them take hold of me.

When I got to the airport, I collected my single bag, and tried to bolster myself as I got a car. His mom had been so sweet.

I didn't even realize she knew who I was. But she did. Because Ryan talked about me a lot, apparently.

The way that his love for me spilled over into other places in his life left me in awe.

I told her that I had made a mistake.

She said that was up to the two of us to solve.

She said she wouldn't tell him I was coming.

I was grateful to her. Because I wasn't sure I deserved that level of support.

But I was just taking it. All of the things that I didn't deserve. All of the things that I needed, regardless of whether or not I had earned them.

Because I had spent my whole life feeling like I wasn't enough. And now I was just having to accept the fact that maybe I wasn't on my own. But I didn't need to be. Because I had people who cared about me. And they were what made everything work. They were what made life so beautiful.

They were what made me complete.

I just had to get to Ryan. I needed him.

Maybe I would be living out of hotels for a while. If he would have me. I really wanted him to have me. I really wanted to have him.

I wanted everything.

I had been so convinced it was something nobody got to have, but I wanted it. Because he'd loved me from the beginning. Through everything. He'd been there the whole time and I was the one who hadn't seen it.

I was the one who'd had it all right there all along.

I took a breath and walked into the lobby. I couldn't believe it. He was there. That same black backpack on, those clothes that I associated with his treks out and about with his camera. His dark hair messy, like he had run his fingers through it multiple times.

"Hi . . ."

He looked stunned. I might as well have walked up to him and kissed him. Or slapped him.

"Hi," I said.

"You can't be here," he said. "You're supposed to be in Pineville. And you hate flying."

"I *do* hate flying," I said. "I really hate it. And I really like to know everything that's going to happen before it happens. I don't want to be dependent on one person. I like to be in control of my surroundings, and I like everything to be familiar. I was happy to stay in a relationship that didn't thrill me. Happy to stay with a man who is insecure. Who I made insecure, because I kept him with me even though I didn't love him. Even though I couldn't love him, because my heart belonged to two other things."

"Two things?" he asked, his voice rough.

"Yes," I said. "Two. I am so acquainted with my trauma. I can name it, I can talk about it at length. We've had those discussions. But I made the mistake of thinking that just because I could talk about it, that meant I was managing it. I went and saw my mother. I was looking for some answers. I was looking for a magic word. That would finally mean I could understand what she did, or what was wrong with me. So I could finally get the key and just get over it."

"And did you?"

"No," I said. " Isn't that wild? There is no answer. And there's nothing wrong with me. Just like there's nothing wrong with you. We aren't broken at all, Ryan. But we are made by the people who let us go and the people who held onto us. And it really has to be fate that brought us together. But we also get to choose. We have to choose. And I've come to another conclusion. One I don't especially like."

"What's that, Poppy?"

"Love is scary. It's Shark Week, Ryan. Maybe that's why we're all so fascinated by it. You can't care about some thing or some one with the whole of your being and not risk something. Because the idea of losing something that means everything to you is scary. And if it isn't, then something is wrong with you. I decided it didn't have to be. I took that relationship with Josh, and I made it into something I could control, and something I wasn't that afraid to lose." I wiped a tear away from my cheek. "But that isn't love. I knew that I had to stop prizing my safety above everything else. Because it's actually the biggest thing standing in the way of my happiness. I love you."

It was the most terrifying thing I had ever said. I said those words before, of course. But they hadn't come from a place this deep inside of me. They hadn't meant half so much.

"I can't . . . I can't stay the same," I continued. "I already changed too much. I got home and it wasn't what I wanted. It wasn't what I expected. You weren't there. It's always been you."

He moved to me and wrapped his arm around my waist, pulled me up against his body, and that was when I felt it. That immediate relief.

I was home. In Dubrovnik. Somehow. Because I was in his arms. And that was all that mattered.

"Do you love your bakery?" he asked.

"I loved my gran. I really want to do wedding planning. Where I help with the whole theme. The whole design. I can actually do a lot of that virtually. Pineville could be our base, but I can travel with you. We can both have our careers. And yes, I'm going to have to build this. I'm going to have to step outside my comfort zone. But I need to do that too. I'm finally tired of just being safe. I want everything instead."

He kissed me. And I knew right then it was worth it. That I'd traded safety for love, and I would never look back.

Ever.

"I love you," he said. "And we might finally heal the rift between our families. Well. I imagine your gran would say that I nefariously seduced you."

"I would like to think the seduction was mutual."

He touched my face, and I felt emotion expanding in my chest. I wanted to cry. But for the first time in days, it wasn't a bad feeling.

"All I ever wanted was a home," I said. "It's you now."

I didn't have many words. Because I had been so focused on wanting somebody to keep me safe, to make me secure, to make me feel loved, that I had never before appreciated what an amazing thing it would be to be that for someone else.

Suddenly, I saw every side of love. All its bright, brilliant, magical possibility. Because of him.

"I guess I'm a romantic after all," I said.

EPILOGUE

The Sixth Wedding
Pineville
Two Years Later

I hadn't made the cake myself. The photographer was fantastic, but it wasn't Ryan.

Because it was finally our wedding, and while we could both manage other people's weddings well enough, we had decided it would be best if we didn't try to do too much at ours. Quinn and Noah were our matron of honor and best man. Because after all, they had definitely helped get us together. We had spent the last two years traveling and returning home intermittently. I had gotten to know Ryan's family who had accepted me so easily.

When I asked about the feud between our families, his mother had smiled. "You're breaking generational trauma."

We were. In so many ways.

She had been teasing, and yet I got the feeling she had been serious too.

I didn't invite my mother to my wedding. I sent her a card. I told her that I hadn't wanted her fame to overwhelm the event. I knew that would make her feel good about not being invited. Which I hadn't done to keep her happy with me. I'd done it because I didn't need to do anything else.

I didn't feel the need to make my wedding about her. But I understood some things about weddings then that I hadn't before, in spite of the fact that I had been part of so many. It wasn't actually a burden to include the people you cared for in the planning, to take them into consideration, because they were part of what made you as a couple.

At least, that was true for us.

Because the people that loved us had changed us.

It used to be fear was one of the biggest factors in my life. From Shark Week, which I still loved, to medicating to fly – which I still did sometimes because anxiety was a whole thing – to how much I let myself care about people. With all of myself now, no matter what.

Because one thing I had learned since loving Ryan was that love was worth the risk. Every single time.

Because fate worked hard, but you had to show up with love to make it matter.

We'd decided on a non-destination wedding.

Ryan and I had decided we wanted to get married at home, because for us, having a place to call home had always felt miraculous.

I looked at the empty cake platter, and the emptying dance floor, and smiled. We had done it.

Ryan wrapped his arms around me and kissed me. I finally understood. Love wasn't about being safe. It was about knowing that no matter what happened, you had someone who would always be with you. Someone who would care for you, as you cared for them.

"I'm not afraid of change anymore," I whispered against his lips.

"You aren't?"

I shook my head. "No. Look at all the amazing things change has brought me so far. It made my nemesis into the love of my life."

He smiled. "Oh Poppy, it was always love. We just had to stop looking at the bad things, and look at the view instead."

I knew if my gran were here she would tell us both we'd done all right.

And that was the perfect ending for me.

HEADLINE
ETERNAL

FIND YOUR HEART'S DESIRE...

VISIT OUR WEBSITE: www.headlineeternal.com

FIND US ON FACEBOOK: facebook.com/eternalromance

CONNECT WITH US ON X: @eternal_books

FOLLOW US ON INSTAGRAM: @headlineeternal

EMAIL US: eternalromance@headline.co.uk